The Burial of a Player

A JAREAU FAMILY NOVEL

KIMBERLY BROWN

#BLP

Copyright © 2023 by Kimberly Brown

All rights reserved.

No part of this book may be reproduced in any form or by any electronic or mechanical means, including information storage and retrieval systems, without written permission from the author, except for the use of brief quotations in a book review.

This is a work of fiction. Names, characters, places, and incidents are either products of the author's imagination or used fictitiously. Any similarity to actual events or locales or persons, living or dead, is entirely coincidental.

Love publications
Heart Piercing Swoon Worthy Black Love Stories

Visit bit.ly/readBLP to join our mailing list for sneak peeks and release day links!

B. Love Publications - where Authors celebrate black men, black women, and black love.

To submit a manuscript for consideration, email your first three chapters to blovepublications@gmail.com with SUBMISSION as the subject.

The BLP Podcast – bit.ly/BLPUncovered

Let's connect on social media!
    Facebook - B. Love Publications
    Twitter - @blovepub
    Instagram - @blovepublications

Author's Note

We have made it to book three in the Jareau Family Series! If you haven't read book one and two, I suggest you read them before reading this one.

Reading Order:
Where Love Blooms (Jamison and Aleviyah)
Deep In My Soul (Cartel and Adina)
Signed, Sealed, Delivered: A Jareau Family Wedding

Playlist

1. Something About Ya- J. Howell
2. Triggers- Nelccia
3. Options- Nelccia
4. Forever- Jessies- Reyes and 6lack
5. Bad- Wale and Tiara Thomas
6. Girl Like Me- Jazmine Sullivan
7. Hurt Me So Good- Jazmine Sullivan
8. Cry- K. Michelle
9. Why You Love Me- J. Howell and Dondria
10. Deserve- J. Howell
11. Expiration Date- Sammie
12. About U- Savannah Re
13. Homies- Saint Harison and Tiana Major9
14. What We Do- Rotimi
15. Yvette- Vedo and Inayah Lamis
16. I'm a Mess- Anthony Hamilton
17. Never- Jaheim
18. You Get On My Nerves- Jazmine Sullivan and Neyo

Introduction

"Create a hostile environment and a player will repent and reform."

—How To Be a Player 1997

Prologue

WALKER

Jamison and Aleviyah's Reception

WATCHING my brother dancing with his bride made me smile.

For a while, I didn't think he was ever going to accept love again, then here came my good sis Aleviyah. The beautiful nanny was now the second Mrs. Jamison Jareau. Their wedding was so beautiful and intimate. My nigga was shedding tears before she even got down the aisle. As soon as the doors of the venue opened, that lip started trembling. I had to admit that Liv looked beautiful in her wedding dress.

It was some shit I'd never seen before. It was this beautiful, strapless, mermaid style gown. Instead of a veil, she had cape-like sleeves. The top portion of it was covered in jewels. The shit was bourgeois as hell, but she was killing it.

"Just look at them," Jorja said in awe.

She sat next to me at the wedding party table, resting her back against me as I draped an arm over her chair.

"They look so happy," she continued.

"They do."

"I can't wait to get married."

I looked down at her. That was news to me. The Jorja I knew was a wild card. She loved her freedom. She loved to party. And she loved to fuck. I didn't see her as being the type to ever want to be anybody's wife.

"Since when?" I asked.

She'd been making comments about finding her a man for a minute now, but I always brushed that shit off. A few times, I thought she might have been serious when she stopped talking to me for a few days, but she always came back. At this point it was just a routine to me.

"Since my career has been taking off," she answered. "I'm in a good place in my life, and I think I'm finally ready. I mean, my sister found her happiness. Watching her and Jamison over the last year opened my eyes to how beautiful love can be. Watching Cartel and Adina finally get their happy ending… I want to experience that."

"I guess that means this between us is over then?"

She frowned. "Why does it have to be over?"

"Didn't you tell me this was over when you decided you wanted to settle down? You trying to fuck on me with a husband?"

"Ain't you tired of just fucking?"

I laughed. "Hell no. That's what this was made for," I said, grabbing my dick.

She pushed off of me and sat back in her chair with her arms crossed, staring straight ahead. Was she seriously upset? In the almost two years we'd been dealing with each other, marriage was the last thing to be brought up.

I kissed my teeth. "Come on, Ja. I know you ain't mad."

"Nah. I'm not mad at all."

"Then what's with the tight face?"

She turned to me, slowly batting her long lashes as she looked me up and down.

"It wasn't until this very moment that I realized I deserve so much more. To think I was open to exploring shit with you. Now I know better."

She got up from the table and walked away. I pushed my chair back, stood, and followed her. She ended up walking outside. The smoke from her vape pen kept hitting me in the face as I trailed her all the way to her car. As she tried to open the door, I closed it.

"Jorja."

"Walker... move."

"Why are you tripping on me right now?"

"Because I was stupid enough to think that after all this time we've spent together, your feelings might have changed. We've literally done everything together for almost two years, Walker. I thought maybe you saw me as more than a piece of ass."

"I don't think you're just a piece of ass. You're my best friend, Ja."

"I don't want to be just a friend anymore! I want something meaningful. I'm not about to fight with you on that. I can take my L and move the fuck around. I let you get the milk without buying the cow for so long, and that's on me. I accept that. But what I won't do is accept *this* anymore. Take a good look."

She slowly spun on her heels before stopping face to face with me.

"Remember and relish in the last time you got some of this pussy. Treasure that memory because after tonight, that's all you have of me."

She pushed me out of the way and opened her car door.

"Jorja," I said as she climbed inside and closed the door.

The tint on the windows was so dark that I couldn't see inside. When she cranked up and "N.A.S" by Inayah blared through the speakers, I took that as my cue to back the fuck off. When women started that subliminal shit with music, things were bound to get petty. This wasn't the time or the place for it. Ja got mad at me all the time. She'd ignore me or mean mug me for a while, but it was never long before she was knocking on my door or hitting my line on some *come over* shit, and we'd make up.

That was our routine.

Even as I tried to convince myself otherwise, something about her goodbye felt so final. Jorja and I had never discussed being a couple. I had love for her. She was good people and like one of my homies. I never even entertained the relationship side of things because neither of us were on that type of time. That was established the day I met her.

We'd just left Aleviyah's apartment in search of food.

She was sitting in the driver's seat of her blacked-out BMW i7 looking good as fuck in those little ass shorts and tank top combo. I couldn't keep my eyes off her, especially those thick thighs and toned ass legs. I was glad the line at Rush's was long as hell because it gave me time to fully take her in.

The blue hairs growing from her scalp fit her perfectly.

She smirked as she looked over at me.

"You gon' stare all day?" she asked.

"Shit, I could. You know how fine your ass is, baby?"

"I do, actually." She had an air of arrogance, and that shit was so damn sexy.

"You must stay in the gym..." I said, touching her exposed thigh. "This body is fucking perfect."

"I'm a dancer."

"A stripper?"

"You know, stripping shouldn't be the first thing that comes to your mind when someone tells you they dance."

"I mean, I like strippers, so it's no problem."

"I like strippers, too, but I don't shake my ass on anybody's pole. I'm a professional, and you're gonna put some respect on my name."

I grinned. "I got something to put on your ass alright."

"Baby, you couldn't handle me. I'll have you somewhere in a corner sucking your thumb wondering where you went wrong. Your best bet is to keep you and ya lil dick away from me."

"Lil dick? You must not know about me, baby."

"Let me guess. You're the pretty boy, the self-proclaimed player and ladies' man. You probably have a roster full of women waiting to fuck on you, but you only keep a few in rotation, switching them out when you feel like it."

I smirked. "What makes you think that?"

She touched my nose with her fingertip. "Game recognize game, baby. I could see it in your eyes the moment you stepped into my sister's apartment. A man in heat is my favorite smell."

I licked my lips. "You nasty as hell, ain't you?"

"Wouldn't you like to know?"

That was the start of an almost two-year affair. At first, it was just sex. Somewhere along the line, we created an unconventional friendship. There was an unspoken love between us. I wouldn't say I was in love with her, but I did love her in a sense. I loved her enough to not want to hurt her intentionally. I loved her enough to fuck a nigga up if they stepped to her the wrong way. But again, I wouldn't say that I was *in* love.

Sighing heavily, I stepped away from her car and headed back inside. I'd leave her alone, for now, because I didn't want to ruin the good vibes of my brother's wedding. But eventually, she would come around... at least I hoped she would.

One

JORJA (GEORGIA)

Back at Walker's House

HE WATCHED me packing up my things from the doorway of his bedroom.

Once he left me in the parking lot, I decided to dip out early enough to get my shit and go home for good. For the last couple of months, I'd barely seen the inside of my apartment. I'd practically moved in over here, and that was proving to be a mistake.

After Cartel got shot, he was distraught. I could only imagine how he was feeling. If that had been my sister, I wouldn't have been able to function. I stayed with him to keep his mind right. Shit shifted between us. The more time I spent with him during that time, the more it felt like we were in a relationship.

Walker and I were always together. He was more than just my best friend. I didn't know when or how it happened, but somewhere along the line, I caught feelings. Maybe it was the fact that I went to sleep and woke up to him. Maybe it was because our families meshed, and we were always around each other. Or maybe it was because this man sexed me like crazy and it was always so damn good.

I found myself doing shit I never did before, and he just let it happen. For example, he allowed me to lay up on him in both public and private like he was my man. At any given time, no matter where we were, I could plant my ass on his lap. He could be mid-conversation, and his arm would slide around my waist, or he'd kiss my arm. I didn't even think that he was aware that he did it.

When we slept together, he was okay with being the little spoon. In fact, that was when we slept the most peacefully. We had inside looks. I wore his clothes. I had a key to his home and was free to come and go as I pleased. There were his and her sides of his bed, his closet, and his bathroom sink. The man kept all my favorite foods and snacks in stock at his house.

How was I not supposed to think I meant more to him than some pussy? Tonight solidified that the shit was all in my head. I saw what I wanted to see, and now I was paying the price for it emotionally.

"You just leaving?" he asked from the door.

"That's what it looks like."

"You really that mad at me, Ja?"

"I'm not mad at all, baby. I'm just enlightened."

I zipped up my suitcase and placed it by the door with the rest of them. Grabbing my duffel bag, I began tossing in all of my lotions, perfumes, hair products, and whatever other small things I'd stored here over time.

"I should have seen this coming," I mumbled as I moved around. "I was crazy to think there would ever be something between us."

"Jorja."

"Leave me the fuck alone, Walker. I just wanna get my shit and go home."

"Home? You been here for months. This might as well be your home. Stop tripping and put your shit back."

"Fuck. You."

He came over and snatched the bag from my hands.

"Walker, give me my shit."

"Not until you talk to me."

"What do I need to talk to you about? You made it very clear where we stand. We are moving in two different directions, and I don't have any more time to waste on a nigga that doesn't want me the way I want him."

"Whatchu mean I don't want you? You realize I've been dealing with you and only you, right?"

"That doesn't mean shit if there is no intent behind it. You say one thing and act another way. You brush off my feelings about us in front of your family, yet every time... every single time, you follow me, begging me not to leave you. You expect me to keep giving you some pussy with no commitment? Am I good enough to fuck but not good enough to claim?"

He rubbed his temples. "Ja... I really think you're being emotional right now because of the wedding."

"Emotional!" I yelled. "You think I'm being emotional about wanting to be more than a cum bucket? All the shit I've said about finding a man, you thought I was playing? I'm gonna show you better than I can tell you."

I snatched my bag back and grabbed two of my suitcases, storming out of the room. Quickly, I made my way down the stairs and out to my car, to throw them in. When I returned to the bedroom for the last suitcase, he was sitting on the edge of the bed with his elbows resting on his knees, watching me.

"Ja, can we talk about this? I'm sorry, okay? Just don't leave."

"I'm gone."

I grabbed the last suitcase and walked out of the room. I could hear his footsteps behind me on the stairs, but I didn't turn to face him. Instead, I headed straight out to my car, tossing the last suitcase in. As I opened the door to get in, he grabbed the top of it.

"So you're really leaving me?"

I scoffed. It was just like a nigga to keep asking obvious shit.

"To leave you, I'd have to first be yours."

"Come on, Ja. You know how I feel about you."

"I do. If I remember correctly, I'm just your friend... your nigga... a bitch you enjoy fucking. Now let me tell you something. I am so much more than the good pussy between my legs. Somebody will appreciate that."

After taking his key off my ring and throwing it at him, I climbed into my car and slammed the door. If he hadn't pulled back his hand in time, I would have taken off his fingers. He stepped back, shoving his hands in his pocket as I backed out of the driveway. I didn't look back, because if I did, I knew I was going to cry, and I hated to cry. Crying over a nigga made me feel like a weak bitch, and I was anything but that.

While I had it in my mind to go home, my car ended up taking me to my mama's house. The light was still on in her bedroom as I pulled into the driveway. Leaving everything but my keys in the car, I got out and headed up the front steps. Using my key, I let myself in and locked up before going up the stairs to her room. I gave a soft knock on the door and waited for her to acknowledge it.

"Come in."

When I opened the door, I found her sitting up in bed, reading a book.

"Jorja? What are you doing here, baby?"

I stood, shifting from foot to foot. In that moment, I felt like a little girl again. Any time I needed a hug, I could go to her or my granny and get all the love I could soak up. I was feeling emotional and vulnerable, and all I wanted her to do was hold me.

"What's wrong?" she asked, setting her book down.

"Can I sleep here tonight?"

"Of course you can, sweetheart. Come here."

I needed no further invitation. I closed her room door and kicked off my shoes before climbing in bed and wrapping my arms around her. My head rested against her chest. The moment she kissed my forehead, I broke. I could hear the confusion in her voice as she spoke.

"Did something happen, Jorja? Talk to me, sweetheart."

I couldn't get the words out through my tears, the same tears I didn't want to shed to begin with.

"Is it Walker?"

All I could do was nod.

"Did you have a fight?"

Again, I nodded.

She was quiet for a moment before she lifted my chin to meet her eyes.

"You finally came to terms with it, didn't you?" she asked. "You accepted that you had real feelings for him."

"Mommy, I feel so stupid!" I wailed. "I should have known he'd never see me as anything but a piece of ass. I don't even know why I wanted him to."

"Jorja... baby, it's okay to feel something for a man. It's okay to want love and companionship. You know what your problem is, Jorja?"

I sat up and crossed my arms, waiting to see what she had to say. I just knew she was about to call me out.

"You like having control over your heart, and you exercise that control with your vagina. I understand that may sound offensive, and I don't mean it that way. You don't want to catch feelings because you're afraid of commitment. You're afraid of getting hurt. I know love isn't supposed to hurt, but we don't all find our Prince Charming the first go round. You also don't find them by having meaningless sex for the sake of temporary pleasure."

She grabbed my hand.

"I'm proud that you are fiercely independent. I'm proud that you don't let anybody run over you. I'm proud of how confident you are. You are everything that I wasn't when Eric left. It's a blessing and a curse. You break your own heart when you tell yourself you don't need to feel anything for anybody. Everybody needs or at least *wants* somebody. That includes you."

"I don't want to want him."

She chuckled. "It's like that sometimes. You know when I knew this was going left? When you started making the boyfriend comments. Once is a joke. Several times? It means something."

"It means I should have left him alone. He told me I was being emotional because of the wedding. He invalidated my feelings. After two years of dealing with each other, he brushes my genuine feelings off as hormones. I don't have anything else to say to him."

"Well, y'all will be around each other because of the family. Take some time to cool off, and then talk to him without all the attitude and cursing, because I know you."

I rolled my eyes, causing her to playfully thump me.

"Don't roll your eyes at me. You ain't too grown."

I sighed. "I just don't see a conversation happening, Ma. I'm gonna treat him like any other man. When I see him, it's blinders up."

"That's not gonna solve anything."

"Maybe not, but I'm not talking to him. There's nothing he can say to make me come back again."

My mother sighed, knowing this was a losing battle.

"Get some sleep, Jorja. Mama is cooking tomorrow, and you know she likes to get up at the crack of dawn to go to the grocery store."

"Granny is always up with the chickens." I fell back against the bed. "I guess I can eat a good country dinner and then go work it off Monday morning."

"Girl, please. If I had your metabolism, I would eat what the hell I want. If I do that now, gravity will have its way with me. I can't walk around here with a saggy booty."

I giggled. "Ma, you know you thick fine. I saw the way those men were looking at your booty when you walked Liv down the aisle. You have a dump truck back there, woman."

"Take your ass to sleep," she said, turning over and shutting out the light in my face.

I laughed to myself as I turned over and snuggled close to her, draping my arm around her.

"I love you, Mommy."

"I love you too, baby."

I knew she was right about everything she told me.

I was afraid and for this very reason. I didn't remember my father when he was in my life. What I did remember was my mother having sleepless nights because she was up crying with worry. I remembered her working sometimes eighteen-hour days to make ends meet. I remembered being with my grandparents so much that I called my grandfather 'daddy' most of the time. It was all because of my father.

He left her, left us, and went on to live well without a care in the world about us or our well-being. He didn't care if we had food or shelter. He didn't care if we were sick or healthy. His focus was on the woman he left us for and their children. If it weren't for old pictures in a photo album, I wouldn't know what he looked like.

He knew who we were, however. Whenever we saw him in town, he quickly went the other way or looked right past us as though he expected any of us to say something to him. Imagine my surprise when I learned he lived in the same neighborhood as the Jareaus. I was driving through to their house one day when I pulled up to a stop sign. Just as I was about to turn, he came out of the house.

Our eyes met, and for a long time, he stared at me with a stupid ass look on his face. He took one step toward my car, yet the moment the front door opened, and his wife and younger children stepped out, he backtracked. That was the best thing for him to do. I was not above showing my ass if he'd said anything to me.

His absence taught me from a young age to never let a nigga have enough of me to hurt me. I broke my own code when I met Walker Jareau. I went further with him than I did with any guy. He knew personal things... intimate things. He knew *me* intimately. I willingly gave him all the ammunition because our chemistry was so fire and natural. Now it was blowing up in my face.

Leaving tonight was the best thing for me to do.

I couldn't just wean myself off of him like a drug. I had to stop cold turkey. What could be so hard about that?

Four Months Later

Two

WALKER

CLUB VEGAS WAS LIT.

The women were rolling deep through here tonight. Titties were up, ass was out, and they were on twerk team status on the dance floor. Ass was shaking everywhere, and I was loving it. Besides. My baby brother Reese, my boys Savon and Mikel, and I were posted up in the VIP section, popping bottles and passing a blunt around as we vibed to the music.

"Man, where are the type of women I like?" Reese asked with a frown.

"Here you go with that shit," Savon said, kissing his teeth. "They are at home in their house dress with their bonnets on."

Reese shoved him. "Fuck you. You act like I'm out here dating somebody's granny. I just like my women a little seasoned."

I laughed as I took a shot of Patrón to the head.

His women weren't grandmothers, per se, but they were definitely somebody's mama. I had to give it to him, though. They may have had years on him, but every one of them was a bad muthafucka. He almost had me reconsidering my own taste.

"Seasoned like Ms. Alicia?" I asked, referring to Liv's mama.

He grinned. "Just like that, with her fine ass. She still thinks I'm playing with her. I want her, and I'm gonna get her."

"Didn't she already curve you?" Savon asked.

"I'm gonna wear her down, eventually."

"Alright, now. Liv and Jorja are gonna fuck you up about their mama," I said.

He kissed his teeth. "Whatever." He looked out onto the dance floor. "Speak of the devil. There's Jorja right there."

I followed his gaze to see Jorja grinding her ass up on some nigga, in a dress so short that if she bent over, those cheeks would show.

Jorja Sandifer...

My not so sneaky, sneaky link. I met her when her sister, Aleviyah, was hired as my brother Jamison's nanny. We'd been fucking with each other heavy ever since. Shit was cool until about four months ago, when she told me she was tired of the same old routine, and she wanted something serious. The confession threw me for a loop, because Jorja had been adamant about being single for a while to come.

That was fine with me.

It meant no expectations. If I was being honest with myself, I had love for her; I just wasn't trying to settle down. I was a successful, twenty-eight-year-old black man. I didn't have any kids and no crazy baby mamas. I ran an award-winning physical therapy clinic, in addition to having a contract with the local university athletic department.

Life was good. Money was plenty.

I could come and go as I pleased.

Why would I want to give that up?

Besides, she'd told me too many times that I wasn't ready for what it would take to make her my woman anyway, so why was she upset? She hadn't even been the settling down type when I first met her. She was just like me. She liked to fuck, and I liked to fuck her. I mean, I even cut off the rest of my hoes to fuck with her exclusively. That in itself was a commitment, because my house had somewhat of a revolving door.

Women were always in and out.

Some of them knew about each other, some didn't. I never sugar-coated anything. I never gave false hope that things would be more than they were. I just did me, and that was that. Those who were cool with the arrangement stuck around; those who weren't kept it pushing. One thing was for certain: Nobody was held against their free will.

I kissed my teeth. "Forget her," I said, taking another shot to the head.

"You ain't hitting that no more?" Mikel asked.

"Nah. She decided she wanted a commitment, and I ain't ready for that right now."

"So she's single?"

I frowned. "Not to you."

He laughed. "So you don't want her, but you won't let me have her?"

"Chill with that shit," Reese warned him. "She's family. Sis ain't no fucking pass around. When you look at her, think of Alaina and how I'd bust you in yo' shit if you ever tried her."

Mikel held up his hands in surrender. "I hear you, bruh."

"Make sure you do," I said, glaring at him.

Just because she wasn't fucking with me anymore didn't mean that I would just pass her off to the next nigga or let them talk crazy about her. I focused my gaze back on the dance floor. Jorja was fucking it up out there. I loved to watch her dance. She moved so fluidly, doing calculated routines. Many times, I'd gone to the dance studio to watch her and her team practice.

All of them were good, but Ja was a beast. She danced like it was her life source. In fact, she had recently taken on the job of assistant coach to my niece's dance team. Last year, she'd gone on tour with a few big-name acts. I heard through the grapevine that she'd been offered a choreographing gig. Shorty was really doing her thing, and I was proud of her.

I could see why she wanted something stable. I just couldn't give it to her right now. I did miss her mean ass though. Aside from sexual compatibility, she was one of my best friends. She knew me inside and out. I would never lie and say we didn't have great chemistry. If I had to choose a woman to call myself being serious with, it would definitely be her. Who couldn't use a lover and a homie wrapped in one?

She didn't have to cut me off completely the way she did. I'd been in my feelings about it for a minute, and seeing her brought me right back to them. My feet involuntarily moved before I could stop myself. I left the VIP section, my boys and my brothers calling my name. Making my way to the dance floor, I maneuvered through the crowd toward her.

When she saw me advancing, she frowned and walked in the other direction. I almost lost her in the sea of people, but I managed to catch her by the bathroom.

"Jorja," I said, gently taking her elbow.

She snatched away. "Walker, get the fuck out of my face," she spewed venomously.

"You still treating me like an ain't shit ass nigga."

"Baby, I'm treating you accordingly."

I sighed. "I miss you, Ja."

"Good. Miss me with that bullshit while you're at it."

"You out here acting like we weren't friends, Jorja. Just 'cause you don't wanna fuck me no more, don't mean we can't be friends..."

She laughed. "It means exactly that."

"That's backwards as hell."

"Walker, you know what I realized? We were never really anything but two people who enjoyed sex with each other. Nothing between us was real or serious, and it's now painfully obvious. I set myself up the moment I met you. You were supposed to be a quick fuck. I was never supposed to feel shit for you because you are incapable of ever being anybody's man, let alone a friend."

That shit was like a stab in the heart. Maybe I wasn't the same for her, but I genuinely thought of her as my best friend. She kept shit real with me. We clicked and vibed on a level I never connected with anybody else on. I could deal with not fucking her, but I still missed my homie.

"How you gon' say that shit to me, Ja?"

"The same way I'm saying this... Leave me alone. I'm done with you, this, and us. Don't talk to me when you see me. Stop calling me. Stop texting me. We have nothing to talk about."

Without another word, she pushed the bathroom door open and went inside, leaving me standing there with my ego in my hands. I'd never been dismissed like that. Most of the time, it was me giving women the boot. I had to admit, it didn't feel good at all. Picking my face up off the floor, I walked back into my section.

"I take it that didn't go so well?" Reese said, noticing my face.

"She trippin'."

"She tripping, or is she sticking to her guns?"

"She's really done with me, dawg."

"I mean, y'all had a good run. It lasted longer than I expected it to, especially after Liv and Jay got engaged."

"It's cool; whatever. Women come a dime a dozen. She can easily be replaced."

Reese chuckled. "That's the hurt talking. Pops and Jay both would tell you every woman ain't replaceable. If you didn't feel something for her, you wouldn't be in your feelings right now."

I waved him off.

I wasn't trying to hear that shit. Nobody said I had to be in a rush to settle down. I wanted to enjoy life to the fullest, whether it be traveling the world, partying every weekend, or enjoying the company of multiple women. The player in me just wasn't ready to retire yet.

* * *

I MADE it back to my house around two.

I was fucked up and still in my feelings. After Jorja dismissed me, I spent most of the night just watching her. Niggas were flocking to her, and for a while, she was turning them down like pages, all except one of them. For the last two hours, she allowed him in her space. I watched with a frown as she laughed and talked with him. Her hand was flirtatiously placed on his knee while he held the other one.

The more he leaned into her, the more shots I took to fight the urge to go snatch him up. It didn't help that they were in a section just a few spaces down from ours. I'd finally had enough and told my brother I was ready to go. It was a good thing he was driving because I was too fucked up to get behind the wheel.

I stumbled into my house and made it upstairs to my bedroom. After discarding my clothes, I hopped in the shower to sober up. A good thirty minutes later, I was drying off and lying in my bed, ass naked. My dick was rock hard, and I couldn't sleep like that. I thought busting a quick nut in the shower would have done the trick, but I was mistaken.

Reaching for my phone, I scrolled through my contact list, trying to decide who would all be up this time of night. I settled on Merissa. She was usually out with friends at this hour, so I was sure she'd be awake. I pressed the call button and waited for her to answer.

"I know the fuck you ain't calling me," she said on the third ring.

"Don't be like that, Riss."

"Don't be like what? You cut me off, remember? What happened?"

"Ain't nothing happened. I just wanted some company."

"You wanted some pussy."

I shrugged. "That too."

She laughed. "I can't believe you. You have a lot of nerve."

"You don't miss me, Merissa? You don't miss the way this dick used to have you climbing the walls?"

"If you would have asked me that a year ago, I might have said yes, Walker. The thing is, I've grown and evolved into a grown ass woman. I did some soul searching. I got the therapy I needed, and I realized my self-worth isn't tied to my pussy. I found a man that makes me feel good about myself and good about being with him. So no, I don't miss you or that demon dick. You can take me off your roster. Call your other hoes."

She hung up in my face, leaving me stunned.

I guess I deserved that. I didn't bother to call back or call any other number, as I was sure I'd get different variations of the same "Fuck you." Tossing my phone on the dresser, I closed my eyes and rested my head against the pillow. Maybe the player in me wasn't ready to throw in the towel, but from the looks of it, I might not have much of a say in the matter.

Three

JORJA

"JORJA, I know you don't have my baby on this stripper pole!" Liv exclaimed as she walked into my apartment. "Anais, get down!"

"Relax, sis," I said as I helped my niece flip from the pole and onto her feet. "She's learning muscle control and stability. She's gonna need both if she's gonna be the baddest dance captain Millwood High has ever seen."

My baby had been working hard. She was a freshman in high school now and had just made captain of the junior dance team. I was such a proud auntie. I'd been waiting for Liv to have kids, and she blessed me with four of the sweetest babies with the Jareau children. I could see why she loved them so much.

"See, Mama Liv. She gets it." Anais slapped me five.

"I get it," Liv said, hands on her hips. "Keep the pole work to a minimum. And, Anais, don't even think about asking your daddy for one."

Anais laughed. "Daddy would have a whole conniption, and then my uncles would get involved. I don't want that smoke."

"Good." Liv waddled over and took a seat on the couch.

"You are getting big, boo," I said, sitting next to her and rubbing her belly. "Hey, Titi baby!"

She was almost six months pregnant with baby Jareau number five. Pregnancy looked so good on her. She was practically glowing.

"I feel big too," she said, rubbing circles on her belly. "This little boy is gonna be as big as his daddy."

"Well, you like climbing trees, so it was inevitable—"

She slapped my arm. "Jorja, how many times do I have to tell you to watch it in front of the kids."

"I'm not a kid, Mama Liv," Anais protested. "I'm a young lady. And talking about sex is healthy. I take sex education, so I know all about climbing trees."

"You better keep it at just knowing and not experimenting," I warned her. "I like to fight, and them little boys are no exception."

Anais playfully rolled her eyes. "You two are definitely sisters. Boys are the last thing on my mind."

I shook my head. "That won't last. You have to be careful with them, Anais. Boys will tell you one thing and show you another. Never let them take advantage of your heart. And never let them talk you into anything you're uncomfortable with."

"I know, Auntie Jorja. Mama Liv and Daddy stress that to me all the time."

"I know they do, boo. You're just a beautiful girl. When you start showing interest in boys, make sure you give your attention to the one that wants you for more than your looks. Even if you're only fourteen, you have so much more to offer them than your body. Take it from me... Know your worth and act accordingly."

I stood to go into my kitchen before I started crying... again. My apartment was open concept, so it wasn't like I could hide from them in there. I just needed a little space.

"Anais, why don't you go wait in the car," Liv said. "Your aunt and I need a moment alone."

"Yes, ma'am." She packed up her things and came to hug me. "I love you, Auntie Jorja."

"I love you too, baby."

I kissed her forehead then released her. She walked out of the kitchen as Liv walked in.

"You wanna tell me what that was about?" she asked, standing next to me.

"I saw him again Friday night, Liv."

"Why don't you just talk to him, Ja?"

"And say what?"

"For one, that you miss him."

"I don't care that I miss him. I have to stick to my guns. Walker doesn't want a relationship, and I've never been the bitch to beg a nigga to act right or want me. I don't need him in my life that bad."

"You know he's gonna be around. I mean, we came into his family, not the other way around. I'm not saying you need to be with him. I'm saying get closure. You abruptly cut him off without getting everything you needed to say off your chest."

"I said too much to begin with, girl. I knew his ho ass wouldn't take anything seriously. We were once the same. I know the game because I played it for so long. Watching you…"

I paused for a moment to regulate my emotions. I hated feeling like this. Once I got myself under control, I continued.

"Watching you fall in love with the man of your dreams and being welcomed into a beautiful little family all your own… it made me soft. I realized the way I was moving wasn't fulfilling to me anymore. I wanted something solid. I wanted a love of my own."

"You deserve that."

I could feel the tears stinging my eyes.

"Why did I think I could have that with him, Liv? Almost two years have passed. I haven't been with another man because I've been so wrapped up in Walker fucking Jareau. He did all the boyfriend shit without ever having the intention of being my man. That man paid my rent for the entire year, to take the burden off me. He came to my practices and my shows. He rubbed my feet or gave me full body massages when I was practicing extensive routines. He cooked for me or made sure I ate. The man did so much for me, Liv. What else was I supposed to think other than he had real feelings for me?"

"I honestly think he does have real feelings, Ja."

"Not real enough to change. He doesn't want to be tied down. I said that shit to him when I first met him. Why buy the cow when you get the milk for free? He enjoyed all the perks without the commitment or the title. If he wanted to fuck another bitch at any moment, he could have because I wasn't his girl. I allowed shit to continue, even when I knew I was catching feelings. That's my fault. Now look at me—in love with a man that can't and won't love me like I need him to."

"Wait... you love him?"

"Yes, I love him, Aleviyah." I wailed, dropping my head back. "Ms. Nina was right. I couldn't keep sleeping with him and not catch feelings. I love him, and I hate it."

Liv pulled me into her arms, hugging me tightly.

I had never uttered those words to a man. I hadn't even uttered them to him, and I wouldn't dare say it now. I spent the last four months trying to get him out of my system. I stopped going over to his house after I took all of my shit from over there. I didn't answer his calls or text. Any time we were in each other's presence, I looked right through him.

Then the other night, he admitted he missed me.

Part of me felt like he wanted to say more, but I couldn't wait around for him. We'd been dealing with each other long enough for him to say what he was really feeling. He knew me. He knew me better than any man. That was the shit that hurt. Why go through the trouble of getting to know the ins and outs of Jorja Monae Sandifer if he wasn't going to use it properly?

I pulled away from my sister and wiped my face.

"I'm sorry. I'm crying all over you."

Liv waved me off. "I've had snot and throw up on me, girl. Tears are the least of my worries." She took my hands in hers. "You deserve happiness, little sister. You deserve the kind of love you want and need. If you can feel love for Walker, you can feel it for another man, one that knows what he has when he has you."

I sniffed and smiled faintly. "You're such a mom these days."

She laughed. "I really am. And a mother's work is never done. I need to get home. My pot roast should be done in the slow cooker, and my kids are gonna act like they haven't eaten all damn day. I'll call you later."

"Okay."

She pulled me in for another hug. "I love you, Jorja."

"I love you too, Liv." Stooping down, I rubbed and kissed her belly. "See you later, Titi's baby."

She left the kitchen, and a few seconds later, I heard the front door close. I sighed as I retrieved a glass from the cabinet and poured me a nice helping of wine. Sauntering back into my living room, I began to clean up from my session with Anais. Liv's words played over in my head. I could find love with a man who knew what he had when he had me.

She was right.

I'd done a lot of growing. I learned myself over and learned to love myself more. I'd had my fun... sometimes too much fun, and now I was ready to focus on the future. I deserved someone who was ready for the same thing. At this point, I had to put Walker and the time we spent together out of my head. That was a done deal.

My king was out there, and whether I found him or he found me, I needed to be free of the hold I allowed Walker Jareau to have on me.

* * *

TODAY WAS the day of Cartel and Adina's baby shower.

My good sis was ready to pop. From the back, she looked normal, but baby, when she turned to the side, she was all belly. It was crazy that the doctor misread her ultrasound. She was actually further along than we initially thought. She was due any day now, and those twin girls were wearing her down. I watched her with an almost euphoric look on her face as Cartel stood behind her, lifting her stomach to give her back some relief.

"That's gonna be you in a few months," I told Liv.

We were sitting on the tree swing that hung in the backyard at the Jareau estate. The yard was packed full of people. Adina's family had come up from Charleston. The staff from Cartel's restaurant was here along with some of Adina's non-profit workers. Isaac, the family lawyer, and Dino and Jefferson, Adina's former security, were in attendance as well. Of course, the entire Jareau clan was here, and so were my mama and granny.

"Girl, that's me now," she said, rubbing her belly. "I feel like a damn whale."

"Maybe you should have swallowed," I jested.

She playfully pushed me. "I swallow plenty, thank you. You see how clear my skin is?"

I had to laugh at her. Before meeting Jamison, she was an avid spitter. I guess the nasty doctor turned her all the way out.

"Look at them," she whined. "They look so happy."

"After all that shit, they deserve it. That right there is pure, unconditional love. Must be nice."

I knew that last part sounded a little bitter, but I really was happy for them. They had gone through hell and high water to stand in this moment. It was absolutely something worth celebrating. I couldn't wait to love on their girls. My baby fever had been out of control for months now. Going through hers and my sister's pregnancies at the same time, was a journey for myself.

I got to go on shopping trips and helped decorate baby rooms. I got to help them come up with names. I rubbed on their stomachs and talked to the babies as much as they allowed. I was simply in love with the fact that they had created lives. At twenty-six, I never thought I'd be looking forward to experiencing that myself.

Before I found my way into this family, I was all about Jorja. Of course, I loved my mama, my sister, and my granny. I'd go to war behind any of them. But my main focus in life was my dance career and making my money. Dancing came easy, and because of that, the money came easy. People assumed that when I said I danced, I was a stripper.

While I knew my way around a pole, I never took my clothes off for money. I didn't knock the girls who did because I'd thrown dollars at some bad bitches twerking their ass on stage. It just wasn't me. I was a trained dancer, studying at Art in Motion Dance Studios since I was twelve. I was proficient in modern, contemporary, ballet, dancehall, and hip hop. Honestly, I could dance to anything.

That was why I ended up in the club the other night. I just wanted to dance and feel good. I went by myself and ended up running into a few girls I danced with on occasion. The last person I was expecting to roll up on me was Walker. I was under the impression that he finally got the hint that I was done with him. My mistake.

Seeing him stirred up everything I tried to bury.

Even while with the guy I sat with for two hours, talking to me, I could feel his eyes on me. I saw him when he left, looking like a puppy with his tail tucked between his legs. He was obviously bothered. I half expected him to show his ass like he did any time men openly flirted with me. I had to shake my head. He didn't want to be my man but didn't want anyone else to be mine either.

Make it make sense.

"Anyway!" I said, clasping my hands together. "I'm starving, and I'm trying to sneak some of those meatballs Granny brought over here. You want anything, baby mama?"

"No. I'm about to go find my man so he can rub my feet. I'll catch up with you."

"Okay, boo."

I snuck over to the food table, searching for the pan of meatballs. My eyes lit up with excitement as I found them. It might have been fat of me, but I grabbed one of the plastic drinking cups and filled it to the brim before covering the pan back up.

"Whatchu doing?" came a deep voice from behind me, causing me to jump.

I turned to see Alaina doubled over in laughter. She'd been coming home a lot more the past year, and we'd grown pretty close. That was my boo, and I loved her. It was a vibe every time we linked up.

"Bitch, don't do that," I said, my hand over my heart. "You scared me."

"You over here sneaking food and shit."

"That edible is kicking in." I picked up a fork and popped a meatball into my mouth. "How long are you here for this time?"

"I don't even know, girl. I've been here so much this past year that I'm considering moving back."

"You should! I miss you. I know your parents and your brothers miss you."

"I miss you guys too. My brothers only want me to come back to be a pain in my ass. How am I supposed to find a man with four overgrown, overprotective ass niggas behind me?"

I giggled. "Well, at least two of them will be too busy with new babies to really get in your business."

"That still leaves Tweedle Dee and Tweedle Dumb," she said, rolling her eyes. They landed on the back door. "Speak of the devil."

I looked up to Walker stepping out into the yard. A deep frown formed on my face when I realized he wasn't alone. At his side was a woman. She was pretty with beautiful, flawless, dark skin, a low haircut, big titties, and a fat ass. I couldn't even hate on her because she was gorgeous. He, however, wasn't shit for bringing her here. Who brought a date to a baby shower?

It wasn't until I heard the cup crumbling in my hand did I realize I was squeezing it.

"Breathe, boo," Alaina said, taking it from my hands. "Look at me."

I couldn't.

My eyes stayed trained on Walker. As though he sensed me watching him, he glanced in my direction. My frown deepened. He wanted to play games, and he was playing with the wrong bitch.

"You're gonna be down a sibling when I get my hands on him," I said, brushing past Alaina.

She grabbed my arm and pulled me back. "Remember where we are? This day is for Cartel and Adina. I know my brother is being petty right now, but don't ruin this baby shower over his ignorant ass."

"He's playing in my face right now, Alaina. Just the other week, he was begging me to talk to him. For a second, I thought maybe he was actually getting it. Maybe he was actually growing the fuck up, and now he's bringing a new bitch here?"

"He's just trying to get a rise out of you. Don't let him see you upset. I'm gonna go talk to him. Do not approach that girl, Jorja."

I kissed my teeth. "I'm not gonna bother her. She doesn't know any better. He damn sure does."

"He does."

"I'm not doing this shit."

"Just sit tight. I'll make him get rid of her."

"Don't even worry about it. Your brother is showing me who he really is. Fuck him."

I stormed off toward the house, brushing right past Walker and his toy. I needed a moment to gather myself, a moment to breathe, because if I didn't take it, I was going to flip my shit.

Four

WALKER

JORJA damn near took my shoulder off as she brushed past me to go into the house.

Right after, I saw my sister storming toward me, a scowl on her face. I rolled my eyes. I got that they were friends, but she needed to mind her business.

"You're in trouble," said Margo, the woman standing beside me.

"I got this."

Alaina stepped in front of us. Her eyes passed over Margo before she turned to me.

"I need to borrow my idiot brother for a minute. Let's go."

She grabbed me by my ear, just like our mother used to do when we were younger, and pulled me into a quiet section of the yard.

"Laina, let me go," I said, prying her fingers away.

She punched me in the chest. "What the hell are you doing?" she asked, crossing her arms.

"Whatchu mean?"

"Now you wanna *act* stupid too? Why would you bring that girl here, knowing Jorja was gonna be here? You really don't have the sense given to a fucking goat."

"You need to mind your business."

"My girl is my business."

"I'm your brother. You forgot that?"

"My grown ass brother that is acting like a teenager right now."

"Look, Ja don't wanna fuck with me. She stopped fucking with me four months ago. Why shouldn't I see anybody else? She was all up on niggas in the club. I watched her smiling up in some dude's face for damn near two hours, yet she gets to throw a temper tantrum because I brought a plus one here?"

"To a baby shower. This was family and friends only. This ain't the place to showcase your latest jump off."

"She ain't a jump off."

"What's her name?"

"Margo."

"How long have you known her?"

"Alaina, stay in your lane, baby sister."

"No. You need to stop acting like a fucking dick. Did you see Ja's face? That hurt her, Walker."

I wiped my hand down my face as I blew an exasperated breath.

I *did* see the hurt beneath the anger. I wanted to piss her off, not hurt her already hurt feelings. Ja had a way of getting all the way up under my skin. I was used to fighting with her and making up a few days later. It was toxic, I knew that, but it was what I'd become accustomed to. This was the longest she'd gone without coming back to me, and I was beside myself.

I hadn't even fucked Margo. She started working with me around the time Cartel started physical therapy, and she was an essential part of his care. She was cool people. On top of that, she was gay a fuck. I never even tried to get at her like that. Still, I knew what it would look like bringing her here. I wasn't about to disclose that to my sister though.

"Look," I said, shoving my hands in my pockets. "She doesn't want me. We're gonna be around each other because of our family affiliation. We might as well get used to seeing each other with other people. I'm done talking to you about this. Excuse me."

Turning on my heels, I walked back over to where Margo stood.

"You good?" she asked.

"I'm fine."

"Listen, I sense some tension, so I'm gonna go. I don't need anybody giving me dirty looks, and I'm too pretty to fight."

"You don't have to leave."

"Yeah, I do. Honestly, I feel like you brought me here to piss that girl off. Mission accomplished. I'm gonna go speak to Cartel and Adina, give them their gift, and then I'm leaving. I'll see you at work."

Without another word, she turned and walked away from me. I silently cursed under my breath as I headed inside to my father's bar area. I needed a drink to calm my nerves. As I stood pouring myself a glass of whisky, I heard the downstairs bathroom door open. A few seconds later, Jorja came around the corner, dabbing her eyes.

I set the bottle down. "Ja."

When she saw me, she frowned. "Leave me the fuck alone."

She tried to hurry out of the room, but I caught her in time to grab her arm. Immediately, I was met with a hard shove to the chest.

"You don't get to touch me!" she yelled. "Never touch me again."

"I just wanna talk to you—"

"Talk to your date. That's why you brought her here, right? To mix and mingle with the family? I find it funny that you were just begging me to give you the time of day, last week, and now today, you pop up in here with Big Titty Brittany. You think this shit is cute?"

"That wouldn't have been my best idea to get you to speak to me," I mumbled.

"So you admit it? Walker, grow the fuck up. That was childish as hell, but you know what? It's all good. These are the types of games you wanna play? Fine. You forget that I'm a player too, baby. But when I play, you're gonna feel that shit in your fucking chest. I promise you that."

"Jorja, I'm sorry, alright. Honestly, I just wanted to make you mad. I don't want that girl. Even if I did, she's gay. We work together, and she was a part of Cartel's therapy."

"That's the shit I'm talking about. You intentionally tried to fuck with me in a space where I couldn't act the fuck up. You take my feelings as a joke."

"I don't!" I yelled.

She crossed her arms and stared at me.

"Fuck, Ja! I miss you. It's been me and you for almost two years. I see you more than I see my damn blood. You're the only woman I deal with, and that in itself should tell your ass something. Come on, baby. You know this is what we do. We fight, we argue, we make up. That's us."

"I don't want that anymore! I want to be loved, not that toxic shit! I don't want to be some man's concubine for the rest of my life. I don't wanna settle for being good enough to fuck but not good enough to make someone's woman. And I don't want to be somebody's baby mama. I've changed, Walker. As easy as it would be to fall back into that toxic shit, my head ain't it, and I won't continue to leave my heart with you."

Her eyes passed over me before she walked away. I followed her movements to see Liv and Ms. Alicia standing at the back door, watching us. They both reached for Jorja, ushering her into the back room. Silently, I cursed myself. I was a whole fucking idiot.

* * *

IT WAS time for pictures with Cartel and Adina.

I wasn't in the mood to smile for the camera, but my mama had already thrown me *the look*, so I pulled myself together. Cartel rented one of those big ass throne chairs for her to sit in, and she'd been lounging in it all day. I could see why. Sis was about to tip over with that big ass belly. I was surprised the doctor hadn't put her on bed rest or my brother hadn't put his foot down.

Then again, from being around them as a couple the last almost year, he was putty in her hands. I'd never seen that nigga be so soft. He was happy, though, and I loved that for him. With all that shit that went down with her husband and us almost losing him, they both deserved to be happy.

"Hey, big mama," I said, leaning in to kiss Adina's cheek before kissing her belly.

"You're lucky I'm not hormonal right now," she said, thumping my head.

I chuckled. "You look beautiful today, sis. You glowing and shit."

"It's this heat. I'm sweating bullets. As soon as these pictures are done, I have to go in the house for a little bit. I need a nap."

"In other words," Cartel said, "pose your ass for these pictures so my baby can get comfortable."

"I'm here, nigga, damn."

The rest of our siblings, Jamison's bunch, and our parents joined us for this last shot. After a few clicks of the camera, we were done.

"Wait!" Adina said, halting the camera man. "I need one with just my girls. Where is my prego twin? Liv! Jorja! Come here!"

They made their way over, Aleviyah waddling the whole way. Cartel helped her into his chair, and she blew out a long breath.

"You are trying to take me out, girl," she said, playfully slapping Adina's hand.

"I've already said I'm taking a nap after this."

I shook my head as Cartel walked over to where I stood.

"You and your pimp walk are gonna catch hell trying to get her ass up off the couch," I said.

He playfully pushed. "Fuck you. If I'm still having issues, that's on you as my therapist."

"Nah, that's on you for not continuing the strength training regimen I created for you."

"Relax. I'm on my shit. I had to be after I almost dropped her ass."

"Bruh!"

He gazed at Adina with a grin. "Listen, pregnant sex hits different. That's all you need to know about that."

"I'll take your word for it."

"You could have been next, but you fucked that up." He looked over at me. "The fuck were you thinking bringing Margo in here?"

"Man, you know Margo is gay. That girl don't want me, and I can't have her."

"You know that, and I know that. Ja doesn't, so why would you do some childish ass shit like make it seem like more than it was?"

"Bruh, I literally stepped outside."

"You know what I'm talking about, Walk. The appearance of shit can get you fucked up. You're lucky Ja didn't spazz out on her or you."

35

"Trust me, I felt her anger," I said, rubbing my chest. "I still feel that shit."

"You better stop playing games before you're the one crying in a corner."

"I'm not crying over a female."

"Alright, but that one," he said, pointing at Jorja. "That one is gonna make a liar out of you, playa."

He slapped my shoulder as he walked away.

I stood watching the photographer snapping pictures of the four beautiful women. They were in their own little world, just smiling and laughing it up. Ja had a beautiful smile. It was one of my favorite things about her. Most of the time, she was the happiest person and always a vibe. It wasn't until this very moment did I realize her smile no longer touched her eyes. It was the same look I'd been seeing for months now.

Realizing it made me feel like the stankest piece of shit because I was the cause of that. Even more so, I realized there might not be any coming back from this.

"Ooooo!" Adina hissed, holding her stomach. "Cartel!"

He rushed to her side. "Contraction?"

"Yeah. I've been having them all day. That one really hurt."

"Maybe we should get you to the hospital."

"I'll be—Ooooo shit!"

"You're going."

He helped her to her feet. The moment she stood upright, her water broke.

"Oh shit!" I said, fist to my mouth.

Everybody started moving.

"Walker, help me get into the truck," Cartel said.

"I need my purse," Adina said. "It's upstairs."

"You get the purse, I'll put her in the car." I walked over and wrapped Adina's arm around my neck, scooping her up bridal style. "Come on here, big mama."

"I'm in pain and I will hit you," she said through gritted teeth as I started walking back toward the house. "You better not drop me."

"Nobody is gonna drop you, woman. You've got two of my future favorite people in there. I'll handle you with care."

"That's sweet, but Walker?"

"Yeah?"

"Walk faster before I deliver these babies in the car!"

I chuckled as I picked up my pace. I guess one silver lining for the day was being able to meet my nieces. If nothing else put me in a good mood, it was the kids in my family. No matter how much of a fuck up I was right now, to them, Uncle Walker was the shit.

Five

JORJA

CARMELLA AND CARINA JAREAU were absolutely beautiful.

As I sat holding Carmella, I fingered her head full of curly, jet-black hair. She was wide awake, looking up at me while she sucked on her fingers. My heart was bursting at the seam. She wasn't even my niece, yet the love I felt for her and her sister was just as potent as the love I felt for their cousins.

"You are absolutely precious," I said, gently stroking her cheek. "She's so chilled."

Adina giggled. "This one is the hell-raiser."

They had been home from the hospital for a week now and were slowly getting into a routine of doing things. Since I didn't work a full-time job, I split my free time between helping both Liv and Adina. Cartel was doing a load of laundry while we sat in the twin's room, chopping it up.

I looked up to see Adina standing at the changing station with Carina. "Girl, that ass is getting fat!"

She looked back at it. "Girl, you can thank these babies and their daddy for that. They made it from scratch."

"Your mommy's so silly," I said to Carmella. "How are you feeling? You are still glowing."

"I'm really happy, Jorja," she said, smiling. "Even with sleepless nights, leaking titties, and bags under my eyes, I'm really happy. I never knew I could love two little people as much as I love my babies. After having this taken away three different times, I just... I just wanna sit and stare at them all day long. They are my perfect labor of unconditional love."

"You're gonna make me cry," I said, wiping the corner of my eye.

She giggled. "You said thugs don't cry."

"Well this thug has been very emotional lately."

"Are you..."

"No, girl. I'm not pregnant. I'm just very overwhelmed with life right now."

"Walker?"

"Is it obvious?"

"Kinda. I hate this for you. I mean, I've seen you two together. You have amazing chemistry."

"Next to Liv, he was my best friend."

"You don't think you could still be friends?"

"Could you just be friends with a man you're in love with?"

"No, I couldn't. Wait... you're in love with him?"

"I've *been* in love with him, Dina. Ms. Nina told me a long time ago that I couldn't continue having sex with him and not develop feelings, but it's so much more than that. I was gonna tell him the night of the wedding, but then we had a fight, and it seemed pointless. Why tell him I love him if there is clearly no future between us? I've changed and he hasn't. We want different things now, and I don't want to settle or compromise anymore."

"You shouldn't. You deserve your heart's desires too. If you know he can't give you that, you shouldn't settle for what you *can* get from him. I will say, I feel like you two should have a heart to heart and get it all out so you can both move on."

"I know you're right..." I whined, tossing my head back. "Liv said the same thing. It's easier being mad at him. I won't fall victim to his charm, and by charm, I mean that fact that arguing with him used to turn me on once upon a time. I don't need to fall back into toxic shit. One minute we're arguing, the next, he's got me face down, ass up on some random piece of furniture. I haven't even had sex in four months, and that is a record for me. My coochie is mad as hell right now. Those toys aren't doing it for me anymore, boo."

She giggled. "Maybe you aren't doing it right."

"Trust me, I know what I'm doing. It's just not satisfying. After almost two years of top tier penis, a substitute isn't cutting it."

"Whoa, whoa, whoa!" Cartel said, stepping into the room. "I don't wanna hear nothing about my brother's dick."

"Well, you shouldn't have been ear hustling," I said, moving Carmella to rest on my chest.

"I wasn't. You just have no filter."

"You're just figuring this out?"

He kissed his teeth. "Give me my baby." He came over to scoop her up. "Hey daddy's pretty girl," he said, kissing her little cheeks. "You hear your loud-mouthed auntie?"

I smiled. It felt good that he recognized me as their aunt, even if I wasn't.

"Switch with me?" Adina said. "She's done."

He carefully switched out the babies. Carina was a little fussy as he maneuvered her around to take off his shirt.

"I can hold her," I offered.

"I got it."

He managed to get the shirt off and rested her on his chest where she immediately stopped crying.

"That's daddy's princess right there," he said, grinning. "You love skin to skin, don't you?"

"Can I just say the softie in you is adorable?" I asked as I relocated to the floor, allowing him to sit with his daughter.

He frowned. "Nigga, I ain't soft."

Adina giggled. "Baby, with me and these girls, you're puddy."

"Y'all trying to play me. You see this, Carina? Your mama and your auntie are some haters."

There was that word again. This time when he said it, I teared up. What the fuck was wrong with me?

"You good, Ja?" Cartel asked.

"I'm fine. I'm just... I'm really honored that you see me as their auntie. Other than my mama and Granny, Liv and I don't really have much family, at least not that we are close to. I've grown to love this family so much."

"Which is why you'll always be their aunt," Cartel said. "No surrogate, no play auntie, just auntie. I appreciate you, Ja. My nieces and nephew took to you, and kids know good people. You welcomed my lady with open arms, and you were right there her entire pregnancy. Why wouldn't I let my babies get in on some of that love?"

I was in full blown tears at this point. This over emotional side of me was sickening.

"You sure you're okay, Ja?" Cartel asked again. "I've literally never seen you cry. You sure you aren't pre—"

"I'm not pregnant!" I exclaimed, tossing my head back with a laugh. "Trust me. I've taken tests. I'm just emotional. All these babies and happy people are turning a thug soft. I guess... I've been re-evaluating myself in a sense. I'm on a journey of love and happiness."

"Well, we hope your journey is successful," Adina said. "Also, Carmella and Carina said they look forward to being the big cousins in the future."

That definitely wouldn't be in the near future. I was ready for a relationship, but dancing was still a huge part of my life. Now that I was coaching, I realized just how much I loved it as well. My girls were no joke. Sometimes they slacked off, but when they hit it, they hit hard. There was so much fire inside of them. I wasn't quite ready to put any of that on the back burner.

For now, I was fine with loving on everybody else's kids.

***

"ALRIGHT, girls. Run that for me one more time, and you're free to go."

They all groaned. We'd been practicing this routine for the last two hours. Some of them had it down, while a few of them still seemed to be struggling.

"Don't give me that. This is a team. One band, one sound. If one of you looks bad, all of you look bad. That means I look bad, and baby, that's one thing I don't do. From the top."

Murmurs went up amongst the twelve of them as they got into place.

"We can always do suicides," Coach Love said. Immediately, they quieted down. "That's what I thought. Now, like she said, from the top."

She started the track and counted them in. As I stood back observing each of my girls, I was surprised that they were all in formation this time around. I smiled to myself. I knew they were all capable; they just needed a little push. When they were done, Coach Love and I gave them a round of applause.

"That's what I'm talking about!" I said. "You dance like that next Saturday and you are sure to win first place."

That really got them smiling. The first competition of the year was coming up, and up until this point, I wasn't sure if they were even excited about it. This win could set the tone for their entire season, and I wanted greatness for them. Even though the twelve of them together worked my nerves at times, these girls were my babies.

"You're dismissed. Have a good weekend."

As they filed out of formation, the gym doors opened. I didn't pay it any mind because it was usually their parents or whoever was picking them up, coming to claim them. We had a strict policy. The girls had to be signed out of practice by someone on their approved list. It ensured that they showed up and that they got home safely.

"My my my," came a deep voice from behind me.

I squinted because it was vaguely familiar. Turning around, I was greeted by a tall, dark, and handsome man. I never forgot a face. Names, maybe, but never a face.

"I remember you. Um... the broadcaster?"

"Tyson... We met the other night at Vegas..."

I slapped my forehead. "That's right. Tyson."

He placed a hand over his heart. "I'm a little sad you forgot my name."

"I apologize. Charge it to the drinks. It's nice to see you. What are you doing here?"

"Oh, Millicent is my niece," he said, pointing her out.

"Really?"

"And you're her coach. Small world."

"Very small."

I couldn't help but look him up and down. The white button-up he wore looked so damn good against his chocolate skin. It was neatly tucked into a pair of brown dress slacks that hugged him in perfection. His hair was low cut and wavy, and I just wanted to run my fingers over it. Focusing back on his face, I admired his full lips and possibly the kindest eyes I'd ever seen. How could I forget him?

I shifted my weight from one foot to the other. "Um, you can sign her out," I said, handing him the clipboard.

He took it and scribbled his name down. "So, Ms. Jorja, I'm assuming you're still single?"

"You assume correct."

"Good for me. I let you get away at the club, but now that I have you, you think I could get your number? I'd like to take you out sometime."

I found my face heating up. He was so damn fine, and he was still a gentleman.

"Sure."

He handed me his phone, and I programmed my number in.

"I look forward to getting to know you," he said as I handed it back to him. "Are you busy this coming weekend?"

"Not that I can recall."

"Can I take you to dinner?"

My mouth hung open as I prepared to answer. "Sure. I'd like that."

"Do you have any allergies?"

"Oh no, baby. I just love food."

He chuckled. "Good to know. I love a woman that loves to eat. I'm a big boy, and my appetite can be hefty."

My eyes trailed him once more. "You wear it well."

It was his turn to blush. "It was nice seeing you, Jorja. Hopefully, after our date, I can talk you into seeing me more often." He gently grabbed my hand and kissed it. "I'll be in touch. Come on, Millicent."

He backed away from me with a smile that left me feeling all giddy and shit. I could feel eyes on me and turned to see Anais with a slight frown and Coach Love grinning at me.

"What?" I asked.

"Now that was a fine man," Coach Love said. "You know you have to be a bad bi—a baddie to pull a man that fine when you're covered in sweat."

"First of all, I met him when I looked like somebody, so he's seen me at my best."

"Did he ask you out?" Anais asked.

"He asked for my number."

Anais looked disappointed. She was rooting for her uncle and me. I hated to disappoint her, but that ship had long since sailed.

"Anyway, I have to get out of here. Come on, Anais. I'm dropping you off."

"Okay."

She sulked as she walked up ahead of me. My poor niece wanted love for everybody she held near and dear to her. I loved that she was so passionate, but love wasn't easy to come by. Some people spent their whole life searching for it and never found it.

Some had it and still didn't know what to do with it. And for some, love had hurt them. Love hurt me more than a few times. Even though I didn't remember much about my father, I had to believe I loved him at some point because what little girl didn't love their daddy? I realized my father had given me my first real heartbreak when I wasn't even old enough to process it.

He left when Liv and I were young and hadn't looked back. I didn't understand how a man could father children with one woman and then abandon them to raise a family with another. Furthermore, I couldn't understand how she could be okay with that shit. Bitches were just as trifling as these niggas.

In the car, Anais sat with a sad look on her face as she scrolled through her phone. Jamison mentioned she was a bit of an empath. I hated that she could feel so much of other's pain. It had to be exhausting.

"Talk to me, boo," I said.

"It's nothing, just... you're going on a date. I guess that means you're over Uncle Walker."

I sighed. "Baby... I'm gonna be real with you. I love your uncle, but we aren't any closer to getting it right than we were when we met. Sometimes, two people just aren't meant to be together."

"But you are. I feel it, Auntie Jorja. Just like with Daddy and Mama Liv."

"Liv and your father were kindred spirits. They belonged together. Walker and I feel toxic, and I don't want toxic love. It's draining. I'm ready for something he's not, and I can't force him to be. I don't want you dwelling on our situation. You're a kid—"

"I'm not a kid."

"A young woman," I corrected. "You should focus on school, dance, and becoming the beautiful human being you are. No matter what, you'll always have me. We're family."

That made her smile a little. The rest of the ride to her house, we made light conversation. By the time we pulled in the yard, she seemed to be in better spirits. We said our goodbyes, and I watched her walk inside before heading home to give myself a much-needed self-care session. As I drove, I thought back to Tyson.

He seemed like a nice guy, but then again, that was based off a two-hour conversation in a club with plenty of liquor between us. Of what I remembered, he was a news broadcaster. When he told me his name, it clicked because my Granny was forever raving about the good-looking broadcaster on the morning news. In the two hours I spent talking to him, I remembered getting to know a lot about him.

I didn't remember half of it now because, once we parted ways, I was taking back-to-back shots. By the time I got home, I passed out and didn't remember much else. Maybe this was the universe giving us a chance to do it over. I'd just have to wait and see if he'd call me. Maybe a date was just what I needed.

Six

WALKER

I BLEW a breath as I knocked on Margo's door.

She'd been avoiding me at work since the baby shower, and honestly, I couldn't blame her. We were pretty much done with the morning sessions we had, and there was about a two-hour window before our afternoon appointments began rolling in. I decided I was going to apologize for bringing her to the baby shower in the first place. Other than my own selfish agenda, Cartel wouldn't have minded her coming.

The door opened, and Margo stood with a frown on her pretty face.

"What?"

"Can I rap to you for a minute?"

"I'm kind of busy, Walker. Is it work related?"

"It's personal."

"Then you can catch me on personal time, *if* I have it to spare."

She tried to close the door, but a set of long nails stopped it.

"Baby, that's rude!"

A short pecan tanned beauty stepped around her, buttoning her shirt. Baby was one of the most beautiful women I'd ever seen. She looked at Margo with a hand on her hip.

"If the man is bringing it to you at work, it might be important. I should get going anyway."

"You don't have to leave, baby," Margo protested.

"I have to get back to work anyway." She cupped her face and gave her a kiss so nasty that even I knew what they were in here doing. "I'll see you at home and we can finish... this."

She winked at her before turning to me. "Nice to meet you, Mr....?"

"Jareau. Walker Jareau, and you are?"

"Lacey, Margo's girlfriend... I'm sorry, fiancée." She wiggled a ringed finger in my face. "You two play nice. Behave, baby."

She blew Margo a kiss before heading out of the office. Margo stared at me for a moment then kissed her teeth.

"Come in."

She opened the door wider, and I stepped in. The first thing I noticed was the disarray on her desk. She reached for the container of disinfectant wipes.

"Were y'all—"

"Minding our grown, gay ass business."

I raised my hands in surrender. "Duly noted. Look, Margo, I wanted to apologize for the baby shower."

"Tell me specifically what you are apologizing for. 'Cause if I remember correctly, you allowed your ex to think that we were fucking."

"I didn't let her think we were fucking."

"You allowed her to create a narrative in her head, Walker. What if that girl had attacked me? Then I would have been well within my rights to sue your ass."

"I know, and I'm sorry. I cleared it up after you left."

"I'd be more impressed if you cleared it up before then."

I was quiet as she wiped down her desk and rearranged her items before sitting.

"You're right," I finally said. "I wasn't shit for that, and I apologize. I also apologize for perpetuating a hostile work environment. No matter how fucked up my personal life is right now, this is my business, and I take it very seriously. You're an asset to my team, and I never want you to feel uncomfortable here. From the bottom of my heart, I'm sorry."

Her face relaxed some.

"Just so we are clear, if it happens again, I'm gonna own this place."

"Understood."

"Be honest with me. What in the hell would make you think that would work? What kind of women are you dating?"

"We weren't dating. We had more of a friends with benefits type of deal for a while…"

"For a while? How long is a while?"

"Almost two years."

She hurled a stress ball at my head. "You are an idiot, you know that? Just like most men, you think with your dick. How many women do you know that are going to continue to allow you to penetrate them with no commitment?"

"She was on the same shit, Margo. That's why I don't know why she's tripping."

"Don't give me that. As a woman, I can tell you we give signs, even when we don't directly tell you. How many times has she shown you she wanted more from you, and you just brushed it off like y'all tend to do?"

I was quiet. She was already reading me, and I couldn't dispute anything she said.

Margo smirked as she leaned forward. "You're very quiet. How long has she not been fucking with you, Walker?"

"Four months."

"And you miss her?"

"I do."

She kissed her teeth. "So you couldn't just tell her you missed her without doing the shit you did?"

"She will barely talk to me, Margo. If she does, it's always to tell me how done she is."

Margo shook her head. "Then maybe you should try doing some shit you've never done. Like listening and being honest with yourself to start with. For a man with book smarts, you lack common sense."

"Are you calling me stupid?"

"Stupid is as stupid does. Now, if you would please get out of my office, I want to enjoy my actual lunch."

"So Lacy wasn't your lunch?"

"She's breakfast, lunch, dinner, the snack in between, and dessert."

"I hear you, playa." I stood and walked to the door. "I didn't think you went for pretty girls, Margo. I always saw you liking studs."

"Pretty girls like pretty girls. Bye, Walker."

I chuckled as I left her office and headed out to my Range Rover to go find me something to eat. I had a taste for barbeque, and I had a coupon in here somewhere. As I dug through the glove compartment, I found it, along with one of those photo booth pictures of me and Jorja. We'd gone with Liv and Jamison to take the kids to the fair. She was like a big ass kid, wanting to get on rides and eat all kinds of weird ass food.

I entertained her, and we actually had a good time. After we ate that edible and I relaxed, I was down for most anything she wanted to try, even squeezing my big ass in that tiny ass booth. She ended up sitting on my lap, striking various poses. One was a little provocative. There was one of us showing off our slugs. In the third picture, I was giving my best mean mug as she looked at me, smiling. The last one was what felt like a gut check. She held my face in her hands, and her lips were pressed against mine.

I remembered how many times she kissed me like that in the months before she cut me off. I remembered the longing in her eyes and how gentle she was. It was crazy that I could vividly play those kisses back in my head but didn't notice it while they were happening. I couldn't pinpoint when shit in our relationship shifted, but now that she wasn't fucking with me at all, maybe it was time to reevaluate things. Her not being in my life at all wasn't feasible.

We were family at the end of the day.

The problem was, even if I wanted to, I'd burned the bridge to going back to being anything but that.

* * *

AFTER FINISHING UP A LATE APPOINTMENT, I decided I was going to try one last time to talk to Jorja. She'd been on my mind all day, and I was going to drive myself mad if I didn't say something to her soon. It was Tuesday, and I knew she would be at the dance studio prepping for an upcoming homecoming show she was dancing in.

Knowing Ja, when she was in dance mode, she forgot to eat. I stopped and picked up her favorite wing combo and a few of her favorite snacks before heading to the studio. I was prepared to be cursed out, but I was also prepared to make my case. As I pulled up to the two story building, I could see her going hard from the window. For a moment, I sat watching her.

I'd sat on that floor watching her practice more times than I could remember. I especially remembered the times when she'd made me part of her routine, and it ended with us getting busy all over the dance floor. There would be none of that tonight though. I'd be lucky if she let me in the door.

Hopping out of my Range with the bag, I headed inside.

"Under the Influence" by Chris Brown was now blasting from the second floor as I made my way upstairs. From the door, I could see Jorja sliding, grinding, and winding across the floor. I just stood there watching, captivated by the fluidness of her movements. This was one of my favorite songs, and the way she danced to it had me in a trance. So much so that I didn't even notice when she cut the music.

"What are you doing here?" she asked, storming over and grabbing my hand, pulling me back to the stairwell.

"I wanted to ask you to give us a chance to talk about things."

"I don't have anything left to say, Walker."

"Well I do. I have a lot to say."

"I'm busy."

"I know. I know your schedule. I also know you probably haven't eaten, so I brought you your favorites."

I handed her the bag. She snatched it, opening it to look inside.

"You think wings and a few snacks is going to grant you an open invitation back to me?"

"No, I don't. I just wanted to make sure you ate. I know how hard you push yourself in here, and I don't want you to pass out from not having anything on your stomach. That's all."

She looked at me with a frown. "Thank you."

"No problem. Can I call you tonight? If you aren't too tired, maybe I could come over and we talk?"

"You mean come over so you can finesse me out of my panties?"

"Just to talk. On my mama, I just wanna talk."

I stepped closer, taking her hand. Much to my surprise, she didn't pull away. She didn't flinch or curse at me for touching her. She simply looked at me with hurt in her eyes... hurt that was because of me. That fucked with me. If she gave me the chance to say what I needed to say, I wouldn't fuck it up this time.

"Please, Ja."

Her face softened. "Fine. I'll text you when I leave here."

I dropped her hand and gently cupped her chin. "Thank you."

Leaning in, I place the most tender kiss dangerously close to her lips. If I was sure she would have gone for it, I would have kissed them. Fuck... I missed kissing them.

She shuffled in her stance. "Drive safe," she mumbled as she walked off back into the studio.

For a moment, I stood in the stairwell, giving silent thanks to God. Getting her to talk after all this time was nothing short of a miracle. I just hoped that she was open to talking. It would be just my luck to let her get me alone and then she beat my ass.

Seven

JORJA

I WAS dog ass tired by the time I left the studio.

It was only around eight, but it felt so much later. All I wanted to do was get home, wash my ass, and lie up in my king-sized bed with all seven of my throw pillows. This was a busy week. I had a performance Friday night, so my team and I were hitting the studio every day to practice. Anais's dance team had their competition Saturday morning, so we were having extra practices this week to prepare.

My body was so sore as I walked my stiff ass into my apartment. Tossing the keys on the coffee table, I headed straight to my bathroom for a good soak in my tub before I took my shower. While the tub filled, I stripped down and went into the kitchen to get me a glass of wine. I lit a few candles around the bathroom, turned off the lights, and put on some soft music to create a relaxing ambiance.

I needed that.

Walker showing up to the studio threw me off for a second. I wasn't expecting him to try speaking to me again so soon, not after his blatant disrespect of my feelings. Something in his aura felt different. I couldn't pinpoint what it was, but I wasn't sure I wanted to get close to him again to find out. That man had a way of sucking me back in every time I told myself I was done.

This was the longest I'd stuck to my word, and I was proud of myself. I didn't need him coming over here and my stupid ass fall victim to his whim again and again and again. If I made up with him, I was gonna fuck him for lost time. Now *that* I didn't need. Maybe my body craved it, but my mind was telling me, *Bitch, think again.* I'd decide on calling or inviting him over by the time I got out of the shower.

After sliding my naked body down into the tub, I rested my head against the wall and closed my eyes. Peace and quiet... exactly what I needed. That was until Siri announced a call from an unfamiliar number. Sighing, I told her to answer.

"Hello?"

"Jorja?"

"This is she."

"It's Tyson. I hope I'm not catching you at a bad time."

"Hey, Tyson. You're fine. I just got home. Soaking my aching bones before I climb into bed for the night."

He chuckled. "How old are you again?"

"Almost twenty-seven."

"You must have been hitting those steps pretty hard."

"I was. I have a performance on Friday."

"Oh? If I was in town the night, I'd come see you. I don't get back until Saturday morning. I'm trying to make it to Millicent's competition. How's she looking?"

"She's doing great, actually. One of my most promising dancers."

"Good to know. She really admires you."

"That's so sweet. She's a good kid."

"I didn't really call to talk about my niece, you know."

I smiled. "Then to what do I owe the pleasure of this call?"

"I just wanted to hear your voice. I'm sorry it's been a few days. Work has been hectic, and then there's the family. I wouldn't have been able to give you my full attention like I wanted."

"I get it. Between dance, coaching, helping out with the new babies in the family, and helping my sister, I've been spread thin. It's nice to hear from you though. I thought you forgot about me."

"How could I forget you, beautiful? Are you busy after the show on Saturday?"

"I don't have anything planned."

"Would you like to have dinner with me? I know it's last minute but—"

"No, it's fine. I'd love to have dinner with you."

"Really? Great. I know you said you loved food, so I'll plan accordingly."

"Should I trust you with my stomach, Tyson? You sure I won't have to go grab fast food afterward to suffice my hunger?"

He chuckled. "Food is one thing I don't play about, beautiful."

"Yeah? Well, what else don't you play about?"

"My family, my career, my woman should I have one."

"Do I have to worry about a random female walking up on us at dinner? I can fight, you know."

He laughed out loud this time. "I promise, there is nobody for you to have to buck up at. I'm *single,* single. Millicent can tell you that."

"Like she wouldn't lie for you. You're probably her favorite uncle."

"Actually, I am. But nah, she wouldn't lie for me. My mama didn't play that. If one of us tried some sneaky shit, and she knew we were in relationships, she snitched on us."

"I would have loved her. More mothers need to be like that and tell you when their kid ain't shit."

"I think that responsibility falls on the ain't shit individual and the person ignoring the signs. Sometimes, things are right in our face, and we choose to ignore the red flags. We have this version in our heads of who we want people to be."

I found myself growing quiet.

Without knowing it, without knowing *me*, he read my ass like a book. When did I become gullible? Normally, I was good at reading people, especially men. Then again, I hadn't been trying to get to know these niggas either. Once they served their purpose, we moved around. It wasn't until I met Walker did I ever really give a man a glimpse of me beyond the bedroom.

He managed to infiltrate my system, and no matter how hard I tried to rid myself of him, I couldn't. He knew the deepest, most intimate parts of me, yet in actuality, he didn't know me at all. Not this version of me, not the woman I'd become since before I dropped him. Things between us had grown stagnant and complacent. I'd been good with what we were until I wasn't.

It wasn't that I hoped or thought I could change him. I just thought maybe I meant a little bit more to him to make him even reconsider. That was my mistake, and I learned my lesson the hard way.

"You okay over there?" Tyson asked. "You got quiet on me."

"I'm fine... I just needed to hear that."

"Are you sure you're okay, Jorja?"

I shook the thoughts from my head and put on a smile as though he could see me.

"I promise I'm fine. So, Tyson... tell me a little about you."

He began talking, and I listened with interest. He was actually pretty funny, and I loved that. I like to laugh, and if it was really funny, I was gonna scream. His personality seemed pretty chill, and his vibe seemed like we would get along fine. I ended up talking to him until the water grew cold in my tub, and I talked to him while I showered. A few times, Walker called me, but I decided that I didn't want to hash out our issues tonight. Maybe another day, but not tonight.

"It's been nice talking to you, Jorja," Tyson said as I settled into bed.

"It's been nice talking to you too."

"I don't wanna take up too much more of your time. I know you said you were tired from dance, so I'm gonna let you get some rest."

"Okay."

"Can I call you tomorrow?"

"I'd like that."

I could hear the smile in his voice as he spoke. "I can't wait to see you Saturday."

"Me either. I haven't been on a date in forever. What should I wear?"

"Something formal. Do you have something like that? I realized I didn't give you two to five business days in advance to find something to wear," he added with a chuckle.

"You got jokes, Mr. Funny Man? Yes, I have formal attire, and I will be looking exceptionally beautiful Saturday night."

"I know I've only seen you twice, but I can't imagine you looking anything less, no matter what you wear."

I found myself blushing. "Look at you, fishing for brownie points."

"Maybe just a little. Goodnight, beautiful."

"Goodnight, Tyson."

We ended the call, and I plugged my phone into the charger before settling into my mountain of pillows and allowed the sounds of *Martin* playing in the background to lull me to sleep.

* * *

THE INCESSANT KNOCKING at my front door broke me out of my once peaceful slumber. I looked over at my phone to see that it was almost midnight. Who the hell was knocking at my door at this hour? Tossing back the covers, I grabbed my gun from the bedside nightstand. I slipped on my robe and left my bedroom and headed up front. As I looked through the peephole, I found Walker standing on the other side of the door.

"Shit," I mumbled.

He stepped closer, putting his eye to the hole.

"I see you, Ja. Open the door."

He was drunk, and as red as his eyes were, I knew he was high too. He banged on the door again.

"Open the door, baby!"

He was getting loud, and I didn't need my neighbors reporting me for a disturbance. Unlocking the door, I snatched it open.

"What the hell are you doing here?" I snapped at him.

He looked down at the gun in my hands. "Why you got the blicky? You gon' shoot me, ma?"

"How was I supposed to know that it was you? And I should shoot you for coming over here like this."

"You were supposed to call me."

"Walker—"

"You didn't answer my calls, Ja. I just wanted to talk to you, baby."

"You're drunk and high, and I can't believe you drove over here like this. You could have hurt someone, Walker."

"I already hurt somebody." He slurred, leaning against my door frame. His hand cupped my chin. "I hurt you."

THE BURIAL OF A PLAYER

I slapped his hand away. "It's almost midnight."

"I know. I was waiting for you, and I had a little too much to drink..." He pinched his fingers together for emphasis.

I ran my fingers through my hair. I didn't want him here, but I couldn't let him get back behind the wheel of his car. If anything happened to him, I'd never forgive myself. With a heavy sigh, I grabbed his hand and pulled him inside.

"We gon' talk?" he asked as I locked the door.

"No. You're gonna sleep this shit off, and in the morning, you're getting the fuck out."

He kissed his teeth as he kicked off his shoes. "Whatever you say, boss."

"You can sleep on the couch. I'll bring you a—"

"Nah, I wanna sleep with you," he said, stumbling down the hallway to my bedroom.

"You're not sleeping in my bed!" I called after him.

"Stop playing with me. You know I sleep better next to you. Bring your ass to bed."

He disappeared into my room. I had a mini tantrum right there, stomping my feet and all before I marched toward my room. There was no way I could move his beefy ass if he laid down. Even with it being a short walk, by the time I made it to my bedroom, he'd stripped down to his boxers and beater and was climbing his drunk ass under my covers.

I frowned as I went around the bed to put the gun away, and then into the bathroom and grabbed the trashcan to put beside the bed.

"You better not throw up in my damn sheets."

"Stop fussing at me, mama."

"I shouldn't have to fuss at you like your mother!" I snapped, my hands on my hips. "You know how fucking stupid it was for you to drive over here drunk? What if something had happened to you Walker? What if—"

"Come on, Ja," he whined. "I get it, baby. I do. You can curse me out in the morning. Just get your ass in this bed and let's go to sleep."

"You are infuriating!"

I stomped around to the other side of the bed since his big ass decided to climb in where I was sleeping. Technically, it was the side he always slept on whenever he slept over, but it didn't belong to him anymore. Shedding my robe, I crawled under the covers and turned my back to him. Just as I closed my eyes, to attempt to go back to sleep, I felt one arm under me and the other slid around me, pulling me back against him.

"Walker."

"You know I need you close to me," he mumbled into my hair.

His lips kissed my neck as his hand palmed my breast before slipping under my sports bra to cup one. I shuddered as my nipple grew hard against his palm. I was used to this. This was how we slept together damn near every night. He loved to touch me, and once upon a time, it gave me comfort to fall asleep in his arms. Right now, all I could feel was my body about to betray me.

I tried to go back to sleep. For a while, all I could hear was his hard ass breathing and light snores. Again, I was used to it, so before long, I felt my eyelids grow heavy. That was until the hand draped over my stomach inched lower until he was caressing my thighs as he pinched that same hardened nipple.

"Stop." I whimpered as his hand slipped into my shorts.

"I miss you, Ja." He growled into my ear as his fingers made contact with my clit. "Fuck... I miss you."

He stroked my clit as he sucked on my neck. Even if I was mad at him, my pussy missed him. She was crying out for him right now, and I didn't have the willpower to fight the glorious sensations flowing through me. My hips involuntarily thrusted against his hand as I gasped for air. I could feel the hardness of his dick pressing against my ass. Just as I was about to reach my peak, he pulled his hand away and pushed my shorts down.

Eagerly, I kicked them off. His dick slipped between my closed thighs with ease due to the juices my body had betrayed me by expelling on his behalf. The pressure of it rubbing up against my clit was too much. My leg had a mind of its own as it lifted. The next thing I felt was him entering me from behind.

He grunted as he filled me. "Fuck, Ja!"

The hand once groping my breast was now gripping my throat. He knew I loved that shit.

"Tell me you miss me." He whispered in my ear as he slowly thrusted into me. "Tell me I can come home, Ja. I just wanna come home, baby."

I couldn't formulate a sentence. He was stroking my pussy so good that if I voiced anything, it would be to agree to the toxicity we shared. This was that demon dick. Dick so good it would have a bitch retracting her words and betraying her morals; dick so good that even when I was mad at him, my pussy always got wet for him; dick so good that even while I hated him and myself for allowing it to get this far, I still threw my ass back at him.

"Shit!" I cried out as he pummeled me, his fingers working overtime on my clit.

I was so wet that even buried beneath the covers, I could hear the sweet sounds of him sliding in and out of me. He pulled his hand away and sucked my juices from his fingers. He turned my head to the side and captured my lips, feeding me the essence from his tongue. Dirty muthafucka. He knew I loved that shit too.

"You gon' cum for me, Ja?" he asked. "Can I feel this pussy rain for me one more time?"

His thrusts went deeper and harder. I could feel his dick throbbing, and I knew he was going to cum right along with me.

"Fuck!" I gripped the hand restricting my airway.

"I know you feel it," he said, gripping my flesh. "I wanna feel it too. Give that shit to me. Act like you know this is my pussy."

She betrayed me like the triflin' bitch she was.

My pussy released for him without hesitancy, and his warm seed invaded my walls as he came with a deep, guttural growl.

"Fuck!"

For a minute, we lay there panting. I felt the overwhelming feeling of being suckered wash over me. I was doing it again. I was allowing him to have me without any commitment. We weren't even friends right now. We were nothing but two people seemingly trapped in an entanglement we didn't need to be in.

I removed his dick from me, and he rolled onto his back. By the time I stood from the bed, this muthafucka was snoring. Shamefully, I walked into my bathroom and locked the door. I headed to my shower and turned the water on as hot as I could stand it. I needed to wash him off of me. I needed the shame and stupidity I felt all over me to wash away with my tears right down the drain. This was a horrible idea, and now I was back at step one with trying to get him out of my fucking system.

    I must have stayed in the bathroom for a good hour. By the time the water ran cold, I was sitting in the corner of the shower with my knees to my chest, crying my eyes out. I had to rid myself of Walker Jareau. There were no ifs, ands, or buts about it.

Eight

WALKER

MY HEAD WAS POUNDING.

The bright ass sun beating down on me wasn't helping. As I opened my eyes, I realized that I wasn't at home. Sitting up, I looked around, realizing I wasn't in my own bed, but Jorja's. She was nowhere to be found. Memories of last night came flooding back. I remembered getting shit faced after Ja ignored my multiple attempts to call her. She'd never texted me or given me the okay to come talk to her.

I remembered being in my feelings as I climbed into my Rover and drove here with the windows down, blasting "Forever" by Jessie Reyez and 6LACK as I drunkenly sang along. It was one of her favorite songs. I'd been torturing myself with the playlist she created in my phone while I waited for it to ring, but it never did.

The fact that my dick was still hanging over my boxers let me know that something happened last night that definitely shouldn't have. Tossing back the covers, I swung my legs over the bed and stood upright. I didn't bother tucking my dick away, just headed in the bathroom for my morning piss and a shower.

Unless Ja had trashed my shit, I had clothes over here. After a sobering shower, I dried myself off and went in search of them. I found boxers, a shirt, and a pair of sweats tucked away in one of her drawers and slipped them on before I went in search of Jorja. I found her in the living room, sleeping on the oversized sectional under her favorite blanket.

She looked peaceful, but I could feel the difference in her spirit.

I rounded the couch and sat next to her, staring down at her beautiful face. Gone were the blue tresses she had when I first met her. She was now rocking brown and honey-blonde, and her natural curls were splayed over her face. Gently, I pushed them aside, allowing my fingers to gently graze her soft, supple skin.

I missed her more than I could understand. For so long, women came in and out of my life like a revolving door. I had my share of freak nasty, kinky sex, and not once did I catch feelings. Then here she came, matching my energy. There were no expectations, no blurred lines. It was supposed to be just sex until it wasn't. We started hanging out outside of the bedroom.

I got to know her. She got to know me. Somewhere along the line, I grew attached to her. I loved having her around. I loved the roasting sessions we had. I fell in love with sleeping next to her. I fell in love with the silence between us in the moments when she was just laying up on me. Not having any of that for months fucked with me heavily. Not having her at all... that shit touched my heart.

She stirred slightly, her eyes slowly opening.

"Good morning," I said softly.

She looked at me, a frown soon to follow. "Get out."

"Ja, baby, please."

"Walker, get out of my apartment. I let you sleep here after you came over drunk as fuck. You got what you wanted from me, so now you can go."

She tossed the blanket off of her and scrambled to her feet.

"I wanted to talk to you," I said, standing as well. "I waited for hours while you ignored my calls."

"Because I didn't want to talk anymore!"

"Why not! I'm trying to communicate with you, Jorja, and you're being so fucking unbearably bull headed! How are we supposed to get past this—"

"There is nothing to get past, Walker. We are done."

"No. No, I don't believe that."

"If you don't believe shit else I tell you, you need to believe *that*."

"That's bullshit. If you didn't still have feelings for me, you wouldn't be this mad."

"I'm this mad because you won't leave me alone! It's been almost five months. Five! What part of I don't want anything to do with you don't you understand?"

"You don't want anything to do with me, yet last night happened?"

Shit, I shouldn't have said that.

She looked at me in disbelief before she walked off to her bedroom. A few seconds later, she stormed back into the room with my clothes from last night.

"Take your shit and get the fuck out," she said, shoving them into my hands. "I'm packing up everything of yours that's still here, and I'm taking it to your parents. Never darken my doorstep again, Walker."

She walked over to the front door and opened it. I stood there for a moment, trying to think of what to say next.

"Get out!" she screamed.

With my head hung, I dragged myself to the door. I felt her hand on my back as she pushed me out and slammed it in my face. I pressed my forehead to the door, contemplating if I wanted to beg again, but I felt eyes on me. I looked up to see Ms. Cooler, the old woman that lived next door, looking at me. She was a funny ass old lady and used to always joke with Jorja and I about how loud we would get at night.

I straightened my posture and walked over to her. "Good morning, Ms. Cooler," I said.

"Good morning. I haven't seen you in a while. I gather you're in the doghouse."

I shook my head. "I'm not even allowed on the property."

"Whatever you did, you better fix it. My girl hasn't been herself."

"I'm trying, Ms. Cooler. Almost five months, I've been trying."

She nodded. "Can I offer you a piece of advice?"

I shrugged my shoulders. "You usually don't ask so... go on."

"Try harder."

"What kind of advice is that, woman? I've been trying my hardest."

"Obviously, your approach isn't working. You don't apologize with your dick, young man." She side eyed me. "I could hear you last night."

"That... wasn't planned."

"It never is."

"This is insanity," I said, resting against the wall.

"You know the definition of insanity is doing the same thing over and over and expecting different results. Maybe it's not working because you keep using the same approach."

"Well you tell me what I should do, Granny Knows It All."

She punched me in the chest.

"Be you... but better."

"Ms. Cooler, I can't with the vague statements this morning."

She laughed. "What I'm saying is, be the man she wants by becoming the man she needs. Be honest with that girl. No man is gonna chase a woman for months if he doesn't love her. Pussy is powerful, but it ain't *that* powerful. You love her, don't you?"

"I... I love her. I'm *in* love with her."

Hearing the word fall from my lips effortlessly made me stand up straight. It was the first time in all of this that I admitted it to myself. It was the first time I said it out loud. I loved Jorja. I was in love with Jorja Monae Sandifer.

"You look like that shocked you," Ms. Cooler said.

"I uh... I need to go." I leaned in and kissed her cheek. "Thank you."

"Come back to see me, handsome!" she called after me.

I made it downstairs and to my car in record time. Once I climbed in, I relaxed into the seat. My fucking chest was tight. I felt like I had an epiphany. No woman—other than my mama, my sister, and my nieces—could say I ever uttered those words to them. It wasn't that I didn't know love or how to love. I was a player. I wasn't one of those niggas that didn't double dip.

There had been about six women I dealt with on a consistent basis. Up until I met Ja, I knew only enough about them to say that at least I wasn't sleeping with a stranger. I knew Jorja like the back of my hand, a testament to how much time I spent with her. I didn't have to wonder how I fucked around and fell in love. I knew exactly what happened.

THE BURIAL OF A PLAYER

* * *

"AYO!" I called as the front door to my parents' house opened.

I was greeted by the frowning face of my father.

"I'm gonna start leaving your ass at the gate."

"I'll just shout it over the intercom until you let me in." I slapped hands with him. "How you doing, old man?"

"I'm still kicking." He headed back into the den where I assumed he'd been watching a game.

"Where's Ma?"

"Spoiling her new grandbabies. Cartel had to go check on the restaurant, so she went over to help Adina for a bit."

"It's opening in a few weeks, right?"

"Yep. I hope you got your suit ready."

"Come on, Pops. You know your boy always cleans up nice."

He rolled his eyes as he focused back on the game. "What brings you by?"

"I um... I need to talk to you, man to man."

He side eyed me. "You got somebody pregnant?"

"What? No, Pop."

"Is somebody *claiming* you got them pregnant?"

"No. Damn, Daddy. That's what you think of me?"

"No. That's what I think of what you do, but that ain't my business."

I kissed my teeth. "I'm serious, man."

He raised his hands in surrender. "Alright, alright. What's going on?"

I took a deep breath, preparing to share my self-revelation with him.

"I'm in love with Jorja."

He looked at me, not batting an eye.

"You gon' say something?" I asked.

"Oh, that was it?"

"Whatchu mean, Pop!" I exclaimed.

"I thought you were gonna tell me some shit I didn't know. All that weed you smoke is killing your brain cells, son. It's killing your brain cells. Everybody knows you love that girl, and she loves you. It's sad as hell it took her cutting you off for you to finally admit that to yourself."

"I know, I know. You know what's even sadder? I didn't admit it until after she put me out this morning."

Pops shook his head. "You're the smartest dumbass I know, you know that? You slept with her, didn't you? Don't try to deny that shit either. I know your yella ass."

"I didn't go over there for that, I swear. It just happened."

"Your dick just happened to fall between her legs?"

"Let me explain."

I ran him the events of last night without being too graphic. He sat watching me with a blank expression on his face.

"I'm still trying to figure out why you slept with her. All of that... all of what you're saying is an excuse. There was no excuse for that, Walker. Women are not objects. Their bodies shouldn't be used as a ploy to get forgiveness. I don't care how good you think your dick is, I bet when she woke up this morning, she felt like shit about it. For months, I've watched that girl look like she wanted to cry every time you came into the room. I watched her put on a that hard ass front and, honestly, I was proud of her for sticking to her guns with you. She did that for herself, to avoid settling for less than *she* felt she deserved. You took that from her last night, intentional or not."

I hung my head. I felt like a child being scolded again, and I deserved that.

"What are you gonna do now?" he asked.

"I don't know what else I can do. I know I need to let her cool off for a minute after this."

"That, you do. Let me tell you this. That's my baby girl. I look at her, Liv, and Adina just like I look at your sister. You fucking with my baby, and I don't like that shit. Get your shit together, Walker. If you can't appreciate her and do right, leave her alone. Don't be surprised when someone that's willing to step up to the plate claims the woman you thought was only for you."

He turned away from me and focused his attention back on the game he was watching. I sank into the couch, my thoughts plaguing me.

How the fuck was I gonna come back from this shit?

Nine

JORJA

I SILENTLY WATCHED the crowd pouring in from behind the curtain sectioned off for my girls. There were already so many people, and the show wasn't starting for another thirty minutes. My nerves were getting to me. I should have been on a high from the performance I gave last night. I killed my show, and the payment I received for dancing behind the artists was sitting pretty in my bank account.

Still, I was a little on edge. I knew they were ready for this, but it was their first competition of the season. Even if they didn't win, I wanted them to give it everything they had. If they did that, they would walk away with something so much more valuable than a trophy.

"Don't look so scared," came a deep voice from behind me.

I turned to see Tyson walking up with Millicent. I smiled. He'd been a welcomed distraction for the last couple of days. Whether it was text messages, phone calls, or video chats, he always managed to put a smile on my face.

"A thug is never scared," I said, crossing my arms. "Hey, Millie."

"Hey, Coach. I'm sorry I'm late. Somebody here passed the exit."

Tyson chuckled. "I said I was sorry. You made it in time."

"It's fine. Go on over there and start your warmups and stretches."

"Yes, ma'am. Bye, Uncle Ty."

She bounced off to join the rest of the girls. I turned to face Tyson, and he reached for my hands.

He leaned in to kiss my cheek. "It's good to see you, beautiful."

"It's good to see you too. Are you ready for our date?"

"I'm anxiously waiting. You are gonna love this restaurant."

"I don't know now," I jested. "Formal attire to me says high prices, low quality food. You promise I'll be full and satisfied?"

He chuckled. "I promise, you and your stomach will be very satisfied. If not, I'll cook for you myself next time."

"You think there will be a next time?"

"I'm hopeful." He flashed me that sexy ass smile. "I'm gonna go find a seat. If I don't catch up with you after the show, I'll see you tonight."

"Okay."

He kissed the palms of my hands before walking off to the bleachers.

"Skeeert! Bring that back!" I heard behind me.

I turned to see Liv and Alaina watching me with wide eyes and grins.

"Hey, y'all," I said.

"Don't *'hey, y'all'* us," Liv said. "Who was that?"

"And why is he kissing you all intimate and shit?" Alaina piped in.

"That was Tyson. I met him a couple of weeks ago."

"And you're crying over my brother when you have that fine ass man in your back pocket?"

Aleviyah elbowed her. "Alaina!"

"I'm sorry, boo. That wasn't tasteful."

"It's fine," I said, pulling my fresh faux locs up into a bun. "Anyway, I have a date with him tonight."

"Why didn't you tell me!" Liv exclaimed.

"I don't know."

She raised an eyebrow. "Are you not feeling him or something?"

"It's not that. It's just a lot has been going on this week, and it's clouded my excitement."

"A lot like what?" my sister asked, rubbing her belly.

"I... I slipped up."

"You slipped up?"

"She slipped and fell on my brother's dick," Alaina said, crossing her arms. "Didn't you?"

"Would you keep it down!" I hissed, pulling them away from the kids. "I feel like shit. Not because of Tyson but because I disappointed myself. I promised myself I wouldn't allow him to get that close to me. I had the weakest lapse of judgment. I've been in my feelings ever since. Tyson has been the light at the end of a few very dark days."

"Well you know I know all about weak lapses in judgment," Aleviyah said, referring to her history with her ex, Amir. "Did y'all at least get to talk?"

"No. I slept on the couch and put him out the next morning. I haven't talked to him since. He's been radio silent."

"I think y'all really need to talk," Alaina said. "I don't wanna sound biased because that's my brother, but no man chases a woman as long as he's been chasing you, girl. Have a heart to heart with him, Ja. He might have something to say."

"No offense, Laina, but your brother is full of shit."

"I know this entanglement isn't ideal. But I also know him. He has real feelings in there somewhere."

I shook my head. "You know him as your brother. I know him as a man. He's used to fighting, fucking, and then making up. He's not gonna get another chance to finesse some pussy out of me again. I'm good on him. I'm gonna go on my date. I'm gonna enjoy myself, and I'm not going to think about Walker Emilio Jareau."

Alaina raised her hands in surrender. "Okay, okay. Since we're using full government names, I won't push." She crossed her arms as she looked around. A smile broke across her face. "Is that the gardener?" she asked, nodding behind me.

I looked back to see Roosevelt holding the hand of the cutest little girl with big, bushy pigtails.

"That's him," I confirmed.

She bit her lip. "He was fine covered in dirt, but good God does he clean up well."

I had to admit, she was right about that. Sweat and dirt was sexy as hell on him, but in street clothes, how fine he really was should have been a shame. He smiled when he noticed us watching and made his way over.

"Afternoon, ladies," he spoke.

"Hey," we all greeted him.

"And who is this cutie pie?" I asked, pinching her cheek.

"This is my daughter, Juniper."

"Well, hello, Juniper. My name is Jorja. This is my sister Aleviyah and my friend Alaina."

"Hi!" she said excitedly. "Daddy, I see my team."

"Go on. I'll be over in a minute."

He kissed her forehead and sent her on her way.

"Who knew you were somebody's daddy?" Alaina said, her eyes slowly passing over him. "How old is she?"

He chuckled. "Six going on twenty-six. That's my baby though."

"How long has she been in dance?" Liv asked.

"Officially, two years, but she's been dancing since she could walk. She's my own little superstar."

"Where's her mother?" Alaina asked. I elbowed her. "What? I just wanna know if he's single."

Roosevelt chuckled. He didn't answer the question about Juniper's mother, but did respond with, "I'm very single."

Alaina's smile widened. "Good to know."

I rolled my eyes. She'd been dying to ask that since she first met him. For the entire three weeks she'd been home, she'd been lusting after him every time he came over to tend to her mother's garden.

"Daddy, come here!" Juniper said, waving him over.

"Duty calls. You ladies have a good evening. Ms. Alaina, I'll be seeing you on Monday."

"I'll be waiting."

He left us with a smile as he walked away.

"Is it bad that I just wanna throw my coochie at him every time I see him?" Alaina asked, gazing after him. "He's so damn fine."

"And he's somebody's daddy," I reminded her.

"He can be my daddy too," Alaina boasted, flipping her hair.

"Here you go being Aleviyah number two."

"First of all... fuck you," Liv defended. "I love my husband and our babies, and he's definitely daddy in more ways than one."

Alaina gagged. "That's disgusting."

"Oh, he's filthy," Liv teased.

I giggled. "Speaking of daddy, here he comes."

"Baby, you said five minutes," Jamison said as he walked up. "You need to get off your feet."

Liv rolled her eyes. "Jamison, I'm fine."

"Until your feet are swollen. Come on and sit down."

"You heard what daddy said," I joked.

She flipped me the middle finger. "Bye, bitch," she said as she allowed him to pull her away.

Alaina clasped her hands together. "My boo looks like he's going to find a seat, so I'm gonna see if I can squeeze my pretty ass next to him. Good luck. Kick ass, girls!"

She kissed my cheek and switched off to catch up to Roosevelt. I took a deep breath. It was time to focus my attention back on the competition. Everything else could sit on the back burner for now. I had to be present for my girls.

* * *

THE COMPETITION WAS AMAZING.

My girls took names and kicked ass, coming out number one in their age group and number two overall. That was a great way to start the season. While Jamison and Liv were taking Anais out to dinner to celebrate, I had a date to get ready for. At home, I took a long, hot, cleansing shower. When I was done, I thoroughly moisturized my body and strategically sprayed my favorite perfume.

For my dress, I chose this bad ass, strapless, red dress that hugged my body and accentuated my curves. The red heels and silver jewelry brought the whole look together. I admired myself in the mirror, snapping a few pictures for my Instagram account. By the time I finished posing, there was a knock on my door. Grabbing my clutch, I headed out of my bedroom and to the front. Checking the peephole to make sure it was Tyson, I opened the door.

"Damn..." he said, his eyes slowly passing over me. "You have far exceeded my expectations tonight."

"Well, you said formal, so I wanted to look as good as I knew you would in this suit."

He was looking dapper in a tailored, all-black suit. The man could have been on the cover of *GQ* he looked so damn good.

"All eyes will be on you." He took my hand and kissed it. "You ready to go?"

"I'm all set."

I stepped into the hallway and closed my door behind me. Of course, Ms. Cooler with her nosy ass was watching.

"That's a fine one, Jorja," she said as we made our way down the hall.

"Ain't he though?" I tossed over my shoulder.

Tyson led us outside to where his car was parked and opened the door for me. I climbed in, settling into the smooth peanut butter colored seats. When he cranked up, the sounds of 2Pac's "Hit Em Up" blared through the speakers. He reached over to turn it down as he pulled out of the parking space.

"My bad. I tend to listen to music like I'm deaf in one ear."

"It's okay. I love me some Pac. Though I must admit I didn't take you for a fan."

He laughed. "You literally met me in the club."

"I know. You just have this aura. Like you were a good boy who did what he was supposed to do."

"So you like roughnecks?"

"I will admit, that's what I tend to attract. I guess that's what I put out there or something."

"I'll have you know, I'm not that much of a cookie cutter. I stole a pack of gum once when I was a kid."

I laughed. "Look at you living on the wild side."

"Nah, my mama beat my ass before she took me up there to take it back and apologize. But seriously, though, I'm safe. Most women find that kind of boring, to be honest. They want the thrills."

"Thrills get old, tired, and played out. I've had my share of thrills.

These days, I'm okay with safe. Besides, you aren't boring at all. You make me laugh."

"And sometimes, I make you scream."

"If you decide you want to date me, scream laughing is something you have to get used to, baby. Once I'm tickled, that's it."

"I'm sure I can get used to the laugh. I love the smile that comes along with it."

I found myself blushing. He was smooth with his flirting.

"Sooo... tell me where we're eating."

"The Ivory Spoon."

"Okay, big spender. Remember, I told you I like to eat."

"I remember, doll face."

"I'm kidding. Not about the eating, but I promise I won't break your pockets."

He smirked. "You can order whatever you want. I'm good for it."

"I'll tell you what. You treat me tonight, the next date is on me."

"I'll take the second date, but in no way am I allowing you to pay for it. If you're gonna bless me with your time, the least I can do is treat you."

"You know, you say all the right things, Mr. Elmore."

"This is just who I am, Ms. Sandifer. Give me the time, and you'll see I'm as genuine as they come."

He reached for my hand and kissed it but didn't bother to let it go. I had to admit, I liked holding hands with him. He had me feeling like a teenager riding around town with my boyfriend. The difference was, I wasn't fifteen, and this right here... this was a full-grown man who exuded confidence from every pore, and I couldn't wait to see what he had in store for me tonight.

Ten

WALKER

I SPENT my Saturday morning working a therapy shift at Whimsical Pines Nursing Home. Two Saturdays out of the month, I volunteered to assist with patients needing ongoing care. I loved old people. Most of the ones I worked with were funny as shit and said whatever was on their mind, especially the little old ladies.

They saw my handsome, black ass with the tattoos peeking out of my scrubs, and they were in love. I couldn't count how many times I've had somebody's granny or great granny flirting with me. It was all in good fun though. I entertained their antics, and it usually put a smile on their faces and made our sessions run a lot smoother.

They always put me in a good mood and a good headspace. After the last couple of weeks I had, I needed that. When I left today, I was feeling so good that I called my mama and asked her to go to dinner with me. Paloma Jareau was my first love. Even though she could spoil herself, every now and then, I liked to take her out and show her off.

Tonight was no different. I pulled up to the gate of my childhood. After all the drama with Cartel and Adina, they added a gate to the already fenced-in property, and it was annoying as hell having to press that intercom every time I came to visit.

"Ayo!" I called.

"Must you do that every time?" my father asked over the intercom.

"At least you know it's me."

"I'm gonna leave your ass sitting right there."

"Come on, Pops. You're gonna make me and my date late for dinner."

He didn't answer, just opened the gate and allowed me entry. I made my way up the long driveway and parked in front of the door. Roosevelt was outside, packing up his truck. My parents had hired him about a year ago when my mother decided she wanted to do some beautification to the property.

"What's up, Rose?" I spoke as I got out of my Range Rover.

"What's good, Walk?" He met me with a slap of the hand. "You looking casket sharp, my brotha."

"I try, I try."

"Date tonight?"

"Taking my favorite girl out. I hope she's ready. You know women have to change their outfits at least five times."

He chuckled. "I know how that can be. Trust me, you learn to move on their time. Don't let me hold you up. I'm about to head out. I just had to bring these flowers by your mama asked for right quick. Might step out for a little bit myself."

"You seeing somebody?"

I eyed him suspiciously. I knew my sister couldn't stop looking at him, and part of me wondered if she had thrown him a line yet.

"Nah, man. I'm going to grab my baby girl from the babysitter's. I had to drop her off for a few while I took care of this. I'm thinking a little daddy daughter date tonight."

"That's what's up. Y'all have fun. Be easy."

We said our goodbyes as I headed in the house. My father rounded the corner with his signature cognac in his hands.

"I just wanna know how you invited your mother to dinner and leave me out."

"You jealous, old man?"

"Hell yeah. I want a free meal too." We shared a laugh. "But for real, she's been looking forward to this since you called her. It makes her day when y'all spend time with her. So you treat my woman right tonight."

"I hear you, Pop. Is she almost ready?"

"She should be down in a minute. You look nice, son. I haven't seen you this clean since your brother's wedding."

"Well I thought I'd treat her to a nice, fancy dinner, so I had to look the part. Somebody might mistake me for her man instead of her son."

My father rolled his eyes. "Don't flatter yourself, Walker. I swear you have the biggest damn ego."

"I don't. I'm just very confident. I mean, look at me. I got the best of both you and Ma. All of this is a reflection of you."

"Edwin! Is he here yet!" my mother called from upstairs.

"Hey, Mama!" I called back.

"Hey, baby! Let me grab my purse, and I'll be right down!"

A few seconds later, I could hear her heels clicking against the stairs. When she appeared at the bottom, I frowned while my father grinned. Paloma had lost her mind. She wore an all-white wrap dress that hugged her sixty-two-year-old curves entirely too much for my liking.

"Mama."

"Don't I look good?" she asked, doing a little twirl.

"Damn right you do," my father said, going over and pulling her into his arms.

Right in front of me, he kissed her like he had plans to make another Jareau when I finally got her back home. I loved that he still loved on her after all these years, but I wouldn't be me if I didn't give them hell about it. I pretended to gag.

"I don't know where you got this hating ass spirit from, Walker Jareau," my mother said. "It's not cute. Just for that, I'm ordering the most expensive thing on the menu tonight."

"I got it, woman. My pockets are laced."

"Since you got it, bring me back whatever expensive dish she orders," my father said. "With dessert too."

I shook my head. "OK, old man."

"And stop calling me old. If you live to be my age, you'll learn that things only get better with time. Ain't that right, baby?"

I gagged for real this time when he slapped my mama's ass before grabbing a handful.

"Okay, that's enough of that," I said, closing my eyes and reaching for my mother's hand. "Come on, Ma. You two can do whatever nasty shit you do when you're alone when I get you back. I just don't want to see it."

She and my father laughed as they shared a final kiss before she gave me her hand.

"Te amo, mi amor," she said as we walked toward the door.

"I love you too. You drive like you got some sense, boy. That's precious cargo."

"Damn, Daddy. I don't get no love?"

He sighed as he walked over to the door. He pulled me in for a hug and kissed my forehead.

"Now get the hell out of my house."

I grinned as I led my mother outside and opened the door to my Range. "Your chariot awaits, madam."

* * *

THE IVORY SPOON was one of the most elite restaurants in the city.

Normally, to get in, there had to be a reservation. To get a reservation, there was usually a waiting list. Lucky for my mother and me, Cartel was friendly with the owner, so he was able to call in a favor for me. The excitement on my mother's face when we walked in was well worth what I was about to drop on this dinner. If there was ever a woman who deserved it, it was her though.

"Walker, this is beautiful," she said, looking around.

"It is. We definitely have to take a few pictures and flex a little bit."

I pulled out my phone and went to my camera. She instantly fell into model mode, giving me several poses by herself before I snapped a few of us together.

"Excuse me?" came a voice from the waiting area with us. I turned to see a group of women. "I hate to be all up in your business... but are you two together?"

"Honey, if this wasn't my son, he wouldn't be my man," my mother said.

I frowned. "Tell me how you really feel, Ma."

"Baby, if you want him, take him. He's single." The women laughed as she linked her arm through mine. "Just let him pay for my dinner first."

"Nothing is more attractive than a man that treats his mama well," one of the women said, winking at me.

"He's a good boy," my mother said, kissing my cheek. "Hardheaded, but good."

I was happy as hell when the hostess called for their table. Knowing my mama, she would have tried to pawn me off on one of those girls. My head wasn't in that shit right now. If only I knew that my good mood was about to sour. A few minutes passed, and the hostess assured us that we would be up next.

The door leading out to the street opened, and instantly, my nostrils were filled with her scent. Peaches and honey. I would know it anywhere. I looked up to see Jorja stepping in looking so muthafucking beautiful wrapped in a red strapless dress with red heels to match. Her faux locs hung over one side of her shoulder and down her back. Her face was free of makeup, and she had this natural glow.

"Shit," I mumbled, causing my mother to look up and Jorja to look in our direction.

She looked nervous for a second, and the reason was clear once the nigga she was with walked in and grabbed her hand. I realized that he was the same nigga that had been in her face at the club.

"Mama Jareau," she spoke, offering my mother a smile as my mother stood to greet her.

"Jorja. You look stunning."

"Thank you. Might I say, you are working that dress, girl. Papa Jareau let you out looking this good without him?"

"Oh baby, he knows I'm coming home." Her eyes drifted over to ol' boy. "And who might this handsome young man be?"

"This is Tyson. His niece dances for me. Tyson, this is Paloma Jareau. She's Anais's grandmother and like a second mother to me."

"It's very nice to meet you, Mrs. Jareau," Tyson said, shaking her hand as he leaned in to kiss her cheek. "Are you dining alone? You're more than welcome to join us."

"Oh no. My date is my son, Walker." She grabbed my hand and pulled me to my feet, although I tried to resist it.

"Nice to meet you," he said, extending his hand.

I looked at it, then at Jorja and my mother. There was no fucking way I was about to shake this nigga's hand—

"Walker," my mother said firmly.

I kissed my teeth, giving him a lazy shake.

"Ja, can I holla at you outside for a minute?" I said.

"No," she said through gritted teeth. "I am on a date."

"It's okay, love," Tyson said, kissing her cheek. "Handle your business. I can keep Mama Jareau company."

Jorja glared at me as she turned and walked outside. The door damn near slapped me in the face as I walked out behind her. She walked a little ways away before she turned to face me.

"Walker, I thought I made it abundantly clear that I was done with you."

"So you just out here dating niggas and shit?"

"That's what single people do."

"This is bullshit, Ja."

"No, this is what you made it. You wanted to be a free agent, so I freed you. Move on. Clearly, I have."

"I don't believe that. Look me in my eyes and tell me you don't feel shit for me."

"The fact that I'm here with another man should tell you something, Walker."

She tried to walk off, but I gently took her hand.

"Baby, please."

"Baby? I'm not your baby. Never was."

"Jorja, I care about you. I'm begging you to reconsider—"

"Reconsider!" Tears laced her voice. "I gave you too much of me with no commitment. I'm not doing that again. Why would I reconsider being an option? Why would I wait for you to decide that you want to get it right when there are men out here that have begged me to stop fucking playing?"

"Like him?"

"He didn't have to beg because he came correct the first time. Now if you'll excuse me, I have a date to get back to."

She tried to walk away again, and again, I held her back.

"Jorja, I love you."

Her eyes widened.

"I've never said that to any woman I've been with, but that's what I feel for you. I'm sorry it took me so long to see that. My world ain't right without you, Ja. I miss you, and I miss us. I don't want you to move on, and I *can't* move on. I want to come home."

She shook her head. "No. No, you don't get to do this."

She snatched away from me and stormed back toward the entrance.

"Ja!.. Fuck!"

All I wanted to do was punch the air. I'd royally fucked up our friendship and anything else that could have been between us. Her cutting me off was one thing, but her actually being on a date with another man... that shit had my chest hurting. I might just have to accept the fact that she was really done with me for good.

I sulked back inside to find my mother waiting with the hostess to take us to our table. I didn't say another word to Jorja or make eye contact with her or her date. I kept my head down as we were led to our table and seated. My mother remained quiet until after we had placed our drink and food orders and the waitress returned with our drinks. I quickly downed my first one before she even left the table, telling her to keep them coming.

"Baby?" my mother said, covering my hand with her own.

"I'm fine, Ma."

"You're not. Seeing her really bothered you, didn't it?"

"It doesn't matter. She told me she's done with me. I guess she meant that."

"Why is it so hard for you to tell that girl you want to be with her? For months, I've watched you two sulk every time you get around each other. It's clear as day you miss each other."

"She doesn't want anything to do with me, Mama."

"Now you know that's a lie. She wants what any woman who isn't lying to themselves want. Commitment. She wasn't asking you to marry her tomorrow. She just wanted to know you shared something that goes deeper than you between her legs. She's not wrong for that."

"And I was, for not being ready before?"

"No. But I don't believe that you didn't notice when things changed between you two. I told you long ago that your ways were gonna catch up with you. You can't be out here having sex and making soul ties with all these women. You were bound to fall for one of them, and look what happened. You fell for the one who ain't down to keep playing your games for the sake of catching a nut."

I cringed. "Please don't ever say the word nut again."

"Nut. Nut. Nut. You uncomfortable?"

"Very much."

"Good. Listen to this, son. Women are not obligated to wait until you are ready to commit to them. You don't get to be mad when they find someone willing to give them everything they wanted with you. Take a good look at her, baby."

She pointed in the direction of Jorja and Tyson. It sickened me to watch him touching her. There he was, leaning in close to her, holding her hand, wiping away tears that I was the cause of. He was already better for her than I was.

"If you cared the way you said you do, you wouldn't put her in a position to have any other man comforting your woman the way you're supposed to. You wouldn't be sitting here looking like you're ready to cry either."

I sniffed as I sat blinking back tears. "I messed up, Ma. She doesn't even want to be friends. I can deal with her not wanting to sleep with me. But she's acting like she never meant anything to me at all, and that's not true. I just told that woman I love her, and she walked away from me."

"So you finally admitted it?"

"Only to be too late. Look at her? She's really on a date with another nigga. All I wanted was a chance to make it right, Ma."

"I hate to be blunt, but this was bound to happen, Walker. Look, you two were once one in the same. You didn't want commitment. You wanted to live life fast, free, and unattached until you became attached to each other. If you just wanted to be friends, sex should have never been an option. You want her to know she was more than a piece of ass, you have to work twice as hard to get back in her good graces."

"How am I supposed to do that?"

"I'm not saying step on that man's toes, but show her you can be the type of man that deserves her. Make your intentions for her clear. Put action behind your words. And keep your dick in your pants. Use the sense the good Lord gave you, son. You watched your father be an amazing husband for twenty-nine years. You've watched Jamison love two women with his entire heart. Hell, you watched Cartel damn near die to protect the woman he loves. Have you learned nothing? I know you have it in you. What do you want?"

"I want her back."

"Then prove it."

That was the last thing she said before the waitress returned with our dinner. I looked over at Jorja, deciding in that moment, I needed to tighten the fuck up. I didn't know what I had in her until she took it from me, and now my ass was sick about it. For months, I played like I was cool, and it was just her being mad at me for longer than she ever had.

I was wrong... wrong as fuck.

It was going to be hard, but one way or another, I was going to get her back... I had to.

Eleven

JORJA

WALKER REALLY DROPPED a bomb on me.

He loved me?

Why would he admit that here? Why now? He had all the time in the world to make his confession, yet he waited until this very moment to be honest with me. It was infuriating. When I saw his face, I just knew he was about to ruin my night. The universe was cruel. What were the fucking chances of my date being in the same restaurant he was dining at with his mother?

If he'd been with almost anybody else, I would have looked right through them, but I loved his mother. She was my mother's best friend, and she'd never done a thing to me. I would have been flaw as fuck to ignore that woman, but her son could go to hell.

"I'm sorry our date got off to such a bad start," I said, wiping my eyes as I sat across from Tyson.

"You don't have to apologize, love." He reached out and cupped my face, swiping at a tear with his thumb. "I can tell you weren't expecting to see him. Is that your ex?"

"He's someone I had dealings with. We were never a couple, but we were intimate for a long time. I wanted more and he didn't, so I ended things where they were. It hasn't been easy because we are family in a sense. My sister is married to his brother. My mother is besties with Mama Jareau. We're always around each other, and I've been putting as much space between us as possible when it comes to engaging."

"Looks like he's regretting that."

"Yeah, well... that's on him. I'm not looking back, only forward. I want to enjoy this night with you. I know this place is hard to get into, and I don't wanna waste your time."

"Full transparency, my cousin owns the place. I wanted to take you somewhere special for our first date. Hopefully, it goes well enough that you'll be willing to see me again."

I smiled. "Well you've been a gentleman so far. Tell me, how is it that no woman has snatched you up?"

He chuckled. "I was a bit of a workaholic until about a year ago. I was always out of town working and finding everything under the sun to do but be with my family. I um... I lost both of my parents within six months of each other. It hit me pretty hard. Time is precious, you know? We're given life, but we never know how much of it. I didn't make the most of the time I had with the people that meant the world to me, and I'll always regret that."

It was his turn to drop a few tears as I reached out to wipe them away.

"I decided to take a position closer to home with a less strenuous schedule. I wanted to be around for my siblings and my nieces and nephews. It was the best decision I could have made."

"I get that. Family is important to me. My mom, my sister, and my granny are my best friends. My father left when we were young. After my grandfather passed away, it was the four of us for so long. My sister got married about four months ago, and I just fell completely in love with her bonus babies. Meeting them made me grow up so much."

"Kids will do that. Do you want children?"

"I do. I've had extreme baby fever since she's been pregnant. I can't stop rubbing her stomach and talking to my nephew. I just know I'm gonna spoil him rotten once he gets here. Do you want kids?"

"I do. Marriage, kids, a fat little bulldog running around, fucking up my shit... the whole nine yards. I've been thinking about it for a while now. I just haven't found the right woman to settle down with. I know that takes time, so I won't rush anything, but I'm dating with intention."

Dating with intention.

Now that was nice to hear. We continued to talk as we waited for our food. I had to admit, the more he spoke, the more I found I liked about him. Maybe I was biased. I hadn't had an actual boyfriend in years, and I hadn't been dating, so I didn't have much to compare him to in ranking. For the first time, I was entertaining someone without the intention of sex, and it was so refreshing.

Tyson was a complete gentleman and fine as hell. He stood approximately six feet three. He was built like he worked out but wasn't a gym rat. His muscles were toned and defined. I was loving his smooth, cocoa skin and that shiny bald head. Perhaps my favorite physical features of his were his deep brown eyes and these juicy full lips. Every time he smiled or licked them, I wanted to melt.

He just had this good energy surrounding him, and I needed that after all this time. I focused all of my attention on him, and he made it so easy to forget that Walker was only a few tables over with his mother. I could feel his eyes on me, yet I never looked back. What I needed in this moment was right in front of me.

When dinner was over, he paid the bill so we could leave. While we were eating, he asked me about my favorite dessert. When I told him it was cheesecake, he mentioned he knew a place that served the best cheesecake in town. Ironically, it was one of my favorite places, so I was super excited to get my hands on a piece.

He stood and came around to pull out my chair and help me to my feet. When he offered me his arm, I happily slipped mine through it, and we walked out of the restaurant. As we were waiting for the valet to bring his car around, he leaned in and kissed my forehead. It was simple and sweet, but there was something so sensual about a forehead kiss.

"If I haven't told you enough already, you look so beautiful tonight, Jorja," he said with a smile.

"Thank you, Tyson." I turned in his arms, wrapping my around his waist. "I could get used to this, you know."

"Stick with me, love. I can show you everything you've been missing."

I smiled. Maybe it was too soon, but I wanted to kiss him. Taking a leap of faith, I tilted my chin and pressed my lips against his. My God, his lips were so soft. His hand came to the side of my face, and his tongue slipped into my mouth. He didn't grope me. He didn't try to cop a feel. His hands remained respectable, but that kiss... that kiss was sexy as hell.

He looked down at me, brushing my hair from my face.

"I've wanted to kiss you since the moment I laid eyes on you, beautiful," he said.

I couldn't help but blush. His hands dropped from my body, but his fingers laced between mine as we continued to wait. Out walked Mrs. Jareau and Walker, standing off to the side of us, waiting for his car. The space became awkward. When I glanced at him, I could tell his eyes were a little puffy like he'd been crying. For a moment, I felt bad. I'd never seen him express deep emotion, let alone shed a tear.

As the valet pulled Tyson's car around, I looked up at him.

"I just want to say goodbye to her," I said.

"Go ahead."

I stepped over to Mrs. Jareau and reached for her hand, pulling her off to the side.

"I know this is awkward," I said nervously.

"Just a little. I know my son hasn't lived up to what you were hoping—"

"No, Mrs. Jareau. He's exactly who he showed me to be. I chose to see something different. I should have left him alone when I realized I was catching real feelings for him."

"He does have real feelings for you, baby. That much I do know. I won't get any further in the middle, but you should know that. I want you to be happy with whoever gives you what you need, whether it turns out to be Walker or that handsome gentleman waiting for you."

"Thank you, Mama Jareau." I pulled her in for a hug and kissed her cheek. "I hope you two had a nice date, at least. I've always loved how he loves you."

"He's a good boy. I have faith in him. He'll get it together. Have a good night, Jorja."

She kissed my cheek as we parted ways, and I headed back to where

Tyson was waiting. For a moment, I looked back, and my eyes connected with Walker. He looked sad and remorseful. Part of me wanted to run and hug him, but I stood steadfast in my decision to end things. We weren't meant to be forever, and I had to remember that.

"You good?" Tyson asked.

I turned to him with a smile. "I'm good."

He leaned in and pecked my lips softly. "Let's get you that dessert."

* * *

AFTER DINNER, Tyson and I grabbed cheesecake and headed back to my apartment for a nightcap. While he chilled in the living room, making drinks at my mini bar, I headed into my bedroom to change into something more comfortable. Normally, I wore boy shorts and a sports bra while I was at home. I didn't want to show off all my goodies, so I slipped into a pair of biker shorts, a tank top, and my favorite fuzzy socks.

When I made it back out front, he was sitting on my couch, scrolling through his phone. The drinks sat on the table.

"I'm back," I said, taking a seat next to him.

He looked up at me with a smile. "Don't you look cute."

"I look bummy."

"I've seen you glowing in sweat, and you still looked radiant."

"So you've been watching me?"

He chuckled. "I'm no stalker... but I've seen you when I picked my niece up a couple times. You just never looked in my direction."

"How silly of me. You have my attention now, though."

"Do I now?"

He reached for the drinks and handed one to me, keeping the other for himself.

"You do."

"What about the guy from the restaurant? I sensed the tension between you. You looked sad when you were talking to his mother."

"I love his mother. She's one of the few people that taps into my emotions."

"Do you love him?"

I was quiet for a moment. Did I want to tell him the truth? No nigga I knew would stay around when a bitch tells them they are in love with another man. Then again, I felt like I had to be honest. If I was honest, he couldn't go around saying he didn't know the deal if shit went south.

I sighed. "I do love him. We dealt with each other for a long time. It doesn't just go away. It's been four months since I ended things, and I've barely spoken to him. I'm not acting on any of those feelings. I'm not around him if it's not family related. I know seeing me is risky, Tyson. I can understand if you don't want the emotional baggage."

"I'm good, Jorja. You were honest and told me what it is. I can't do anything but respect that. All I ask is if you ever feel like you aren't feeling me or this, you be honest with me. I wear my heart on my sleeve, and I don't wanna put myself out there if you have even the slightest of doubts."

I nodded.

I'd already lied about not acting on those feelings. The night I allowed Walker to fuck me still rested in the back of my mind. I shouldn't have let it happen, but it did. All I could do now was not let it happen again.

"Can I ask you what you want, Jorja? What are you looking for?"

I took a sip of my drink as I pondered the question.

"I want to be loved." I paused for a moment, preparing to tell my truth. "I haven't had the best track record with men, starting with my father. I dated in high school, but it was never anything serious. As an adult, I haven't had a serious relationship. I've treated most men like most of them treat women, as an object."

"What makes you want love now?"

"I've had the grounding experience of being around nothing but beautiful, black love for almost two years now. I see the way my brother-in-law and his father treat their wives… the way his brother treats his girlfriend. They don't have perfect relationships, but that love is undeniable and beautiful to witness. It made me realize that I wasn't fulfilled living the way I was. I want to come home and be greeted with warm hugs and tender kisses. After a long day, I wanna lay up under my man and feel nothing but peace.

"I want to feel secure. Not financially because I can take care of myself. I mean I want to feel physically, emotionally, and mentally secure with him. I want a man that knows my weaknesses and doesn't use them against me; a man that says what he means and means what he says, but he also puts action behind that shit. I don't wanna have to wonder or second guess his motive and intentions."

He nodded, seemingly processing my words.

I wasn't sure how he felt about my confession. I wouldn't consider myself a ho by any means. I wasn't out here sleeping with a bunch of men. Not everybody could say that they had me. In all honesty, I'd only had eight men able to say they penetrated me over the course of ten years. There were three others that just loved to eat my pussy, and they were so good at it that I didn't even need the dick afterwards.

He reached for my hand, and when I slid it to him, he pulled me closer.

"I hear you," he said, gently rubbing the back of my hand with his thumb. "I respect your honesty, and I admire that you've embraced growth."

"You don't have any thoughts on my past?"

"You've lived..." He chuckled. "I've done my share of living, too, so you get no judgments from me."

"So you're a reformed ho?" I jested.

He laughed. "I've been delivered." He looked at me for a moment. "Come here."

He pulled me into his lap to straddle him. His hands gently caressed my thighs before moving up my arms to cup my face.

"You know how beautiful I think you are, Jorja?" He tucked his bottom lip between his teeth as he gazed up at me. "How sexy I think you are?"

He pulled my head to his and softly pressed his lips against mine.

"So... fucking... sexy..."

He accented each word with a peck before sucking my bottom lip between his. A whimper escaped my lips. Sitting on his lap and him kissing me like this was turning me on. My nipples hardened, and I could feel the slickness between my lower lips. As his tongue slipped into my mouth, he gripped the back of my neck with one hand and my ass with the other. I was trying to will myself not to pop my pussy for him on the first date, and the way he had me grinding on his dick wasn't helping my case.

I couldn't fuck him, but the way his lips and tongue were assaulting me, I was almost okay with letting him taste me. I just knew his head game was in-fucking-sane.

We ain't doing this, bitch! my inner self shouted. *You can't tell this man you want love and then give up the goods on the first date.*

I forced my lips away from his.

"Maybe we should slow down," I said, rolling back onto the couch.

Damn, I really said that.

"I'm sorry," he apologized. "I got a little carried away."

"It's fine. I just don't want to give you the wrong impression of me. I'm big on actions matching words."

"I get that." He fingered my chin. "I do like kissing you though."

"I like kissing you too."

He leaned over and kissed me again. "How about we settle in for a movie? I'll even throw in a foot massage."

"You any good with your hands?"

He chuckled. "These fingers work magic. Slide those pretty feet over here and watch me work."

Grabbing the remote, I flipped on my television to Netflix where I put on *The Jazzman's Blues* and rested my feet in his lap. The duration of the movie was spent between us commentating, him giving me the most heavenly foot massage, and me resting comfortably against him. By the time the credits were rolling, the itis and those drinks were kicking in, and I was beginning to nod off.

"I'm gonna head out so you can get your beauty rest, love," he said, shifting slightly.

I jumped awake. "I'm up... I'm not sleep."

"You were most definitely snoring over there."

"Whatever. You fed me well, brought me my favorite dessert, and massaged my feet. That's all I needed to fall asleep."

"At least it's not because I bore you." He stood and pulled me to my feet, wrapping me up in a hug. "This was nice."

"It was."

"So that means I can take you out again?"

"Yes."

"That's what I like to hear."

He dropped his hands and linked his fingers through mine as we walked to the door.

"Let me know when you make it home," I said as he unlocked the door and opened it.

"I will." Turning back, he lifted my chin with his finger and blessed me with the single most sensual, arousing, panty wetting kiss. "Goodnight, Jorja."

"Goodnight."

He stepped into the hallway, and I watched him until he got on the elevator. Closing the door, I pressed my back against it. This man had me all giddy inside, and part of that feeling was right in my kitty.

"Calm down, girl," I said to her. "I'm about to take care of you right now."

Twelve

WALKER

A NIGGA WAS SICK.

Not a physical type of sick, but I'd be damned if my heart wasn't hurting. Jorja told me she'd make me feel this shit in my chest, and she didn't lie. For the past three days, after seeing her on a date with that nigga from the club, I'd been locked in my house. I passed off my therapy clients to Margo and the rest of my team. My calls went unanswered, and my texts went unread.

I didn't want to see anybody.

I didn't want to talk to anybody.

I just wanted to be by myself and sulk.

Apparently, that didn't register to whoever was at my door. Here I was, laid out on my couch, smoking my third blunt of the day. I could ignore the knocking. What I couldn't ignore was the sound of my locks disengaging. The chain on the door blocked my intruder's entrance, however.

"Walker!" Alaina yelled. "Open this goddamn door."

I rolled my eyes. I loved having her home, but right now, I just wanted her to leave me the fuck alone.

"Locked doors mean I don't want company."

"Locked doors don't mean shit to me. Come take this chain off."

I didn't move.

"Alright, you wanna play hardball."

She was quiet for a minute. Then I heard the sound of a phone ringing.

"Hello?"

"Mami."

Shit.

"Is he okay?"

"He's in here. He won't open the door and let me in."

"Walker Emilio Jareau!" my mother yelled through the speaker. "*Levanta el culo y abre la puerta.*"

She told me to get my ass up and open the door. I kissed my teeth.

"Did he just suck his teeth at me?"

Damn bionic ears.

"He sure did."

"Don't make me come over there. I sent your sister to make sure you were okay. Come to this phone and talk to me. *Ahora!*" She told me to hurry up.

"Fuck, man!" I mumbled, throwing my feet over the side of the couch. I stood and walked over to the front door, snatching the chain off. Alaina pushed her way in. I snatched the phone from her hand and took it off speaker.

"Yes, Mama?" I answered, returning to the couch.

"Why haven't you been answering the phone? I almost sent the police to your house."

"I just didn't feel like talking, Ma."

"Then you should have said that. You don't just ignore people, especially me. After your brother almost dying, you know how I feel about not being able to reach y'all."

For a moment, I had forgotten all about my brother being kidnapped and attempted to be murdered. My mother had been hysterical when she was told that they found his detail with a bullet in his head in the driveway, and Cartel was missing.

"*Lo siento, Mami.* I'm sorry," I apologized. "I just needed some time to get my head together after Saturday."

Her voice softened. "Walker, you can't let this situation with Jorja depress you, baby. I know it hurts."

"It hurts because I was stupid, Ma. I had her. In my mind, I knew she would come back like she always did. Then days turned to weeks, and weeks turned to a month, and before I knew it, it's been four months. I'm professing my love for her, and she's out here on dates with niggas."

"You told her you loved her!" Alaina exclaimed in the background.

"Mind your business, Laina, damn!" I yelled.

"Hey!" my mother snapped. "Don't talk to your sister like that. You know better."

I heaved an angry sigh. "Ma, I really just want to be alone right now. I'm fine. You don't have to send the calvary for me."

She inhaled deeply. "Okay. But when I call or text, you respond. Even if it's to let me know you're okay. You can't scare me like that."

"I will. I promise."

"I love you."

"I love you too, Ma." The call ended, and I handed Alaina her phone back. "Get out."

"You're not about to dismiss me," she said, flopping down next to me. "You told Jorja you loved her?"

"It doesn't matter."

"Yes it does. That's big. What did she say?"

"She didn't say shit. She left me standing there with my face on the ground and went back to her date."

"I'm sorry, Walker." She rested her head on my shoulder.

"Don't be sorry. I'm just getting what I deserve, right?"

"Well..." She dragged the word, causing me to snatch my shoulder away. "I'm sorry," she said, looping her arm through mine. "I don't like seeing you like this. The Walker I know didn't sweat women or shit like this."

"Ja ain't just any woman. I can't get her out of my system, sis. I tried that shit, and every time I see her, I miss her even more. I haven't fucked another woman since her, and it wasn't for lack of trying. My shit doesn't wanna work for me half the time these days, let alone another woman."

"I did not need to know that. Look, sometimes you have to know when to bow out. Now would be that time."

"If she agreed to a date with this guy, something about him attracted her. I don't like him."

"That's just the jealousy talking."

I shook my head. "Nah, it's something about that nigga. I feel it on him."

"So you're the empath now?"

"No. He just felt off to me. I watched him their entire date."

"Don't tell anybody else that. Look, you can't torture yourself about this forever. You should go back to work. Do what you do best." She looked around my living room. "You should also clean this mess up... and go take a shower. You smell like weed and stale ass."

"Fuck you."

I playfully pushed her, causing her to swing at me.

"Alright, now. I haven't beat your big ass in a minute."

"You ain't ever beat my ass. Let's just put that out there. I let you win because Pops would have killed me if I roughed you up too bad. You held your own though. I never have to worry about a nigga beating your ass before one of us get to him."

"Yeah... you don't. Anyway! I know what will make you feel better."

"What?"

"A tattoo session!" she answered, full of excitement.

I grinned. Tattoos were kind of our thing. Both of us were covered in them. Reese was always joking that we wanted to be Chipotle bags so bad. Every time she came home, we got a new one together, and so far, we hadn't had a session this time.

"I'm down for that," I said, standing. "Since you want to complain about it being messy, why don't you clean up while I wash my ass."

"You tried it. Go on, Funkmaster Flex."

I threw a pillow at her head before heading up to my bedroom to shower and get dressed. Maybe some new ink would lift my spirits.

* * *

AFTER OUR TATTOO SESSION, Alaina and I went to grab a bite to eat.

Although I wasn't happy about her being sent to my house, I was grateful for the distraction. We ended up at Cartel and Adina's because my sister couldn't go a day without seeing our new nieces. She currently had both of them in her lap, talking that annoying ass baby talk to them.

"You see how they're looking at you?" I asked, noticing their wide-eyed expression. "They want you to stop that shit."

"Your uncle is a hater because you're giving me all this little loving," she said, tickling their stomachs.

They were almost a month old, and I still couldn't tell them apart until Carina started raising hell. Adina and Cartel had it down to a science. Fucking with me, these kids would have an identity crisis. As if she read my thoughts, she started up. I reached over and scooped her up, cradling her in my hands like a football.

"You better not drop my baby," Adina said, walking into the room with their bottles.

"I didn't drop you, I'm not gonna drop her," I said, cradling her against my chest and reaching for the bottle. "Carina, tell her you're in safe hands."

"As long as you feed Little Miss Greedy, she doesn't care. I'm happy y'all are here. While you feed them, maybe I can get some cleaning done—"

"Or maybe you can sit down and relax," Cartel said, coming from around the corner. "I told you to stop overdoing it, just like I told you I've got the cleanup once the girls are down for bed."

He sat in the recliner and pulled her down into his lap where she rested her head against his shoulder. He whispered something in her ear that caused her to giggle, right before they shared a kiss. It was like Alaina and I weren't even in the room once she slipped him some tongue.

"Hello!" Alaina said, snapping her fingers. "I don't wanna see y'all working on baby number three already."

Adina laughed. "I have several weeks before any of that can happen."

"I bet he can't wait either," I jested.

He flipped me the middle finger. "I'm glad to see you came out of hiding."

"I wasn't hiding. I didn't wanna be bothered. Your mama sent your sister to Deebo her way into my house."

"I didn't Deebo you. I simply called reinforcement."

Cartel chuckled. "Did she get to speaking Spanish on you?"

"And she used my full government name." I shook my head.

"What's up with you?"

"Jorja," Alaina answered. "He saw her on a date."

"Oh shit!" Adina and Cartel said in unison.

"Mama didn't say all that," he said.

"He also told her he loved her," Alaina added.

"You just gonna tell all my business?" I asked, looking over at her.

"So you finally admitted it?" Adina asked.

"A lot of good it did me. Look, I don't wanna talk about that."

They both raised their hands in surrender, but I could tell they had burning questions. Things grew quiet for a minute. The only sounds that could be heard were the babies sucking on their bottles. The sound of the doorbell ringing finally broke the silence.

"It's open!" Cartel called.

"You are awfully comfortable letting people in here without going to the door," I said.

"The threat is gone. Ain't nobody else coming in here on that type of shit."

The front door opened and closed followed by the sound of flapping against the floor. I looked up to see Jorja strutting in.

"Fuck," I muttered under my breath.

"Hey, y'all."

Then she noticed me. The smile on her face dropped. For a moment, we stared at each other before I broke eye contact and focused my attention back on Carina. Adina and Alaina both spoke, but I remained quiet. As soon as Carina finished eating, I was getting out of here. Balancing her bottle under my chin, I pulled out my phone and booked me an Uber. It said the wait was about ten minutes, and that was about all that I could stomach right now.

As she and the girls talked amongst themselves, Carina and I made silent conversation with our eyes. She looked up at me the entire time she was guzzling that bottle. I studied her features. She and Carmella were such beautiful babies. When I found myself wondering what my own kids would look like, I knew it was time to get the hell out of the house. My Uber notification chimed on my phone, just as Carina let out a good burp.

"I'm about to head out," I said, standing with her in my arms.

"I'm not ready," Alaina protested.

"It's cool. I booked an Uber. I'll see y'all later."

I kissed her forehead and handed Carina to Jorja, knowing she probably only came over for them. We didn't make eye contact or exchange words. After kissing Carmella's cheek, I headed to the door then outside. I was back in the mood where I just wanted to be alone. The rest of my blunt was calling me.

Thirteen

JORJA

WHEN I DECIDED to drop by Cartel and Adina's, the last person I was expecting to see was Walker. I didn't see his Range out front, so I had no reason to believe that he would be here. Walking in and seeing him on the couch, feeding Carina, almost made me want to turn around and walk out. Yet and still, I held my ground. It wasn't like I could always avoid him. I mean, this was *his* family. He didn't have to announce every time he was going to be a place so I could avoid him.

I ended up staying over for a few hours. Thankfully, nobody brought up the awkward exchange. That was until Alaina and I were walking out to our cars to leave.

"Sooo... are we gonna talk about it?" she asked, leaning up against her Jeep.

"I really don't—"

"He told you he loves you?"

I sighed. "He did."

"And you're okay?"

"I'm fine, Alaina. Shocked... but fine. It came at a mighty convenient time, so I don't know if I believe him."

"My brother wouldn't lie about something like that," she defended.

"I'm good on him. Listen, I have to go. Tyson invited me over for dinner, and I need to go get ready. I'll talk to you later."

"I guess. Have a good time. I love you."

"I love you too, boo."

I climbed into my BMW, cranked up, and pulled out of the driveway. Thoughts of Walker plagued my mind. Being in the same space with him and saying absolutely didn't even feel right. He tried to hide it, but I could see the sadness in his eyes as he sat silently on the couch.

He looked miserable. With anybody else, that would have made me feel good, but it felt anything but good with him. The part of me that loved him wanted to say something, but the part of me that was ready to move on shut it down. We weren't good together. I didn't want toxic love. Sure, I wanted to settle down, but I didn't want to settle for that.

Ten minutes later, I was pulling into my apartment's parking lot. I got out and headed inside.

"Ms. Sandifer, you have a delivery," Melissa, the front receptionist, said, grabbing my attention.

"A delivery?"

"Yes. One moment."

She disappeared into the back office, returning shortly with a beautiful bouquet of roses and hydrangeas along with an edible arrangement. A smile broke out on my face as I retrieved them from her.

"Somebody has an admirer," Melissa said. "Would this be the handsome gentleman I saw you with the other night?"

"That would be him. Thanks, Melissa."

Securing my items in my hands, I headed to the elevator and up to my floor. Inside the apartment, I set everything on the counter and pulled the card from the bouquet to read it.

BEAUTIFUL FLOWERS FOR A BEAUTIFUL SOUL. *I hope these make you smile.*

--Tyson

PULLING OUT MY PHONE, I dialed his number as I dug into the beautifully arranged fruit bouquet.

"Hey, beautiful," he answered.

"Hey, Tyson."

"How are you?"

"All smiles after receiving your delivery. Thank you. That was so thoughtful."

"You're welcome. I was thinking about you, so I decided to send you a little something."

I found myself blushing.

"Are you ready for dinner?"

"I've been starving myself all day for it, so you better not disappoint me."

He chuckled. "I promise, you'll be satisfied. I just got in from the grocery store, so I'm about to get started. I can't wait to see your pretty face. I've been looking forward to this all day."

"Have you, now?"

"Absolutely."

"Then I guess I better get myself together and make my way over."

"I guess you better. I'll see you soon."

"You will."

We ended the call, and I headed into my bedroom for a shower. The flowers and edible arrangement had been a nice surprise. Tyson was such a nice guy, and it seemed to come from a genuine place. During practice this week, Millicent asked me if I was sure I liked him. I wondered what made her ask that question. My best guess was she was like Anais and wanted love for him. I mean, what else could it be?

* * *

I ARRIVED at Tyson's home around seven thirty.

It was my first time being here, and it was absolutely beautiful. It was an older house, but the upkeep was impeccable. The one-story vintage bungalow was off from the street, surrounded by tall trees that cast a shadow.

It sat in a quiet suburban neighborhood in a corner all its own. The outside was in picture perfect condition, with lots of neatly trimmed bushes lining the front of the property. If it wasn't for the top of the house being visible, you wouldn't be able to see anything.

For a moment, it gave serial killer vibes.

A house hidden from the street gave the perfect setup to drag a bitch's body into the car without being seen. I'd seen way too many horror and mystery movies and shows. I shook the thoughts off as I climbed out of my car and headed up the front steps. Ringing the doorbell, I waited for him to answer. He answered a few seconds later, greeting me with a smile.

"Hey, you," he said, reaching for my hand to pull me inside.

"Hey."

The moment the door closed, he pulled me into his arms and kissed me. It was a little rough at first, but he quickly recovered.

"It's good to see you, love. You look beautiful as always."

"Thank you."

"Can I get you something to drink? I have wine."

"Wine would be nice."

He grabbed my hand and led me into the kitchen. I was greeted by steam and the heavenly aroma of whatever was cooking in his pots. I took a seat on a barstool while he retrieved glasses and an unopened bottle of wine from the fridge. He poured both of us a glass and came to stand next to me.

"To a beautiful night," he said, raising his glass.

"To a beautiful night."

We clinked them together and took a sip. It was possibly the smoothest red wine I'd ever tasted, and it was sweet. When he swallowed his sip, he leaned over and kissed me gently before going back to the stove.

"So what do you have planned for us tonight?" I asked, taking another sip.

"Well dinner, dessert, and I thought we'd just chill and watch a movie or something. Just spend some time together, see where the night takes us."

"I'm cool with that. It's been a long day, and I just want to relax."

"A lot going on?" he inquired over his shoulder.

"Just dance stuff. I had an audition today. I'm sure I could have done better."

"I'm sure you did just fine. If you're half as good as you're teaching my niece to be, you should have nothing to worry about."

"Nah, Millie is already good on her own. She's one of my best dancers. That's why we chose her for co-captain. I'm just helping her expand her skills."

"Don't sell yourself short." He turned off the stove and faced me. "I'd like to see you dance... witness the master at work."

"Well I have a show this coming Friday. I went on tour with GEM last year. He's performing at the university's homecoming."

"You went to school with GEM?"

"You know him as GEM; I know him as Emerald. We grew up in the same neighborhood. His house was right around the corner from mine. Anytime he's doing a local show, I dance for him. He personally asked me to not only dance in this show but choreograph the routine."

"That's big. That'll probably get you a ton of bookings."

"You think? I love choreographing for the girls and my team, and while I know I'd kill this shit, I'm a little nervous. That's a big leap."

I took another sip of my wine. Emerald told me he would shop the live performance to his industry friends in hopes of bringing me business. I'd met with him and his dancers today, and rehearsals were starting tomorrow. I had his set list for the last month, so I had ample time to prepare a few dances. It was the other girls that worried me. I hoped they were receptive because I did not need bad attitudes fucking up my mood or my money.

Women were already catty. Being put in a space where everybody's goal was to get noticed, sometimes, drama was inevitable. I just wanted to do what I was hired for and have a good time.

"Just go in giving your best. Who else has Grammy winning artists name dropping them? If you weren't ready, the opportunity wouldn't be there."

"You are so sweet, you know that?" I hopped off the stool and slid over to give him a kiss. "Where's your bathroom?"

"Down the hall, second door on the left."

"Thanks."

I followed his directions and ended up in a beautiful guest bathroom. Quickly, I handled my business and washed my hands. After drying them, I headed out of the bathroom to go back to the kitchen. As I neared the kitchen, I could hear Tyson on the phone.

"No... no, now is not a good time... We've talked about this."

Who was he talking to? As I got closer, I heard him expel a frustrated sigh as he listened.

"Everything okay?" I asked quietly.

He looked back at me and held up a finger. "As I said, now is not a good time. I'm busy, and we can discuss this at a later date. Goodnight." He hung up and powered off the phone before slipping it in his pocket. "I'm sorry about that. People don't seem to respect that I don't bring work home with me. Are you ready to eat?"

"Yeah... yeah I am."

"Why don't you have a seat and I'll make your plate."

"Thank you."

I shook off the weird feeling I had surrounding the phone call and went to take a seat at the table. He plated us a serving and brought it over. He then brought over the glasses of wine we'd been drinking and topped them off before taking a seat. Reaching for my hands, he blessed the food, and we dug in.

It was a delicious meal of smothered lamb chops over a bed of Jasmine rice, cabbage, and cornbread. When he told me he wanted to cook for me, I wasn't sure if I'd be stopping off to grab a burger on the way home, but this was a pleasant surprise. After we finished eating and cleaning the kitchen, we settled into the living room to watch a movie. I wanted to watch both Black Panther movies and ended up shedding a few tears by the end.

"I know you aren't over there crying," he said, looking over at me.

"You can't tell me that wasn't emotional."

"It was good. I'll give you that." He turned off the television and slid close to me. "You think I can have you to myself for a little bit?"

"You've had me to yourself all night."

"Yeah, but there was the food and then the movies... distractions." He fingered with one of my locs. "I want you with no interruptions."

He leaned in and kissed me softly. His hand traveled up my arm and shoulder to the side of my face. I felt my body being pushed into the soft leather couch and then his weight on top of me. I didn't know what it was about this man kissing me that just set my hormones on fire. When he started kissing on my neck, my legs fell open. If I had on a skirt, he surely would have felt the wetness between my thighs the way his dick was pressed against my mound.

All of the pep talks I gave myself about waiting to share my body with him seemed to be flying at a closed window, trying to break free. I was trying to think with my head, and my pussy kept getting in the way.

"Tyson..."

I moaned against his lips. He pulled the tucked blouse from my pants, and his hand traveled beneath it.

I wasn't wearing a bra, and when his fingers toyed with my nipples, I let out a small whimper. He took that as a green light. I felt the top buttons of the blouse being undone as his lips migrated to my neck. The cool air brushing against my bare skin caused me to shudder as the blouse fell open. He looked down at my hardened buds, licking his lips.

The first swipe of his tongue caused my back to arch slightly from the couch. He captured my nipple between his lips and sucked it into his mouth, moaning as he alternated between devouring each of them.

"I want to taste you so bad, Jorja..." he declared as his free hand unbuttoned my pants.

Just as he was about to slip his hand in, his phone started vibrating loudly in his pocket. He ignored it, and the vibrating soon stopped.

"Where were we?" he asked, turning his attention back to me.

His lips crashed into mine as his hand slipped between the band of my thong and cupped my pussy. He was greeted by the slickness already creating a puddle between my legs.

He moaned. "Mmmm.... You're so wet already. I bet—"

The phone started vibrating again. Whoever it was, was killing my mood. There was no way it was work this time of night. I removed his hand from my pants and pushed him off of me.

"Just answer the phone," I said, standing to fix my clothes. I wasn't even sure when he turned it back on because I watched him turn it off before we ate.

He sighed as he pulled the phone from his pocket. I caught a glimpse of the contact name. Francesca. A frown appeared on his face as he answered it.

"Yes!" he snapped. "No... What do you mean she—" He began rubbing his temples. "Okay. I said okay. I'm on my way."

He hung up as I stood with my arms crossed, waiting for an explanation.

"I'm sorry, love."

"Who was that?"

"My cousin. Her mom was my mother's sister. They just rushed her to hospital. She was complaining of having chest pains then she just collapsed, unresponsive. I have to get to the hospital."

I remembered him telling me that his mother died the same way. My face softened.

"I'm sorry... Do you want me to go with you?"

"No. I know you have a busy day tomorrow, and I don't wanna keep you out any longer. I'll update you."

I searched his eyes. The same weird feeling I had about the first phone call entered my body. I didn't know what it was, but I didn't like it.

"Okay," I said, picking up my shoes from the floor.

As I slipped them on, my eyes never left his. He seemed a little nervous, and I picked up on it; however, I didn't show my hand. Instead, I grabbed my keys and my phone and headed for the door.

"Call me tomorrow?" I tossed over my shoulder.

"Sure thing. Drive safe, Jorja."

"Mmm hmm."

Without another word, I walked out of the house and out to my car.

Fourteen

WALKER

"I DON'T FEEL like doing this shit today," Mr. King mumbled.

I took a seat in front of him.

Julian King was a fairly new client of mine. A year ago, the forty-year-old man got into a hit and run accident, leaving him in a coma for six months. When he woke up, he learned that he was partially paralyzed. As a former firefighter, it was a hard blow for him. To make the new adjustment worse, two weeks after he woke up from the coma, his wife left him, stating she couldn't handle the responsibility of caring for him.

Earlier this week, when his sister brought him in, she told me that his wife served him with divorce papers. My heart went out to the man. That was a fucked-up way to leave somebody she took vows with. Up until then, he'd been trying his hardest to get back to himself, hoping that she would come back to him. It seemed like since he was served, all the fight in him was gone.

I clasped my hands together. "I know you're having a hard day."

He scoffed. "A hard day? Try a hard year."

"I know. I understand."

"You don't understand shit about what I'm going through. Was your life almost snatched from you? Did you lose out on six months of life, only to wake up and find out you're crippled? And now to add insult to injury, did your wife leave you? What reason do I have to wanna do this anymore?"

"You have you, man. Don't you wanna do this for you?"

He was quiet.

"Look, Mr. King. I'm gonna keep it real with you. Sometimes, fucked up shit happens. What happened to you was an unfortunate accident. And your wife leaving afterwards... well, that was just cruel. I know you feel like you have no reason to keep going, but you've still got you. You've still got life, and that in itself is a blessing, man. You been doing good here. I've seen you getting your strength up. You're getting your stamina back. If you put in the work like you did in the beginning, you'll be ahead of our schedule."

I playfully slapped his leg and tried to lighten his mood. "You're still a good looking guy. I see the way the ladies look at you when we're in the gym, playa. Ms. Pam can't keep her eyes off of you. If you are worried about bouncing back when all of this is over, you have nothing to worry about, my guy."

Again, he was quiet. I sighed as I stood. From time to time, I ran into clients who wanted to give up, much like he did now. They were the ones that needed tough love.

"Alright, Mr. King. Get up."

He frowned as he looked up at me.

"Let's go. I'm not gonna allow you to do this to yourself. If you don't wanna do this for any other reason, you do it for you. In this world, sometimes all you've got is yourself. All you can depend on is you. If you can't trust yourself to do what's best for you, then you've already lost before you even get in the game. Fight. You've got that shit in you, and I see it. I feel it. You've got anger. You're hurt. I'm sure you feel rage. Channel it. Turn all that negative energy into strength and endurance. Get. Up."

I reached for his hand.

For a moment, he just looked at it. He hung his head, seemingly in his thoughts. He reluctantly grabbed my hand and allowed me to help him up from the floor.

"We're gonna do this right this time, okay?" I said.

"I got you."

For the rest of the session, I pushed him, and he gave it his best. That was all I could ask for. By the time he left, he seemed to be in better spirits. I retreated to my office to document his progress. Since he was my last client for the day, I had plans to head home when I was done. As I sat behind my desk, my fingers moving like lightning across my keyboard, there was a knock at my door.

"Come in," I said without looking up.

"Hey," Margo said, stepping in.

"What's up?"

"I'm about to head out for the day."

"Okay."

"You sure you're okay? You've been moping around here all week."

"I'm fine, Margo."

"Well... it's Friday. If you don't have anything to do, you should come with me, Lacey, and a few of our friends."

I looked up. "Are they all gay?"

"They are."

"Then no, thank you. If they look like you and Lacey, that's too much temptation for women who don't want me."

"Aren't you trying to turn over a new leaf? Maybe you should be around women that like pussy as much as you do. At least then you won't be tempted to fuck one."

"Nah, Margo. If I get the liquor in me, I'm gonna try to turn one of your friends out just for the hell of it."

She rolled her eyes. "You know pussy isn't everything?"

"Says the woman who has two when she goes home."

"Actually, I have three, but that's a story for a different day."

"I don't even wanna know."

"Anyway! If you decide to come out, we're going to homecoming and then hitting up the afterparties."

"I'll think about it. I'm not feeling sociable these days."

"You have to get out of this funk. I know you miss your girl, but life goes on, Walker."

"Margo, I told that woman I love her the same night she went out on a date with another man. And that was after I fucked her a few days before."

"You can't be serious."

"I was drunk. I don't even remember that shit. And now the more I think about it, I feel like I violated her. That shit has been fucking with me, Margo. I at least want to apologize." I leaned back in my chair and ran my hands down my face. "Seems like all I do lately is fucking apologize. I'm tired of feeling like a sorry ass nigga."

"Then you have to stop doing sorry ass, fuck nigga shit."

"Why do I have to be a fuck nigga too?"

"Don't make me tell you what you're acting like." She threw me a smirk and tossed her stress ball at me. "I'm totally playing. It's good to see you show actual emotion about something."

"I express my emotions just fine—"

"That's a goddamn lie. How many times have you used sex to fix a problem?"

I couldn't answer that because it was too many to count.

"Hence the reason we're having this conversation. You communicate with your dick. That's where your ego lies. I can tell you've smooth talked women out of their panties. I'm even sure you've had a few of them so dickmatized that even when they couldn't stand you, they still loved fucking you. Unfortunately, sometimes, we women love that toxic shit. It turns us *on* until it turns us *off*. That's what happened with your girl. Once we get turned off, you either need to step up or step off. What are you gonna do?"

She offered a tight-lipped smile as she stepped back into the hallway and closed the door. I turned my chair to the window and propped my feet up. Gazing out at the city traffic, I squeezed the stress ball in my hand. Margo didn't have to read me like that. Hearing that shit out loud made it sound as bad as it was.

At this point, I just felt like maybe it was best to just let shit be what it was. I mean, that was the last thing I wanted, but what the hell else could I do?

* * *

THE BURIAL OF A PLAYER

"WHAT ARE YOU DOING TONIGHT?" I asked Reese as I sat across from him, tossing a basketball in the air.

"You know I gotta show my pretty face at homecoming. Why? You wanna go?"

"I don't know. Margo invited me out there with her and her fiancée and some of their friends."

"Margo? That's the bald-headed chick with the fat ass you brought to the baby shower?"

"Margo ain't baldheaded. She has a low-cut fade."

"Whatever. You going or not?"

"I don't have shit else to do. I've been in the house all week long."

"Depressed ass nigga. You know your player card is revoked, right? You broke the number one rule: Don't fall in love."

"I don't wanna be a player no more, man."

"I'm not a playa, I just crush a lot," he sang, dancing in his seat. "That was my shit."

"Nigga, you high?"

"Is that even a question?"

"I'm over here being sentimental, and you're singing and dancing." I threw a pillow at him.

"You blowing my high, man! Look, I got this honey coming through to give me a fresh retwist, and I'm trying to make something shake with that. Go home. Wash ya ass and make yourself look like somebody, and I'm gonna come scoop you up at around nine thirty. The concert starts at ten."

"So you putting me out?"

"I'm saying see you later." He fished a blunt out from under a magazine and lit it. "You know the way out."

I kissed my teeth as I peeled myself off his couch. Grabbing the throw pillow, I pretended to smother him with it.

"I'ma tell Mama you are trying to kill me," he said, snatching it away. "She's gon' beat yo' red ass."

"Fuck you." I slammed the door of his condo shut and headed to my Rover.

Maybe a night out would put me in a better mood.

Cranking up, I backed out of his driveway and headed toward

home. I didn't even realize I was down to almost five miles until empty. I'd been ignoring my gas light for the longest, just driving on a wing and a prayer. Knowing that I wouldn't make it home, I stopped off at the nearest gas station to fill up.

After paying at the pump, I allowed it to fill while I waited in the car. I sent Margo a text, letting her know I would see her at the concert.

As I sat aimlessly, watching the gas station patrons, one caught my eye as he was coming out the store. It was the nigga I saw Jorja on a date with. I didn't doubt his were the hands I saw rubbing her feet in her IG story the other night.

My lip curled in disgust as I watched him walk to his car with his phone to his ear. He looked to be having an intense conversation with whoever was on the other end. He wasn't yelling, but I could tell he was whispering something angry. The deep frown on his face gave away his emotions. He was pissed.

Behind me, I heard the pump click, signaling that my tank was full. I stepped out, my eyes still on him. I guess he felt me staring and finally looked in my direction. For a moment, he stared at me before ending his call and making his way over as I hung up the pump.

"Walker Jareau, right?" he asked, coming to a stop in front of me. "Your father played for the Rippers. Edwin Jareau."

"Yeah. That's him."

"I'm a big fan of his." He cocked his head to the side. "Did you need something?"

"From you? Not a damn thing."

"Well you looked at me like there was a problem, so I thought I'd ask."

I chuckled. "And you walked over here like you knew me and felt safe about it."

"What reason would I have to be afraid? I'm dealing with a *single* woman, so... I haven't done anything to warrant a threat."

"Right..." I nodded as I capped my gas tank. "So who was that on the phone? You looked like you were having a pretty intense conversation. I know Ja, and there is no way she'd sit on the phone arguing with you."

"*That* is my business."

"It might be. But if you are on some funny shit with her, I'm gonna make it mine."

He chuckled. "I don't think you're in a position to insert yourself where you're no longer welcomed. If I remember correctly, she's been done with you for how many months now? That means whatever you two had is done. It also means that you need not worry about anything concerning Jorja or myself. We're good. Even if we weren't, there is no level of comfort that *you* could give her. Let's just stay in our lanes."

His phone rang, and he lifted it in his hand. I glanced quick enough to see the name Francesca.

"Francesca, huh? Looks like she wants to finish that argument."

Again, he chuckled. "You would love to have something to go back and tell Jorja, wouldn't you? Anything to make your case. Let me be real with you about something. There is nothing you can say to her about *me*, that won't make it worse for *you*. It doesn't matter if it's true or not. Nothing that comes out of your mouth will be taken seriously by her. Thank you for that. You should just bow out while you're ahead."

He pressed the answer button on the phone. "If we're done here, I have to take this."

"I've got my eye on you, nigga."

He glared at me before he turned and headed back to his car, phone to his ear. I watched as he climbed into the vehicle, cranked up, and drove away. Everything in me wanted to lay that nigga the fuck out. Something was off about him. He was too cocky, and cocky niggas always had something to hide. Whoever this Francesca woman was might just be it.

Fifteen

JORJA

THE CROWD WAS ALREADY GOING wild for the opening act.

It was a local group that GEM handpicked to share the stage with him. Whenever he did hometown shows, he always selected local talent to open the show. LUXE happened to be a group my girls and I danced behind on the regular.

"They are fucking it up tonight," my girl Kenya said, watching beside me.

"They are. If we hadn't booked this gig, we probably would have been right out there."

"You know they asked."

"As long as they ask when they blow up after this, we can call it even."

We continued to watch the show, vibing and dancing along. I looked out into the crowd. As my eyes passed over the sea of people, I caught a glimpse of a familiar face. There was Walker and Reese with a group of women, one of which was the girl he brought with him to Adina's baby shower. I was about to frown until I saw her all hugged up on the female next to her.

"So he was telling the truth about that..." I mumbled to myself.

"Who?" Kenya asked. I pointed to Walker. "You still giving that man a hard time?"

"I'm not giving him shit."

"You know you miss him, and that square ass nigga you're dealing with now ain't it."

"Tyson is a nice guy."

"He may be nice, but he's not for you. Don't get me wrong, he's fine and all. But you and Walker... y'all had something—"

"Toxic."

"I wouldn't even call it toxic. It's just the way you two were with each other. You can say what you want, but I know that man loves you."

"According to him, he does."

"And you love him."

"That doesn't mean I should be with him, Kenya. Looking at our entanglement as a whole, love wasn't enough. I was ready for commitment, and he wasn't. I told him a long time ago this would be over if that happened. He waited until I was moving on to tell me he loved me or want to show any interest in wanting that. You know what he told me the night he came over and we had drunk sex? He wanted to come home. *Home*, Kenya. When did I become home?"

"You were probably always home for him, Ja. Niggas aren't as sentimental as we are, girl."

"That's a lie. My brother-in-law is sentimental. Cartel is sentimental. His father is sentimental. You know when Walker has no problem expressing himself? When he's fucking me. Don't express your feelings only when you're in my guts. Be just as loud about that shit when you aren't."

"Ja."

I rolled my eyes as I heard his familiar voice calling my name. I turned to see security blocking him from entering backstage.

"Looks like somebody wants to talk," Kenya said. "I'm headed to the dressing room. Don't be too long. We are on in thirty minutes."

She walked off, leaving me standing there with my arms crossed. I motioned for security to let him through. He came up the stairs and stood in front of me.

"What do you want?" I asked. "Make it quick."

"Can we go somewhere quiet?"

I kissed my teeth as I walked off backstage, with him following close behind. I found an unlocked, unoccupied room and led him inside.

"What?" I asked closing the door.

"Jorja... I just wanted to apologize."

"Not this again."

"Just hear me out. I promise it's the last time. I won't bother you. I won't show up unannounced. I'll just take my L."

I sighed. I waved my hand toward the set of chairs, motioning for him to sit down. We sat across from each other, and he reached for my hands. Reluctantly, I gave them to him.

"I know I've apologized a million times for the way things went, and you don't want to hear that, so I won't say it. I do want to apologize for my recent behavior. The night I came over... what we did... that wasn't my intention. I honestly just wanted to talk to you. I was vulnerable. You were vulnerable, and I feel like I took advantage of that. I feel like I took advantage of you, and that's been haunting me, Ja."

He looked down at his feet, sadness written all over his face.

"I never want to hurt you. I never want you to feel like I took something from you. That whole experience made me feel like I violated you—"

I thought I was tripping until I saw the tear slip down his cheek. The frown on my face relaxed. Walker didn't cry often, and for him to do so, that had to have been weighing heavily on his chest. Maybe it was time we really sat down and had this talk.

"Look at me," I said, lifting his chin. "You didn't violate me. I could have slept on the floor or the couch or anywhere but in bed with you. I could have moved when you touched me. I had options. The truth is... as much as I hate that I allowed it to happen, I craved it. It wasn't just you I was mad at. I was mad at myself for having a weak moment."

"I don't like this space we're in, Ja. I miss the fuck out of you, and I know there's no chance in fixing it. We're gonna be around each other because of family. I don't wanna fight with you. I don't want you to look at me in disgust every time you see me. I just want us to be friends, if I can't have anything else. I love you enough to let everything else go but that."

I searched his eyes. His tone felt sincere, and when I looked into his eyes, I felt like he was telling the truth. While I could have taken it at face value, I had questions that needed answers.

"Why did you wait until I was seeing someone to tell me you loved me?" I asked.

"Because I didn't admit it to myself until the morning you put me out. You wouldn't have received it if I told you then. I didn't wanna tell you the way that I told you, but I was desperate, Jorja. Seeing you with him..." He shook his head. "You deserve to be loved, and I'm sorry that I couldn't give that to you when you wanted it from me."

For the first time in months, I actually believed him. There was nothing for him to gain by lying about his feelings now. Hell, I was shocked that he was telling me this to begin with. Once upon a time, getting this out of him would have been like pulling teeth. I wasn't sure how to feel right now.

He looked at me, gently rubbing the back of my hand with his thumb. "Do you love me, Ja?"

I didn't want to answer that. Answering it would make it too real, and I was trying to move on from what we shared. Yet, when he asked again, I knew my silence wouldn't suffice.

"Ja... do you love me?"

"Yes," I whispered, pulling my hands away. "I was afraid to tell you. You made it a point to tell people that I was just your nigga, that we were just friends, and neither of us wanted commitment. It was my own fault for sticking around as long as I did when my feelings for you started to change. I just kept hoping that you would wake up one day and realize we could have been more than what we were.

"I look at Jamison and Liv... Cartel and Adina... your parents... they all share such a beautiful love. No man has ever loved me like that. I never thought I'd desire to be loved like that, but I do. And I deserve it without one day wondering if this is the day you decide you don't really want me."

"I want you, Jorja," he said, cupping my face. "I've been chasing you for months, baby."

"But we wasted two years 'just fucking around'," I said, quoting his own words.

"I'll admit, in the beginning, that's all it was. But I got to know you. I know I love sleeping next to you. I know I love the twinkle in your eye when you eat good food. I love your obnoxious laughter when you find something funny. I love you roasting my ass when we're high. I love watching you dance, because it gives you so much life. I love the way you love my family, especially the kids. You haven't been just pussy to me in a long, long time, Ja. I'm sorry it took me so long to realize that."

He dropped his hands but kept his gaze on me.

"I love you, and I'm in love with you. I love you enough to let you find what you deserve. But that nigga you are entertaining... he ain't it."

"Tyson is a nice guy."

He frowned, and venom laced his words as he spoke. "He's a cocky muthafucka, and he's hiding something. Don't fall for that shit."

"Okay, Walker," I said, throwing up my hands as I stood. "I don't wanna talk about Tyson with you. I have a show in ten minutes. You have to go."

He nodded as he stood. "Can I hug you?"

Even though everything in me was telling me not to, I stepped closer to him and allowed him to pull me into his arms. He held me against his chest, gently stroking my back. The familiar feeling flooded my body as my head rested near his heart. I tried to fight those feelings, but it was no use. Then I did it. I looked up at him. His eyes met mine, and for a moment, we just gazed at each other.

When his head dipped and his lips pressed against mine, I couldn't stop myself from kissing him back. His hands came to the sides of my face, and his tongue slipped into my mouth. He kissed me with passion... with lust and desire... with love. Why couldn't it have been this easy months ago? Why did it have to be a battle when adult conversations could have prevented all of this?

He pulled away from me, wiping the corners of my mouth.

"Have a good show. I'm proud of you."

He kissed my forehead before letting me go and walking toward the door. I wrapped my arms around myself to fill the void. More than that, I did it to comfort myself because if I didn't seek some sort of comfort, I was going to fall the fuck apart.

"I love you, Ja," he said to my back.

I heard the door close, and immediately, I fell back into the couch, crying profusely. He told me that he loved me, and he meant it. He let me go so that I could find the love I deserved. Why the hell was I crying over him?

A knock on the door caused me to gather myself and wipe my face. "Come in."

The door opened, and GEM, AKA Emerald, stuck his head in.

"It's almost show time. I was wondering where you disappeared to."

"I'm sorry. I just had something to take care of."

"Are you okay, Jorja? You been crying?"

"I'm fine. I'm ready for the show."

He looked at me silently for a moment, then nodded his head. "Well, okay. We can talk after the show."

I didn't say anything. I had to get it together. It was time to work, and I couldn't let anything fuck up my check. Not Walker, not my feelings and emotions, nothing. If it wasn't this performance, it had no space in my head at this moment.

* * *

"Y'ALL HAVE BEEN GREAT, MAN!" Emerald spoke to the crowd. "It's always a good feeling when I'm back home in my old stomping grounds. Real quick, I wanna give a few shout outs. First, giving Honor to God. Without Him, there is no me. To my wife, Rhyon, I love you, baby. Thank you for being by my side tonight."

He blew her a kiss offstage, and she blew one right back.

"To my babies, Marisol and EJ, Daddy loves you. I continue to do this for you. Of course I have to thank my family for always supporting my dreams. To my fans, y'all have shown me unconditional love over the years, and I wouldn't be here without you. Thank you to Benedict College for allowing me to come party with y'all for homecoming. Thank you to the talented team on this stage. It's been an honor and a pleasure to work with you tonight. Last, but certainly not least, y'all give it up for one of the hardest working women and the baddest choreographer I know. Please give a round of applause to Jorja Sandifer."

He beckoned me to the front of the stage as the crowd clapped and cheered. When I stood next to him, he grabbed my hand.

"Now I know many of y'all are familiar with her work," Emerald continued. "You may have seen her on tour with me last year, and I know she's got her foot on a few necks around here. Y'all are looking at a legend in the making. Maybe if you give her a little encouragement, she'll agree to come choreograph for me full time."

I blushed as the crowd began cheering again. I really did have the time of my life choreographing for this show. While it would be a dream come true, I think so much time away from my family would take a toll on me. For one, I was *not* missing the birth of Liv's baby. Nothing but death could keep me from my sister. I knew she would encourage me to venture off into the world. I loved the traveling aspects of the job, but honestly, I was mostly content with little ol' South Carolina living.

Columbia wasn't a huge city. I loved going outside of city limits, but this was home. Everything I loved was here. Still, I knew that this was an amazing opportunity. If favorable odds could be worked out, I might just consider it.

After Emerald said his goodbyes to the crowd, we all left the stage as the crowd began to disperse. Backstage, the chatter was loud. I located Emerald and Rhyon heading toward his dressing room.

"You just put me on the spot like that?" I jested.

"Anything to get you to change your mind," he said.

"You did a great job with those girls, Jorja," Rhyon said. "If I had some rhythm, I would ask you to teach me a thing or two."

Emerald offered me a position as his exclusive choreographer a while ago. He recently brought it up again when I booked this show.. I was shocked yet honored that he had that much confidence in me.

I blushed. "Thank you. And for the record, I haven't said no. I'm just weighing my options. You, Mr. Grammy Winner, have been away from home a long time. It's not so easy to leave everything behind."

"Trust me, I know it's not," he said, looking at his wife. "That's why I came back to claim my everything."

Rhyon giggled as he kissed her cheek. "Something or someone holding you back, Jorja?"

"It's a few things... a few people."

"Like the gentleman I saw leaving you before the show?" Emerald asked.

"That is over," I said, looking down at my feet.

"Was he bothering you?"

"No. We just needed to finally talk, and it was emotional. He and I dealt with each other for about two years. It started off as a physical thing, and you know how that goes." I rolled my eyes. "Anyway, I walked away, and now it seems like I'm tempted to fall right back."

"Old habits die hard," Rhyon said with a giggle. "It was all of, I think, three days into him being back in town before I let Em talk me out of my panties. How long has it been?"

"It was *five* months. In light of recent events... a couple weeks. I'm trying to finally move on, and this nigga has me in a chokehold." I looked up at them. "Can I ask you both a question?"

"Of course," they answered simultaneously.

"Why did you break up?"

Rhyon raised her hand. "At the time, we wanted different things. Emerald was just starting his professional career. I was making a name for myself at the law firm. He wanted me to move to California with him, and to me, that meant giving up everything I worked for and starting over. We tried it for a while, and the distance really put a strain on our relationship."

"I think I underestimated this lifestyle a bit," Emerald said. "In my mind, we were about to be living our best life. I saw me out there topping charts and her killing court cases. We'd been a part of each other's lives so long, it never really hit that we might not always be together."

"Life has a way of humbling you," Rhyon said, chuckling. "We changed. We took the time to learn ourselves, to grow."

Emerald added, "When the time was right, we crossed paths again."

"What he means is, he took a sabbatical from the music to come get my ass. The man told me he wasn't leaving town until I was his."

"Looks like he was right," I said.

"He was." She looked lovingly at her husband.

"How did you know things would be different?"

Emerald chuckled. "That took a lot of faith, prayer, and just working at making our relationship what we wanted and needed. If you think it can be salvaged, I say don't give up completely."

"But..." Rhyon added, "only if you both of you feel it in your heart."

"I haven't exactly been the most forthcoming in talking to him. We mostly see each other these days in family settings. He's Aleviyah's brother-in-law."

"That's right!" Rhyon exclaimed. "She did get married!"

"And expecting," I confirmed. "It's her first baby, and I don't wanna miss a second of it. That's the major factor in whether I take this position. Plus, how can I leave Mama and Granny?"

"That damn Ms. Oleena." Emerald smiled as he shook his head. "How is she with her sassy self? Is she still everybody's Grandma?"

"She's still the neighborhood granny and still very sassy. She's been living with my mother for the last couple of years now. You should stop by and see them before you leave town."

"We'll do that. I'd love for them to meet my kids. Maybe I'll luck up and get a slice of her sweet potato pie."

"If she knows you're coming, I promise she'll have one ready."

He clasped his hands together, offering me his million-dollar smile. "You wanna hook an old friend up?"

"I've got you. I'm gonna let you guys go. My feet are hurting, and I'm about ready to get home and get my ass in bed."

We exchanged hugs and goodbyes. As I was walking off toward the back, I heard my name being called.

"Jorja!"

I turned to see Tyson standing with security. In his hands were a bouquet of roses and a smile on his handsome face. I motioned for them to let him through. He made his way through the crowd and over to me.

"Hey, baby," he said, pulling me in for a hug.

"Hey, Tyson."

He handed me the flowers. "These are for you, beautiful."

His lips dropped to mine, and instantly, I remembered that Walker's tongue had been in my mouth earlier. I gently pulled away.

"Thank you. I thought you couldn't make it?"

"I moved some things around. I caught the last three songs. You did your thing out there. It was worthy of that shoutout."

"I was just doing what I love. Thanks."

"Do you plan on enjoying the homecoming festivities?"

"I might go to the game tomorrow. Right now, I'm tired, and I just want to get home."

"How about I follow you? Maybe I could give you a massage before you go down for the night." He pulled me into his arms again. "I've missed you."

He leaned in and kissed me again. It was a quick peck, so it didn't feel as cringy this time.

"A massage does sound good."

"I got you. I'll take good care of you."

"I actually rode here with a friend. Let me grab my things, and I'll be right back."

"Okay, love."

Flowers in hand, I headed for the dressing room to grab my bag. I really did just want to go to sleep, but a massage would be heavenly.

Sixteen

WALKER

HOMECOMING DIDN'T OWE me shit.

After the concert on Friday, Reese, Margo, her friends, and I ended up bar hopping in The Vista and Five Points. It was swarming with college kids and alumni. Of course, it wouldn't be anything without bar brawls breaking out all over the place. After witnessing these two girls drag another one in a bloody fight, I knew it was time to get my ass out of there and head home.

It was Sunday, my normal chill day.

I spent the morning nursing a hangover. Around twelve, I got up, showered, dressed, and left my house. Today was Granny Oleena's birthday, so she was having a small cookout at her and Ms. Alicia's house. I knew my family would be in attendance, and she would have my head if I didn't at least show my face.

After stopping off to grab a gift and some flowers, I headed over to the other side of town. The house was located in a predominantly black neighborhood. It was one of those places where kids were playing basketball in the streets. People were sitting outside on their porch or congregating in the front yard, playing cards and listening to music.

Growing up in a wealthy neighborhood, I didn't experience much like this unless I was with friends after school or on the weekends. I loved the vibe. Since coming over here all the time with Ja, my face was recognizable, mainly by the kids and the elderly people on the block. Jorja took me on several walks around the neighborhood, introducing me to people from her childhood.

I think what I most admired was the whole neighborhood felt like a big family. As I got out of my Range with the flowers and gift, I threw up my hand to wave at a few familiar faces. One of the kids I normally saw playing ball came up to me. She was an adorable eight-year-old little girl named Quani. She bounced over to me with a head full of beads and a mouth full of attitude.

"Mr. Walker, where you been?" she asked, her hands on her hips.

"I've been busy, lil bit. Why? You missed me?"

"I miss you buying us ice cream. You're on time today! Mr. Johnny is coming around the corner in a minute."

Sure enough, I turned my head to see Mr. Johnny's ice cream truck pulling at the stop sign. Kids started coming outside, running to the sidewalk.

"So you came over here to stick me for my paper, Quani?"

"Well, you been gone a long time. You can make it up with ice cream for everybody."

"Everybody! How did we go from you to everybody?"

"We all missed you."

That made me smile. I did miss coming over here. On several occasions, I bought the kids ice cream from Mr. Johnny. They always had me in the hot ass sun, playing ball or some other game with them. To them, I was a big ass kid that bought them sweets. I didn't mind though. I loved kids.

"I guess that's fair then," I said, reaching for her hand. "Come on."

I waved at Tamara, her mother, who was watching from across the street. The kids gathered around me, giving me various greetings and asking where I'd been. As Mr. Johnny rolled to a stop, I led them over to the truck.

"How you doing, Mr. J?" I asked, extending my hand to shake his.

"I'm blessed and highly favored. It's good to see you. It's been a while."

"Yeah, it has. Lil Miss Quani here decided to run my pockets for ice cream for everybody."

"She's always been my best customer." He smiled as he winked at her.

"Whatever they want is on me."

"I got you."

According to Jorja, Mr. Johnny had been the neighborhood ice cream man for about twenty years now. His wife died about ten years ago, and they never had any children. They basically adopted the whole neighborhood. Parents respected them. Kids loved them. Now that she was gone, he'd taken to doing this full time to keep himself busy.

"You here for Oleena's birthday?" he asked as he passed out the ice cream bars to the kids from memory.

"Yes, sir. I couldn't let the day go by without showing my face. She'd never let me hear the end of it."

He chuckled. "I'm glad you know it."

Once he finished giving out the ice cream, he gave me my total. I paid him in cash, tipping him a little extra. After saying goodbye to the kids, I headed back toward the house. Entering through the side gate, I went into the backyard. The cookout was in full swing. The deejay had the music pumping. The grill was going, and the aromas had my mouth watering. I could almost taste the barbecued ribs.

Making my way through the crowd, I located Granny sitting in her favorite spot in the tree swing. She was talking to another older woman I'd never met before. When she saw me, she rose from the swing with the biggest smile.

"There's my baby!" she exclaimed, greeting me with the tightest hug. "Oh I've missed you!"

"I've missed you too, Granny," I said, rocking her from side to side. I kissed her cheek and held her away from me. "Look at you looking so fine on your birthday. What am I gonna do with you?"

She waved me off.

"Who's this... fine, tattooed gentleman, Leena?" the other woman asked, her eyes passing over me slowly. "I definitely would have remembered this face. How you doin', suga?"

Was this woman flirting with me?

THE BURIAL OF A PLAYER

"I'm fine, ma'am. How are you?"

"Please... call me Roxy."

She held out her hand. I, being the natural flirt I am, decided to play along. She was a nice-looking older woman, probably around my mama's age, and very youthful. I kissed the back of her hand and offered her a smile.

"How you doing, Ms. Roxy?" I asked. "It's a pleasure to meet you."

"Ooo, and he has manners. How old are you, baby?"

"He is not looking for a cougar cat, Roxy," Granny said, slapping her hand away.

I had to laugh at her. She never failed to have a comeback.

"This is Aleviyah's brother-in-law, and he's off limits."

"I see no ring on his finger."

"You might see a ring around your eye," Granny mumbled, turning back to me. "How are you, baby?"

"I'm good. You know I had to come see you for your G-day. And I come bearing gifts."

I handed her the flowers and gift bag.

"You shouldn't have!" She reached for them with a smile.

"I can take them back, now—"

"Absolutely not!"

She took the items from me and kissed my cheek. "Thank you, suga. Come with me in the house so I can put these flowers away and see what you got me."

Linking her arm through mine, she led me toward the back porch. I waved at several people I hadn't seen in a while and a few of my family that was already here. Once inside, she placed the flower arrangement in a fresh vase of water. Settled at the table, she pulled the card from the bag first.

Her smile was wide as she read the heartfelt message I wrote inside. Her eyes widened as she opened the check I'd given her.

"This is too much! I can't accept this!"

"You can and you will. Go do something nice for yourself. You can do that while wearing what's in the bag."

"What am I gonna do with you?" she asked, shaking her head as she dug into the bag. When she pulled out the velvet box, she gasped. "Walker Jareau. You did not get me jewelry!"

"These are your golden years, and they should be celebrated in gold."

She opened the box to find a beautiful gold tennis necklace, bracelet, and diamond earring set.

"You are going to spoil me," she said, dabbing her eyes. "Thank you, suga. Put it on me."

I removed the items from the box and quickly latched them into place. She pulled out her phone to see her reflection in the camera.

"Don't I look good!"

I chuckled. "You look fly. The next time I get you a gift, it'll be a grill that matches mine. You gotta let them know how we rep."

She laughed. "Me? With a grill? Chile, I'll be the talk of the bingo hall."

"Give those old ladies a reason to talk about you, girl."

I reached for her hands and pulled her to her feet. She wrapped her arms around me, embracing me in a grandmotherly hug.

"It's really good to see you, Walker. I thought you'd forgotten about me."

"I could never. I've just been trying to keep my distance."

"You and Jorja... I'll tell ya."

As if we'd talked her up, the front door opened, and in walked Jorja. She was looking so damn fine in the white mid-drift top and high waisted brown skirt that hugged her curves and stopped mid-thigh. She dressed the look down with a green baseball cap, matching green purse, and white Forces. She was wearing one of my favorite wigs of hers— long, black, and curly. That shit always smelled so good that I'd bury my face in it. If it was one thing this woman was gonna do, it was change her hair.

"Happy birthday, Granny!" She squealed as her grandmother went to meet her with a hug. "You look so good, girl!"

Granny struck a pose. "I know I do."

"I see you are dripping in diamonds today, as you should be. Go on with your bad self!"

"Well, my suga here gifted them," Granny said, motioning to me.

THE BURIAL OF A PLAYER

Jorja's eyes met mine. "Hey, Walker," she said, smiling softly.

"Hey, Ja."

She turned back to her grandmother. "My little gift isn't gonna compare to Mr. Big Spender over her." She handed her a large gift bag.

Granny waved her off as she took it. "I appreciate all gifts. You thought enough of me to get me something."

"Girl you know I love you! Open it."

Granny sat the bag on the table and removed the tissue paper. When she pulled out the brand new designer bag, she broke into a smile.

"You know I've been eyeballing that bag you carry! I can't believe you got me one!"

Jorja grinned. "It's your world, lady. You can have whatever you like."

They shared a hug and kiss before Ja turned to me.

"You know you're gonna have to top diamonds for her birthday next year, right?" she said.

I chuckled. "Granny can get whatever she wants out of me."

"Well, Granny, if you ever get tired of wearing that, you can slide them over here," Ja said, flipping her hair. "You know diamonds are a girl's best friend."

I shook my head. I'd iced her out a few times when I bought myself new pieces. If we didn't do anything else, we always matched each other's fly when we stepped out. She was wearing a necklace and bracelet I bought her right now.

The door opened wider, and in stepped that fucking nigga. Jorja smiled awkwardly as he closed the door. I could tell she wasn't expecting to run in to me as soon as she walked through the door.

"Who's this?" Granny asked.

"Granny... this is my friend Tyson. Tyson, this is my granny, Oleena Sandifer."

"It's very nice to meet you, ma'am. Happy birthday."

"Thank you, sweetheart. Oh, have you met Walker?"

He looked up at me, smile frozen in place. "We've been acquainted."

"Well... welcome to the party. I'm sure my granddaughter will make sure you know where everything is. Shall we head out back?"

"Yes!" Jorja said, clasping her hands together. "I could smell Mr. Henry's ribs from the street."

She grabbed Tyson's hand and led him toward the back. Granny looked at me, and I looked at her.

"I'm sorry. I didn't know she was bringing anybody."

"It's okay," I said, raising my hand. "Ja and I spoke. For now, I think we cleared a little air. I'm giving her, her space to find what she needs."

"Well, no matter who she picks, you will always be my baby too." She kissed my cheek. "Come on. I want to dance, and I need a partner that can keep up with me."

I smiled, knowing she was trying to distract me. It was cool. I loved dancing with her at functions. It was her birthday, and I wouldn't let the sour taste in my mouth about that nigga being here ruin her special day.

* * *

"SO THIS IS A THING?" Reese asked, motioning to Jorja and Tyson.

We sat at a picnic table playing dominoes and chopping it up with Jamison and Cartel.

"It's something," I mumbled.

I glanced up from the dominoes in my hand to see Tyson with his leg tossed over a bench and Ja sitting between them as he fed her potato salad. They were way too fucking cozy. He was sitting up on her like he'd been in her. The last thing I wanted to picture was that nigga being inside of her.

"You okay watching that shit?" Cartel asked me.

"What am I gonna do? Show my ass? Look, I've accepted where shit went wrong. It's been long enough, man. Ja and I had a talk. We've come to terms with a few things. She's free to be happy."

They all looked at me with wide-eyed expressions.

Jamison slapped me on the back. "Well, I'm glad to see you being mature about this."

"I'm growing, nigga. I have a long way to go to catch up to your ass, but I'm growing."

He chuckled. "I'm still growing, too."

"I hope your old ass is working out so you can chase this baby you're about to have. You're about to be forty."

"We'll see how old you think forty is when you reach forty."

"I have eleven years to find out. For real though. How are you feeling preparing for a new baby again?"

"I think I'm driving Liv crazy. The closer she gets to her due date, the more nervous I get. I just want her to relax, and she won't sit her short ass down."

"You know you can't tell these women what to do," Cartel said, kissing his teeth. "Adina is hardheaded too."

Reese laughed. "Y'all are complaining like y'all aren't their yes men."

Both our brothers glared at him, knowing he was right.

"Mind your single ass business," Jamison said, slamming his dominoes down on the table. "What we have is balance. When the wife is happy, the house is happy."

"Sucka shit," Reese commented. "I love that for y'all though. One of these days, I'm gonna be like that."

His eyes darted off to the side. I followed them to where Ms. Alicia sat talking to my mama and the girls.

"Damn," he said, licking his lips. "She gets finer and finer every time I see her."

"When are you gonna give that up?" Cartel asked.

"I can't, man. She's got me in a chokehold. The things I would do to her..."

"That is my mother-in-law," Jamison said, slapping the back of his head.

"Who's beautiful as fuck," Reese added. "I swear, if Mama, Ja, and Liv wouldn't kick my ass, I'd say fuck it and go for it. She knows she likes me."

"You are literally about half her age," I said. "That lady don't want you."

He kissed his teeth as he waved us off. "Whatever." He looked up again to see Ms. Alicia and my mama walking over to us.

"Heeeey, Ms. Alicia," he said, grinning wide.

She rolled her eyes with a smirk. "Hello, Reese."

"You look mighty fine today. I see you out here breaking hearts, mine in particular."

"*Corta esa mierda,*" our mother said. *Cut that shit out.* "I've told you to leave this woman alone, boy."

"It's fine, Paloma," Ms. Alicia said, blushing. "He never fails to remind me that I've still got it... just not for him."

Snickers went up around the table. Reese grabbed his heart.

"That's cold," he said, feigning hurt.

"Anyway, which one of you wants to make a store run?" Mama asked. "Don't all speak at once."

I sighed. "What do you need?"

"I'll text you."

"You aren't sending me grocery shopping, are you?"

"And if I am?" she asked with her hand on her hip.

I raised my hands. "I was just asking, playa. No need to get rowdy."

"Mmm hmm. Hurry up."

"I'm going, I'm going."

I got up from the table. "One of y'all has to play my hand. I was winning, and these fools owe me some money."

"I got you," Ms. Alicia said, reaching for my dominoes. "If I win, I might hand it over."

"You would play me like that, Ms. A?"

She laughed as she claimed my seat. "I've been playing this game longer than most of you have been alive. I could easily whip any of you."

"Those are fighting words," Cartel said. "How about putting your money where your mouth is?"

"So you're the shit talker at the table, huh? I'm gonna take your money first."

I shook my head as they went back and forth. Fishing my keys out of my pocket, I headed out the back gate that led to the front yard. Knowing my mama, she had a whole list of shit, and I'd probably be gone for a while.

Seventeen

JORJA

"SOOO..." Liv said, dragging the word out. "You and Tyson look awfully chummy. I take it things are going well."

"He's nice."

"You realize you say that every time someone brings him up. Is there more to him? I mean, you must like him to bring him here."

"I do like him. He's a nice guy. He treats me well. He's sweet, and his hands... those hands are magical. Last night..."

"Last night? Did he sleep over?"

"He did. He took me home after my show and gave me a much needed massage. Girl, I was so turned on, the next thing I knew, that man's head was between my legs, and I was running for the headboard."

"I guess it was good then?"

"It was great. The dick was a shocking bonus."

"Well damn!"

"I know, I know. I couldn't help myself. He caught me fresh out of the shower. There was nothing but a towel for him to go through."

I replayed Friday night in my head. Tyson's mouth and that nine-inch monster took me on a fantasy ride. I hadn't expected him to be so damn nasty. I liked freaky shit, and he delivered on my freak level. He spent the night, and with the exception of him leaving to visit his aunt, we'd been together all weekend. I was in such a good mood when we woke up this morning that I invited him to my granny's party. Part of me felt awkward with him loving on me while Walker and his family were in the same space.

The other part of me said fuck that, we're grown, and Walker was never my man. Besides, this was my mama's house. If she didn't have a problem with him being here, fuck what anybody else had to say.

"Well, I'm glad you're moving on," Liv said, rubbing her belly. "I'm surprised Walker is keeping his cool."

"He didn't look too happy when he saw us, but he spoke and kept it pushing. We had a conversation Friday night, and for now, I guess we're okay..."

I looked over at him laughing and playing dominoes with his brother. He seemed to be in good spirits, and I was happy about that. Seeing him cry put me in my feelings for a minute. I hadn't expected this to be hard on him too.

"That look," Liv said, pointing at me. "That look says something happened."

I shifted my eyes as I took a sip of my wine cooler. "He might have... kissed me."

"Jorja."

"And I might have kissed him back."

"Jorja!"

"I know, Liv! I couldn't help myself. It was more like a goodbye kiss."

"It was a gateway kiss. You're gonna be right back in your feelings."

I took the rest of my drink to the head. "I don't wanna talk about him. Let's go check on Adina and these babies."

She gave me the side eye as I stood and reached to help her to her feet.

"If I wasn't big and pregnant, I would have slapped your hand away."

"Come on here, baby mama."

She linked her arm through mine, and we headed toward the house.

THE BURIAL OF A PLAYER

I motioned to Tyson, who'd stepped away to take a call. He acknowledged me with a head nod and went back to his conversation.

"Who's he talking to?" Liv asked.

"He said his aunt is in the hospital."

"Oh no. I hope everything is okay."

"Yeah… me too."

Inside, we found Adina and the babies curled up in my granny's bed, taking a nap. My poor girl had to be exhausted.

"Just look at them," Liv said as she stroked their baby hairs. "So precious. I can't believe one of these is about to come out of me. Damn, I hope my coochie goes back to normal."

I laughed out loud, causing Adina to stir.

"Did I fall asleep?" she asked.

"You were knocked out, girl," I said.

"I'm sorry. I've just been so tired today. Cartel said we could have stayed home, but I really didn't wanna miss the party. Looks like I'm sleeping it away anyway."

"Girl, you popped out two babies who are only a month old. Of course you're tired."

"Is she at least enjoying herself?"

"You know she is," Liv confirmed. "She's been dancing off and on since we got here. Of course, she had to get her dance in with my husband, her personal Kevin Atwater."

"He does kind of look like that man," I agreed.

Liv rolled her eyes. "Whatever."

Adina sat up and gave a good stretch. "I think I'm good now. I can load them into the stroller and take them out. I should probably change them first." She grabbed the baby backpack and began rummaging through it. "Shit."

"What?" I asked.

"I'm almost out of wipes. I could have sworn I packed an extra one."

"I can go get you some," I volunteered.

"You don't have to do that…"

"It's not a problem. The store is literally around the corner. I'll be right back."

"Thank you, boo."

I left the bedroom and headed out front where I bumped into Tyson.

"Ooop, my bad," I said, regaining my balance. "Hey, I'm about to run to the store right quick. Are you gonna be okay here?"

"Actually, I have to go."

"Oh... is everything okay?"

"My aunt isn't doing that well. I'm headed to the hospital."

"I'm sorry."

"It's okay. She's old. She said a long time ago that she's made peace with leaving this world. I'll call you tonight, okay? If it's not too late, I'll swing by."

"Okay. Well at least let me walk you out."

We headed out the front door and down the steps. Since we drove separately, I didn't have to worry about taking him or finding a ride home. I walked him to his car, and he kissed me quickly before hopping in and driving away. I was heading to my own car when I heard my name.

"Ja!"

I looked to see Walker standing beside his Range Rover.

"You leaving?" he asked.

"Oh, Adina needs wipes. I was going to the store."

"You wanna ride with me? My mama is sending me on a store run."

I hesitated for a second before my feet carried me to him. He walked around and opened the passenger door for me, a first.

"Thank you."

He nodded and closed the door. I settled into the seat. It was still in the same position I always left it in whenever I rode shotgun. As he slid into the driver's seat, my nerves settled in. Once again, we were alone. I just prayed I could keep my shit together and my body parts to myself.

* * *

THE SHORT DRIVE to the dollar store seemed to take forever. Walker and I drove in awkward silence the entire way there. Once in the store, we went our separate ways. I grabbed the baby wipes and walked around aimlessly until I found him with a basket full of shit.

"You ready?" he asked.

"Yeah."

Again, the awkward silence returned. We stood behind an older woman who was impatiently waiting for the cashier. When it was her turn, she spoke in a loud whisper.

"Excuse me, I'm looking for something to wash my cat."

"Your cat? Pet products are on aisle five."

"No, not my cat, my *cat*..." She pointed down.

"Oh... oh! That. Um... that's aisle seven, ma'am."

"Thank you."

I tried to hold it in. Then I felt Walker's eyes on me. The moment I looked at him, we broke into loud obnoxious laughter accompanied by the slapping of each other's arm. Moments like this reminded me why he was the person I could never sit by at a funeral. The woman looked back at us with a frown as she hurried away. The cashier finally let out the laugh she was holding in.

"I'm sorry," I said, setting the wipes on the counter. "That was the funniest shit I've ever heard."

"That death glare she gave you both said she didn't find it funny."

"I hope she finds something for that," Walker said, placing his items on the counter as well. "I've got this."

We were all still laughing as the cashier rang us up. As soon as the woman returned, we shut up. I felt like I was going to burst at the seams if I didn't get out of here soon. I grabbed a few bags and walked toward the door as Walker grabbed the rest of them.

"Have a good day, ma'am," he said, looking back at the woman.

"Come on!" I called, bursting into laughter once again as I walked out the door.

Back in the car, we were still laughing at the exchange.

"If she could have backhanded you, she would have," I said as I placed my bags in the back seat.

"The holy spirit would have been in that slap."

We climbed into the front, he cranked up, and we pulled out. He rolled down the windows and opened the sunroof as we cruised down the road. I relaxed into the seat, memories of us like this flooding my mind. I always enjoyed riding shotgun with him. I controlled the music, and most of the time, I had food in my hands, so I was a happy passenger.

"Feeling familiar?" he asked after a while.

"Yeah."

He chuckled. "Remember that drive we took to Miami for one of your shows?"

"You mean the first time you let me push the Rover?"

"You mean the first time I let you flex in my whip and you got a speeding ticket and a noise ordinance because you wanted to blast Stefflon Don through a residential area?"

"We were in Miami, and I was feeling a vibe. You know Steff is my girl. I just want to dance for her once time."

I did a little twerk in my seat, causing him to grin.

"Well if you take this choreographing gig, you might make that happen. Congratulations, by the way. You deserve that."

I blushed. "Thank you. I'm not sure if I'm gonna take it though."

"Why not? This is what you been working for, right?"

"It is, but..."

"Ain't no buts, Ja. You dance like your life depends on it. I watch you transform into a whole other person when that beat drops. I watch you teach, and I see the excitement in your face when it all comes together. I see the confidence you've given Anais. If anybody deserves this shit, it's you."

"I just... I don't wanna have to leave home for good. I can't imagine not having time for my family. Everything I love is here. If I could find a way to teach remotely and still be around, maybe then I would consider it."

"Make that shit work for you. Just don't let a once in a lifetime opportunity pass you by because you're afraid to step outside of yourself."

I was quiet. He was well versed in my love of dance. From the first time he saw me perform live to my practices, to me dancing for him, he always sang my praises. He was always encouraging on that front.

"Besides..." he added, "I get bragging rights to knowing you before the fame."

"I'm sure knowing me wouldn't help you in any way."

"It's a personal matter."

"Hmmm..."

The rest of the ride was taken in comfortable silence. When we got back to the house, we unloaded the car and headed inside. We were immediately greeted by Liv, Jamison, Cartel, Adina, and the twins. They all stared at us as we stepped through the front door.

"Mmm hmm..." Liv said, her eyes passing me over.

"Y'all good?" Cartel asked. "I don't see any black eyes... nothing looks out of place..."

Adina slapped his arm. "Baby!"

"What? I'm just—"

"You're just gonna mind *our* business."

I snickered. "That's why I love you, Dina," I said, handing her the wipes.

She winked at me. "I got you, boo." She turned to Cartel. "You can take the shitty diaper," she said with a giggle.

HE KISSED HIS TEETH. "Come on, Mel," he said, picking his daughter up. "Let's go get you cleaned up while your auntie and uncle pretend we don't see right through them."

He grabbed the diaper bag and wipes, then headed toward the back bedroom.

"On that note," Jamison said, standing and reaching for Liv's hand. "We are going to mind our married ass business outside."

"Huh uh, I'm trying to be nosy," Liv protested.

He gave her a stern look. She rolled her eyes before placing her hand into his outstretched palm and allowing him to pull her to her feet.

"You heard what big daddy said," I shot at her, using the nickname she often referred to him as.

"Bitch," she tossed over her shoulder as he led her back outside. I laughed as I flipped her off.

"I'm gonna take this stuff out to Mama," Walker said, stepping around me.

"Thanks for the ride," I said.

"No problem."

He smiled as he followed behind Liv and Jamison. Adina smirked as she and Carina looked up at me.

"What!" I asked, my hands on my hips.

"You tell me. The other week, you two sat in my living room without saying a word to each other, and today you're taking rides together. Is somebody having a change of heart?"

"We've agreed to be friendly."

She kissed her teeth. "Go'onah. Don't even much play with me," she said, her Charleston accent popping in. "I should box you for lying to yourself."

"You said box, so I'm gonna take it that that is a threat y'all use back home."

"Correct. Where's ya lil ming? Your lil boo?"

"He had to leave for a family emergency."

"Is everything okay?"

"Well, last week he got a late call saying his aunt collapsed and was unresponsive. She's been in the hospital ever since."

"Are they close?"

"I'm not sure. I know he told me that his mother died the same way, so I'm sure it's hitting home for him."

"Well, I pray everything is okay. Liv said he seems smitten with you."

"Yeah... I guess he likes me."

"How do you feel about him?"

"He's..." I was about to say nice but stopped myself. "I do like him. He's sweet and attentive..."

"But?"

"Walker seems to think he's hiding something. I'm not sure if it's jealousy or intuition."

"What do you feel?"

"I don't know. I want to believe he's genuine, but you know as well as I do that you can't put shit past a nigga."

"Say that again."

I did want to believe that Tyson was the man he presented himself to be, but the fact of the matter was, I'd only known him for a month. That wasn't long enough to determine if he was everything he portrayed. I wouldn't lie and say that the shit wouldn't hurt. In spite of lingering issues with Walker, I did like the guy. However, I wasn't sure if I'd be totally upset if things didn't work out. Maybe he was for me... maybe he wasn't. Maybe my lack of feeling about it was a sign. I'd just have to see how things panned out.

Eighteen

WALKER

TODAY HAD BEEN A PRETTY decent day.

After Ja and I got back from the store, the air between us seemed a little lighter. She even partnered with me to whup my brothers' asses in a few games of spades and dominoes. They already had to come up off two hundred dollars apiece, playing with Ms. Alicia. Reese in particular wasn't happy about losing.

"You cheated," he said, frowning.

Ms. Alicia kissed her teeth. "Boy, nobody cheated you."

"Nah, you definitely cheated," Cartel said, an identical frown on his face. "Ain't no way you won that many times in a row."

"Remember when I told you I was going to take your money first?" She held out her hand to the two of them. "Hands up. Cash out."

"Run them pockets, Mama," Jorja said, clapping to enunciate each word.

They both grumbled as they pulled out their wallets and handed her several bills. Jamison had been smart and copped out after he lost the first round. Ms. Alicia counted off my portion and handed it to me. She then handed Ja a couple of bills.

"How are you gonna give her our money, Ms. A?" Cartel asked, popping open a beer.

"Because once it left your hands, it was mine. Besides, that's my baby."

Jorja smirked as her mother cupped her chin and kissed her cheek.

"It was nice playing with you boys," she said as she stood.

"You just breaking my heart and my pockets," Reese said, looking up at her.

"Poor baby." She leaned in and kissed his cheek. "You'll live," she said, patting his head.

She tapped the side of my face as she walked away from the table.

"Ja, you better tell your mama to stop playing with me," he said, grinning as he watched her ass jiggling in the sundress she wore.

"Nigga, my mama don't want you."

"But I want her. She can't be kissing my cheek, getting me excited and shit."

Jorja glared at him. "I'm about to get excited and slide my hand across that same cheek."

He laughed out loud. "That's the hater in you."

"Hater or not, one thing you will never be is *in* my mama."

"That shit would be funny as hell if it came to pass," I said, taking a sip of my beer.

She playfully punched him on the arm. "These hands are rated E for everybody. You want some too?"

I grinned. "Alright now. Remember how we used to wrestle? You don't want these problems."

"Maybe I do."

Our eyes lingered on each other for a moment. Jamison and Reese passed a look between each other.

"Mmm hmm...." they both said.

"What was that?" Ja asked, breaking eye contact.

"*That* was you two flirting," Reese said. "*Maybe I do*," he mocked her. "Y'all ain't fooling nobody. We all know how this is gonna end between you."

"We can be friendly," Jorja protested.

"Well it's not like he has a choice now with ol' buddy in the picture. Where did your little boyfriend go anyway?"

"He's not my boyfriend. He's a friend, and he had a family emergency."

I felt my eyebrows furrow. "Right," I mumbled. "Was it Francesca calling again?"

Ja's head snapped toward me. "Who told you that?"

"Nobody had to tell me. I saw her calling his phone at the gas station a few days ago."

"And how would you be close enough to him to see that?" She put her cards down and folded her arms. "Did you say something to him, Walker?"

"You know what, I did. I told that nigga he was gonna see me if he's on some funny shit with you. I meant that."

Jorja scoffed. "Unbelievable. You need to mind your business."

"You are my business."

"No, I'm not!" She snapped at me. "What I have going on with Tyson is of no concern to you. In case you forgot, you aren't my man, and you never were. Don't play the role of the jealous ex. It's not for you."

"Jealous? I'm looking out for you—"

"Remember that when I warn the next bitch about you with your walking red flag ass."

She stood from the table and walked off into the crowd of people. I could feel my brothers' eyes on me. When I looked at them, they looked away. I threw my cards on the table.

"I'm out," I said, standing.

"You're leaving?" Jamison asked.

"I can't do this shit, Jay. Every time I see her with that nigga or have to hear about him, I get pissed off all over again. I hate thinking about him being in her space. I hate wondering if he knows what it feels like to be inside of her. I hate this whole fucking thing."

"I know you do, Walk," he said, sighing.

I was trying to be cool. I was trying to let her be happy, but about that nigga, I'd lose my damn mind over her every time. Did I deserve that right? Maybe not. Was it a hill I was willing to die on? Absolutely. I didn't like him. It wasn't just jealousy. Something about him wasn't right, and I felt that shit.

THE BURIAL OF A PLAYER

"I'm gonna go say goodbye to Granny. I'll holla at y'all later."

Without another word, I headed over to the swing where Granny, Ms. Alicia, my mama, the girls, and the twins were chattering away. When Granny saw me, she waved me over. I politely eased into the swing next to her.

"Everything okay?" she asked.

"Everything is fine. I just came to let you know I'm about to head on home," I said, leaning in for a hug. "I hope you had a great birthday, Grams."

"I sure did. I'll sleep good tonight, I know that."

"Don't party the night away now. You go to bed at a decent hour, young lady."

She waved me off. "Whatever. Thank you for coming, sweetheart."

"You know you my girl. I'll show up for you every time."

"Don't stay away so long next time. I need to see your handsome face."

"Don't make me blush."

I had mad love for this woman. Ja and I used to be over here all the time. My family didn't do Sunday dinners since we saw each other all the time anyway. Jorja had Sunday dinner with her people every Sunday. Most of the time, our Saturday nights turned into Sunday evenings, so she would invite me to dinner before I went home. Granny was the reason I took my ass to the gym. She always fed me well and sent leftovers home with me.

That was love. We had a bond like she really was my grandmother.

"I promise I'll come by more often."

"Sunday dinners are still open."

"Granny!" Jorja said, frowning. Of course, she had been ear hustling.

"I thought you two were friendly now?" Granny said, looking between us.

"If it makes your granddaughter feel better, we can make Wednesdays our standing dinner date," I said, looking over at Jorja. "That way, nobody has a problem."

She rolled her eyes at me.

"You two will get it right one of these days," Granny said to me under her breath. "Take care, baby."

"Take care."

I kissed her hand and made my rounds of goodbyes to the rest of the ladies, excluding Jorja.

"You know I can't stand you," Ja mumbled as I stooped to hug Liv.

I gazed as I rose to my full height. "You love me, though."

Her frown deepened, and she crossed her arms. "Bye, Walker."

I cupped the side of her face and kissed her cheek. She looked up at me, her gaze lingering for a moment. Her teeth sank into her bottom lip, and her eyes dropped to my lips before she looked back up at me. I let my hand drop slightly to her neck, giving a subtle squeeze as I let go.

"Y'all have a good night," I said to everybody watching the exchange.

I made my way back to the side gate and headed out to my car. By the time I got in the car, she'd sent me a text.

Lil' Baby: Stop playing with me, my nigga.

Me: You stop playing with *me*, my nigga.

She sent back the middle finger emoji. I chuckled as I placed the phone into the cupholder, cranked up, and headed home.

* * *

NIGHT HAD FALLEN.

When I got home, I headed into my home gym to work off both the food I consumed and the tension I was feeling. Being around Ja on some friend shit was proving to be more of a challenge than I anticipated. I was giving this shit my best shot. It had been less than twenty-four hours since our unspoken truce, and I was already regretting that shit.

I wanted her to be happy, but I also simply wanted her. I wanted her worse than I'd ever wanted her since we met. That little exchange between us when I left her grandmother's party was intense. Every hair on the back of my neck stood up when she looked at me. That was how I knew shit between us wasn't over.

My shower was complete. I had my shit ready for work in the morning. All I wanted to do was lay out until I got ready to climb into my lonely ass bed. I headed into the kitchen to grab a beer before going into my living room, plopping down on the couch. With the remote in my hand, I turned on my seventy-inch flat screen and flipped through the apps until I settled on reruns of *The Fresh Prince of Bel-Air*.

This was a classic and one of my favorite shows. The reboot wasn't like the original, but I liked it too. I was about three shows in when my doorbell rang. I looked up at the clock to see that it was around nine. Getting up, I went to the door and looked out the peephole. Much to my surprise, Jorja was standing on the front porch. I quickly took off the locks and opened the door.

"Hey," I said, leaning against the frame.

"Hey."

An awkward silence fell between us. She'd obviously gone home because she was now dressed in a pair of biker shorts, a graphic tee, and her UGG Slides. The scent of her body wash swept around me as a cool breeze blew the night air.

"Are you gonna let me in or what?" she asked.

"Um... sure."

I stepped aside, allowing her entry. She stepped in and went directly to my space on the couch. I was a little confused as I closed the door. Walking over to the couch, I stood over her, causing her to look up at me.

"What?"

"I was sitting there."

"Well, now I'm sitting here." She tossed her phone and keys onto the coffee table and crossed her arms. "Either move me or sit somewhere else."

I pinched the bridge of my nose. The statement fucked me up a little. There were several places I could move her to, including my dick. I was trying to remain respectful, but she was making it hard, figuratively and literally. Stepping around her, I moved to sit on the other end of the couch.

"What are you doing here, Ja?" I inquired.

"I was bored."

"Your little—"

"If you're gonna bring him up, I can leave," she said, cutting me off.

"You get upset when he's around or talked about. Don't fuck up my mood right now."

I raised my hands in surrender. "Fair enough."

Grabbing my beer, I settled into the cushions and popped the top. I took a long sip of it, knowing I was going to need something to take the edge off.

"Must you slurp?" Jorja asked, looking over at me.

"Now my slurping bothers you?"

Her eyes passed over me. "In this moment... yes."

"Get over it."

She scoffed and snatched the beer from my hands. Turning it up to her mouth, she chugged the rest of the can before handing it back to me.

"I'm over it."

I chuckled to myself. "So you came over her just to fuck with me?"

"Aren't we supposed to be friendly?"

"We're supposed to be friendly, but you cockblocking Sunday dinner with Granny. What's up with that? You trying to bring your little boyfriend instead?"

She frowned as she crossed her arms. "Since you insist on bringing him up, please, enlighten me on what it is that you don't like about him, other than the fact that he has me and you don't."

"He's a cocky ass nigga."

"*You're* a cocky ass nigga. It's more to it than that. Be real with me. If it's the whole Francesca thing, that's his cousin."

"Ja, you are too smart to fall for that shit. We used to run that same game. Shit, we compared ho stories all the damn time. How many times have you had to spin shit in your favor?"

She frowned as she looked at me, clearly doing the math.

"You wanna know what he said to me, Ja? You wanna know what really made me look at the nigga sideways?"

"Please... put an end to my suspense."

"He said thank you."

She shrugged. "For what?"

"For giving him an advantage. He's so sure that I've done so much damage that you wouldn't believe anything I said about him whether it's true or not."

Her frown deepened. "He said that?"

"On everything I love, that's what came out of that nigga's mouth."

"And when was this said?"

"The night of the concert."

I saw the anger flash in her eyes. Her fingers flexed in her lap.

"Why are you telling me this?" she asked.

"Because I love you. Maybe I wasn't the best introduction to falling in love for the first time. But I've always been your friend, Ja. I don't want you to go out like that. I'll deal with you hating me before I let you move on with a nigga that may not have the best intentions for you. Maybe I didn't give you the best of me, but you deserve the best of somebody."

Her face softened a little.

"I'll handle it."

"If you need me to throw hands, I got you."

She rolled her eyes. "I'm a big girl. I can take care of myself."

"I know you can, but I've always got you."

I reached for her hand. Reluctantly, she gave it to me. I held it for a moment before pulling her across the couch and into a hug. For a moment, she allowed me to hold her. My emotions were beginning to surface. I missed her. When she pulled away, her eyes lingered on mine before dropping to my lips.

"Stop playing with me, Ja," I said, tracing her bottom lip. "You know how I feel about that look. Stop looking at me like that."

"And if I don't?" she asked, moving to straddle me. "What are you gonna do about it?"

Her fingers wrapped around my neck where she gave a gentle squeeze. She looked down at me with lustful eyes.

"You been drinking?" I asked.

"Shut the fuck up."

She pressed my head into the back of the cushion and her body against mine. That aggressive shit always turned me on, and she knew that. My dick was pitching a tent in these shorts.

"You miss me, right?" she asked, grinding against me as her lips hovered over mine.

"Yeah... yeah, I miss you," I said, licking my lips. "You fucking me up right now, Ja."

"Good."

Her lips fell against mine as she sucked the bottom one into her mouth.

"Mmmm..." She let out a moan as her hips continued to wind in my lap. "Shit."

Again, she kissed me, her sweet tongue caressing mine. My hands moved from her thighs to her ass where I gave a tight squeeze as I pulled her down.

"You asking for trouble," I warned her.

"I can handle trouble... or did you forget?"

"I ain't drunk tonight, Ja. I'm of sound mind and body, and I will fuck the shit out of you on this couch. Stop while you're ahead."

"It's never taken you this long to decide if you wanna fuck me," she complained.

"'Cause if I fuck you now, I'm gonna wanna fuck you again. And again. And again. Before you know it, we'll be right back on the same shit. You can't be mad at me if you put it out there. I want you, Ja. I want you bad as fuck, but I know what it's like to be on the receiving end of your unforgiveness. I'm not trying to feel that shit again."

She sat back on my lap and looked at me.

"You serious? You turning me down?"

"I'm turning you down."

"Wow," she said, sliding off my lap and back onto the couch. "That's a first. I'll respect that."

"Don't let me having blue balls be in vain."

"Shut your ignorant ass up," she said, punching me in the shoulder.

"Seriously though. I love you, Jorja. Admitting that to myself makes me wanna handle you differently. If we are gonna do this shit, we need to do it right. And you gotta drop that nigga."

I looked at her curiously.

"You fucked him?"

She didn't answer.

I nodded. "You did. When?"

"That, I'm not answering."

"You didn't answer the first question."

"I don't have to answer *any* question. Did you fuck somebody?"

"Nope."

"So you haven't had pussy in now five months? You haven't dipped back into any of your old bitches?"

"The only person I dipped back into was you, and I was drunk for that. I don't even remember if it was good or not."

"Nigga, you funny," she said, rolling her eyes. "If I could, I'd snatch all my good pussy back for that comment."

I had to laugh out loud.

"Don't laugh. It's not funny. I bet you beat your dick to memories of me all the time."

"I surely do. I haven't forgotten."

She kissed her teeth as she slid back to her end of the couch and crossed her legs.

"Turn to something else. If I have to sit here with a wet pussy, at least make it worth my while. And get me a drink."

"Don't come over here like you run shit," I said, standing.

"Yet you're moving."

I chuckled as I leaned over her, bringing my face close to hers. "You're lucky I'm turning over a new leaf."

I pecked her lips before standing and going into the kitchen to get her drink. Maybe this shit might work in my favor after all.

Nineteen

JORJA

I WATCHED *him walk out of the party.*

He was so fucking frustrating to me, and he had me feeling all sensitive and shit. When I finally turned my head back to the group, I found all the women looking at me.

"What!" I exclaimed.

"I don't know about anybody else, but I'm about sick of the two of y'all," Mama Jareau said.

"Amen!" went up around the circle.

I frowned. "That's how y'all feel?"

A resounding yes went up, causing me to fold my arms.

"Y'all just don't understand," I said.

"We understand that you love that boy, and he loves you," my mama said.

"Mama—"

"Hush and let me talk. Now I've stayed out of your business for this long because you're grown. But I'm gonna say this and let it go. I don't know what's going on with you two behind closed doors these days, but if you want to be together, y'all have to stop playing these damn games with each other. And leave people like Tyson out of it."

"I actually like Tyson. He's—"

"Nice," Liv and Adina finished for me.

I jerked my head in their direction. "Yes, he is nice,"

"You know you don't want that man," Granny said. "You may like the way he treats you, but that never feels as good as it would coming from the person you really want. The person you really want just walked out that gate."

"Y'all are about to stress me out," I said, rubbing my temples. "Walker and I are done. Okay? We had a talk. We admitted where we both went wrong. We know that we love each other, but maybe it's best we leave each other alone."

"So you both admitted you loved each other?" my mother asked.

"Yes."

"After all this time?"

"Yes."

"And you're okay with moving on so soon after a conversation like that? Jorja, it's abundantly clear that this thing between you two isn't over. Have either of you ever considered if you wanted to try things the right way?"

"I guess the rest of you think we should do that too?" I asked, looking around.

"We all want you to be happy, both of you," Mama Jareau said. "We just don't want either of you to look back and regret not trying again. I can honestly tell you that Walker regrets not manning up about his feelings, just as much as you regret not being upfront about yours. If you feel there is nothing to salvage, so be it. Just know there is nothing wrong with fighting for what you want if both of you want it and both of you want to commit to it. That's all we're saying."

That conversation played in my head all the way home.

It was on repeat during and after my shower. Even as I got into my car and drove across town to Walker's, I could still hear it. What if we gave things a real chance? Could it be something worth having? Could we really be happy with each other? I pondered those questions while I sat on the opposite end of the couch from him Sunday night.

The shock of him actually turning me down wore off after about thirty minutes. That was a first. He loved when I got aggressive with him. It was evident by the hardness of his dick beneath me. If he hadn't said no, I was prepared to give him the ride of his life.

This was especially after learning what Tyson had said to him about me. It was shocking because he didn't present himself as manipulative or the type to capitalize off someone else's emotions. I was definitely planning to address that shit.

It was one thing to be blindsided. It was another to have him openly say thank you for basically giving him the upper hand. That made me question everything. Was he ever even genuine? Was anything he showed me real? Shit, was Millicent even his niece?

I hadn't heard from him in three days. My calls went unanswered, and my texts went unread. Since I was free tonight after practice, I had plans to go over to his place. I knew showing up unannounced was risky, but fuck that.

"Jorja, where are Anais and Millicent?" Coach Love asked, interrupting my thoughts.

I turned and looked around for them. Practice was starting in a few minutes, and they were nowhere to be found.

"They are probably in the locker room getting dressed," I said. "I'll go look for them."

"If they're late, that's five laps around the gym."

"I got you."

Slipping my phone into my bag, I headed for the locker rooms. As I entered, I could hear hushed whispering. Slowing my strides, I tipped toward the direction it was coming from.

"I'm telling you, Anais. I've never seen him so upset."

"Well, was she telling the truth?"

"She had receipts. Not only that, she brought living proof with her. That little girl was his spitting image."

Little girl? I knew damn well Millicent wasn't dealing with some little boy who had a baby.

"I can't believe this," Anais said, frowning. "How are you going to tell her?"

"I don't know if I *should* say something..." Millicent whispered.

"That's my aunt and your coach," Anais said, her frown deepening. "If you don't tell her, I will." That caused my ears to perk up.

"Tell me what?" I asked, stepping out of hiding.

They both jumped, and they turned to look at me.

"Ms. Jorja.... We were just, um..." Millicent struggled to find a lie.

"What's going on?"

I crossed my arms in front of me as I looked between the two of them. They looked at each other nervously.

"One of you better start talking," I warned.

"Well... Sunday, a woman showed up at my house," Millicent began, her gaze shifting. "She had a little girl with her."

She looked from me to Anais and swallowed hard.

"She um... she said that she was Uncle Ty's wife."

"What!"

"She had a marriage license, wedding pictures, pictures of them as a family... all of that, Ms. Jorja. I'm so sorry. We didn't know..."

"It's okay, Millicent," I said, holding up my hand. "I'm sure that was hard on you, and I'm sorry you were put in that position."

"I feel bad. You're so nice, Ms. Jorja. You didn't deserve that."

She started crying, and it pissed me off because she was a child. She shouldn't have had to keep a secret like that because of a grown muthafucka like her uncle. I pulled her into my arms and hugged her tightly until she stopped crying.

"What are you gonna do?" she asked, wiping her eyes.

"Don't worry about that. You two get to practice."

She nodded as she grabbed her bag and headed out of the locker room.

"I'm sorry, Auntie Jorja," Anais said, hugging me. "Are you okay?"

"I'm fine. You never have to worry about me."

"I could tell you liked him."

"Yeah, well... everything that looks and sounds good isn't good. You remember that when these boys start whispering in your ear, baby girl." I kissed her forehead. "Go on."

"Are you sure you're okay?"

"I promise."

She offered me a sympathetic smile before grabbing her bag and leaving the locker room as well. I was alone with my thoughts. I could feel the anger flowing through my body. If there was one thing I had no respect for, it was a married ass nigga that disrespected his wife.

I was angry with myself for not seeing it. I was angry that I let him inside me. I was angry that I defended his trifling ass. He'd really tried to pull the wool over my eyes. How long did he think he could keep that shit a secret? As I stood there, stewing in my anger, I thought about how I was going to handle this.

Practice was about two hours long. There was no way he'd show his face to pick Millicent up. I decided right then that I was pulling up. I didn't care if the wife was there. He was going to answer for this shit.

* * *

"SAY THAT AGAIN," Liv said as we stood outside of her car.

She'd come to pick up Anais, and I had to tell somebody the news that was brought to my attention.

"His wife, bitch. *Wife*. Can you believe that shit?"

"Wow. That is some scandalous shit. What are you gonna do?"

"I'm pulling up on his ass. He's gonna look me in the face and tell me the truth."

"I don't think you should go over there."

"Liv, did you hear the story I just told you? He's got to answer for that."

"You don't know what you're gonna walk into. You don't know that woman and you barely know him—"

"I don't care. He's every bit of our trifling ass daddy. He paraded me around on his arm like he was right, knowing he not only had a wife but a whole fucking kid. He knew what kind of shit he was in. That's why he's been ghost for three days. Who lies like that? Who pretends to have an aunt practically dying in the hospital? How old are we?"

I was pacing back and forth in front of the car at this point. Knowing that I was headed to his house right after she left, had me on edge. I needed a damn blunt. I didn't think that I'd ever been this angry, even at Walker.

"Ja, I think you should go home. Have you a drink and relax. He's clearly not worth this shit, sis."

THE BURIAL OF A PLAYER

I looked over at her but kept pacing.

She sighed. "I have to get the kids home. Please call me later."

It was my turn to sigh. "I will." We shared an embrace. "I love you, Liv."

"I love you too."

She climbed into the car as I made my rounds, kissing my babies.

"I love you, rugrats."

"Love you too!" they all said as I closed the door.

Stepping back onto the sidewalk, I watched as they drove off. Once they were out of sight, I headed to my car. After plugging his address into my GPS, I backed out and headed for Tyson's house. The fifteen-minute drive seemed longer, and I wasn't sure if that was a good or a bad thing. When I got there, I parked on the street where he couldn't see me. After pulling my hair up into a bun, I climbed out of the car and stormed up to the front door.

Inside, I could hear loud voices, one of them being a female. She was yelling at him about finding our pictures in his phone. If this wasn't perfect timing. I didn't bother to ring the doorbell; instead, I banged on the door. The voices quieted down, and a few seconds later, I heard the locks disengaging. Tyson opened the door, looking disheveled and wide eyed.

He stepped out on the porch. "Jorja, baby, this isn't a good time."

"Oh, I think it's the perfect time."

Pushing him out of the way, I entered the house to see it was a wreck. Broken furniture, glass, and a bunch of other shit was all over the place. The woman I assumed to be his wife was standing with a baseball bat in her hand.

"So she's freely coming over here, Tyson!" she screamed.

She swung that bat at his TV, causing the screen to shatter. When she came at me with it raised, I held up my hand.

"Pump your brakes," I warned her. "We are on the same side of this fight."

"Bitch, no the fuck we aren't!"

She went to swing at me, but I grabbed the bat from her hands.

"I said calm the fuck down!" I yelled, pointing it at her. "Your husband, who I'm just finding out lied to me, never fucking mentioned that he was married. I had to find out from his niece who had to confide in mine about your secret." I turned to his wife. "Are you Francesca?"

"So you know my name?"

"I know your name because I've been with him when you called. The lying son of a bitch said you were his cousin calling about his aunt who was supposedly in the hospital."

She scoffed in disbelief. "A cousin?"

"I can explain—" Tyson started.

"You can't explain a muthafucking thing to me," I said. "Niggas like you are exactly why women complain about not being able to find good men. I opened up to you. I shared my feelings with you, and baby, I don't do that. For you to tell Walker thank you for giving you the upper hand lets me know you never actually gave a fuck about me. All of the wining and dining, all the time we spent together... all of that was for what? So you could fuck me? You wanted to sniff good pussy that bad?"

He scoffed. "What about you, huh? You wanted to get over ol' boy so bad you practically handed yourself to me. I showed you what he didn't, and you ate that shit up."

"My struggles with him were not for your gain! I didn't share that with you for you to use it against me!"

He shrugged. "I'm sorry, alright?"

"You're sorry?" I nodded. "You're fucking pathetic, that's what you are." I turned to his wife, handing her the bat back. "This man told me he was looking for marriage and kids, knowing he had you and your child hidden away. For that alone, you should fuck him up and then divorce his ass. Clearly, you can do better."

I strutted past Tyson, and he grabbed my arm. I looked down at his hand and then up at him.

"Get your fucking hand off me," I said calmly.

He glared at me like he wanted to do something. His grip tightened.

"Tyson," I said, slightly raising my voice. "Let... me... go."

He wasn't moving fast enough for me. The fact that he grabbed me in the first place had already pissed me off. I didn't play that shit. When he didn't let go, I brought my leg up, kneeing him in the stomach. He released me with a grunt. Just because he thought it was okay to put his hands on me, I kicked him in the dick for good measure. He immediately dropped to his knees, holding himself as he groaned in pain.

"Oooo, you fucking dirty slut..." he mumbled.

"Fuck you, you community dick ass bitch."

Without another word, I stormed out of the house, slamming the door behind me. As I made my way down the front steps, I could hear him yelling for his wife to stop. Obviously, she'd taken my advice and was beating his ass with that bat. I smirked to myself as I made my way back to my car, praying she broke every bone in his cheating, trifling, lying ass body.

Twenty

WALKER

TODAY WAS WEDNESDAY, and as I'd promised Granny Oleena, I was on my way to her and Mama Alicia's for dinner. She'd called me earlier while I was at work to make sure that I was coming. When I told her I was, her voice filled with excitement. After stopping by the store to grab some flowers and wine, I headed over. Parking my car behind Ms. Alicia's, I climbed out and headed up to the front door.

Just as I raised my hand to knock, it opened, and Ms. Alicia greeted me with a smile.

"Hey, Walker."

"Hey, gorgeous." I pulled her in for a hug and kissed her cheek. "Y'all have it smelling good up in here."

"Mama has been waiting all day to see you. Come on in."

She stepped aside, allowing me entry.

"This is for you," I said, handing her the wine.

"You must have known I needed this. And it's my favorite."

"I remember."

"There's my baby!" Granny exclaimed, coming around the corner.

"There's my girl." I went to her with open arms, wrapping her up in a tight hug. "These are for you, beautiful." I handed her the flowers.

She smiled brightly. "You spoil me."

THE BURIAL OF A PLAYER

"You deserve it. Come on, dinner is ready—"

Before she could finish her sentence, the front door opened, and in walked Jorja. Everyone's eyebrows rose in surprise.

"Why are y'all looking at me like that?" she asked, slowly closing the door.

"Because you made a big fuss about Walker coming to Sunday dinner, yet here you are," her mother answered, folding her arms.

"Well... you always said I could come home whenever I want. I wanted to come home today."

I stifled a laugh as I shook my head.

"Something funny?" she asked, her hands on her hips.

"Nah, baby. I just had a lil tickle in my throat."

"Mmm hmm. So... what's for dinner?"

Her mother and grandmother rolled their eyes as they headed into the kitchen, leaving us alone.

I stepped close to her, cupping her chin. "If you wanted to see me, that's all you had to say, Ja."

She slapped my hand away. "I came for the food. Honestly, I forgot you were gonna be here."

I twisted my lips. "Really?"

"Yes!"

"If that makes you feel better. Give me some love."

I opened my arms to her, and surprisingly, she came to me, wrapping her arms around my waist. She rested her head against my chest and gave me a gentle squeeze. I kissed the top of her head. Next to me, she was a tiny thing with her short ass.

"Did you grow a few inches?" I jested.

She pulled away, playfully shoving me. "I might be short, but you know I'm big dawg, my nigga."

I had to laugh at her. "A'ight, big dawg. Everything okay?"

"Yeah... everything is fine."

"You sure?"

"I promise I'm good, Walker."

I eyed her skeptically. We hadn't spoken since she popped up at my house a couple of days ago. I wondered if everything was handled with ol' boy, but I wouldn't come out and ask.

"Why are you looking at me like that?" she asked, frowning.

I stepped back into her space, peering down at her. "I can't look at you?"

Her eyes shifted slightly from side to side as she looked at me. They then dropped to my lips. She always did that when she wanted to kiss me.

"Ask," I said.

"What?"

"You know what you want. Ask for it."

She shrugged as she brushed past me. "I don't know what you're talking about."

I chuckled, shaking my head as I followed her into the kitchen. She stood at the sink, washing her hands. I walked over and waited to do the same. When I was done, Ms. Alicia handed me a plate filled with smothered cube steak, rice, collard greens, macaroni, and cornbread.

"Here you go, baby," she said.

"Thank you, Ma."

Jorja opened her mouth to say something but shut it when her mother handed her a plate as well with a smirk.

"Don't start your shit," she warned her, kissing her cheek.

Jorja grinned. "I'm on my best behavior."

"Mmm hmm. You two go sit down."

We joined Granny at the table, and Ms. Alicia soon followed. Grabbing hands, Granny said a prayer before we dug in. For the longest time, there was nothing but the sound of forks scraping the plate, filling the space. Granny was the first to finally break the silence.

"Sooo..." she said with a smile. "What's new with the two of you? Something here is different."

Jorja and I looked at each other.

"Well, Granny, I decided it was less effort in being cordial than being angry," she said.

"That's all?" Ms. Alicia asked.

"Yes, Mommy. That's all."

I smirked behind my glass of sweet tea before setting it down.

"I'm just happy she isn't cursing me out at every turn anymore," I said. "I've had enough of that."

THE BURIAL OF A PLAYER

"Don't tempt me," she said, elbowing me.

"I'm gonna get Granny on you. You know I'm her baby."

"Speaking of, I don't like that. Granny, how are you gonna baby him? You're my grandmother."

"The same way my mama spoils you," I shot back. "You can literally go sit on her lap like you're her child."

"I can't help it if your mama loves me."

"Just like I can't help it if your granny and your mama love me."

"Don't bring me into this," Ms. Alicia said. "I am neutral over here."

"Don't act like you don't spoil him, girl," Jorja said, poking her. "You used to bake sweets just for him on Sundays."

"I baked them for you too! I just knew you were going to be with him, so I sent them home with him."

"Tell me anything."

"I smell a hater," I said. "You better be glad I shared with you, woman."

"You didn't have a choice. Share the sweets or none of my sweets for you."

"I could have gone the rest of my life without hearing that," Ms. Alicia muttered. "Especially since I don't have a man."

"You could have a man, Ma," I said.

"Don't you start!" Jorja said, pushing me. "Reese and my mama is never going to happen. Not now, not ever."

"I wasn't even talking about Reese!" I protested. "Look, Ma. You are a beautiful woman. Any man would be lucky to have you. I have a single uncle I can hook you up with. You know what, Isaac is single."

Jorja's eyes lit up. "Oooo, Mama. Mr. Isaac is fine, and he's educated. And he has a little thug appeal to him. You two would be cute together!"

"Aht aht!" Ms. Alicia held up her hand. "I'm good. I don't need any of you playing matchmaker. Lord only knows what you'll send my way. I'll stay single first."

"At least get you some, Alicia," Granny said. "And Isaac *is* fine, chile. Somebody needs to knock the cobwebs off that—"

"Granny!" Jorja exclaimed.

"I wasn't supposed to say that out loud. My bad."

"Okay!" Ms. Alicia said, raising her hands. "Can we change the subject to something that doesn't surround me and my private areas?"

We shared a laugh, and dinner continued on a lighter note. As we ate and talked, my eyes kept drifting over to Jorja. All throughout dinner, she kept rubbing her leg up against mine or touching me when she laughed. I didn't know what to make of that shit, but if she kept it up, she was gonna know something.

After dinner, she and I volunteered to clean the kitchen while Ms. Alicia and Granny relaxed in the living room. We worked in comfortable silence as I washed the dishes and she dried them. When we were done, we headed into the living room with her mom and granny, where we sat talking with them for a little bit.

My eyes started getting heavy. I was tired. Today had been a full day of clients, and now that I had a full stomach, I was ready to get home, wash my ass, smoke my blunt, and then go to bed. I fought back a yawn as I stood.

"I hate to dip out on y'all, but my body is gonna shut down on me soon."

"It's okay, baby," Granny said, reaching for my hand. "You go home and get you some rest. Thank you for coming."

"Thank you for having me. The food was A one, as usual."

I bent down to hug her and kiss her cheek, before doing the same with Ms. Alicia.

"I'll walk you out," Ms. Alicia said.

"I've got it, Ma," Jorja said. "I'm about to head out myself."

She gave them her goodbye hugs and kisses, and we headed out the door, walking to our cars in silence. She stood next to hers, and I stood next to mine as we stared at each other.

"Sooo..." I said, dragging out the word. "What's good?"

"So... you were right," she said, looking down.

"About?"

"Tyson. He wasn't who he pretended to be."

"How so?"

"He's married with a kid."

"The fuck?"

She sighed. "I overheard his niece talking to Anais. His wife showed up at her house, looking for him. She told me the truth, and I pulled up on him. She was there, fucking his house up."

"Wait, you pulled up on him? Why would you do that?"

"Because he played in my face, Walker."

"He could have hurt you."

"I can handle myself. When he grabbed me—"

"That nigga grabbed you?"

"Yes but—"

"Give me his address. I'm about to fuck him up. I should have fucked him up at the gas station."

"I'm not giving you that man's address. He learned his lesson when I kicked him in the dick."

"Don't do that shit again, Ja. Don't say shit to that nigga if and when you see him."

"I hear you."

"And—"

She covered my mouth with her hand. "Walker! I hear you. I promise. I said my peace, and I'm done. I don't need you to protect me or fight my battles. I'm a big girl."

"I know you don't need me, Ja," I said as I removed her hand.

"I appreciate you caring."

She stepped closer to me, grabbing the hem of my shirt. She looked up at me with innocent eyes.

"Can I have it?" she asked.

I smirked. "Can you have what?"

"Don't make me say it," she whined.

"Nah, you have to be specific, because there are several things I want to give you."

She sighed as she rolled her eyes. "Can I have a kiss?" she mumbled.

"Why?"

"Because... I miss kissing you. And... I've been thinking about you."

"And why is that?"

She inhaled sharply, obviously annoyed with my line of questioning.

"Because I'm not mad at you anymore, okay. We talked. You acknowledged my feelings. You apologized. I apologized."

"You realize we could have had this talk months ago if you weren't ignoring me."

"Well it's sad that you had to be ignored to come to terms with shit."

"I'll let you have that as long as you can admit we were both at fault here, Ja. I take responsibility for not owning up to my feelings. But you have to do the same."

She rolled her eyes. "Okay," she mumbled.

"What was that?"

"Okay!" she said louder. "I did the same thing, just with heightened emotions. I was afraid, Walker. I've never been in love. I've never wanted to be in love, and it scared me thinking you could never love me back."

"That shit scared me too, Ja. You not talking to me made me realize just how easy it was to lose you. I can't imagine not having you in my life in any capacity. Even if we never get this shit right and be in a relationship, I need you around."

"Why? So you can fuck up any other nigga that comes my way?"

I chuckled. "No… I'd hate to have to watch it, but I want you to be happy. Even if it ain't with me."

She smirked. "Just not with Tyson."

"Fuck that nigga."

She laughed. "Yeah, fuck him." She looked up at me. "It feels good to not want to choke slam you every time I see you now."

"First of all, you could never choke slam me with your little ass."

Her hand swiftly moved from the hem of my shirt to my neck. Her fingers gave a hard squeeze as she pulled my head to hers. I inhaled sharply as I backed her up against her car.

"What have I told you about me being little?" she asked just above a whisper.

"Alright now. You know I like that shit."

"I know you do. I believe I asked you nicely for a kiss. Now I see I'm gonna have to take it."

I smirked. "Take it then."

Her grip on my neck tightened, and I swear my dick bricked up in my pants. She stood on her toes and kissed my lips softly. When her tongue slipped into my mouth, I immediately picked her up and set her on the hood of the car. My hands moved to the side of her face as I kissed her so passionately that she began to moan. The kiss soon turned nasty when she slipped her hand into my pants and grabbed my dick.

"Don't let your mama and grandmother have to hear how loud you are when that shit is in you," I warned her.

"Mmm... I want it in me..." she said as her tongue snaked out of her mouth to lick the side of my face.

Fuck. I would give my left nut to slide up in her right now. However... I told her I wanted to be different with her, so I needed to follow through with that. Instead of inviting her back to my house like I wanted to, I chose a different approach.

"Let me take you out."

"Like a date?"

"Yes, like a date."

"Like you're gonna plan something?"

"You act like I don't know how to plan a date."

"We've never been on a date, Walker. I mean, we went places together, but it was never a real date."

"The money I spent on those places say otherwise, but I'll indulge you with planning a *real* date."

"When?"

"Friday. Be ready at seven. Wear something nice."

"Okay."

"Okay? No back talk?"

She giggled as she removed her hand and hopped down from the car. "No back talk."

I grabbed her hand and led her around to the driver's side, opening her door. She turned and looked up at me.

"I love you," she said quickly.

I smiled. "Say that shit again... slower."

"I said... I love you."

"I love you too." I leaned in to peck her lips. "Drive safe, and let me know when you make it home."

"I will."

She climbed in and closed her door. I went back to my car and climbed in as well. After waiting for it to pull off from the curb, I followed behind her until she had to turn off. The entire ride home, my thoughts were preoccupied with just what the fuck was going on with us. Things felt different between us, that was for damn sure.

I couldn't help but feel like we wasted a lot of time. Maybe not completely being that we knew everything about each other. But we wasted months because we couldn't have an adult conversation. I felt like I'd grown up a little. Honestly, looking back, I needed to. My mother always told me I was going to run into a woman that was going to force me to change whether I liked it or not.

She'd told me that shit so many times, and I always waved it off. I told myself I was gonna be a player until the day my eyes shut and they threw dirt on my casket. Who knew that what was supposed to be a one-night stand, or a few hook ups, would turn into a whole two-year affair, and now we were here. I didn't want to go through additional months of hell.

Once was enough.

We had to get it right this time.

Twenty-One

JORJA

"I'M STILL THINKING about it, Emerald," I said, sighing.

He'd been calling me almost every day to see if I'd made up my mind about choreographing his upcoming tour. He'd even upped his offer on my salary, and it was too good to pass up. I just needed a little more time to make my decision. If I was honest, I had calculated routines in mind. He'd given me his set list ahead of time, knowing I worked the moves out in my head before I ever put them in motion.

He groaned. "You're killing me, Jorja. How about I throw in an extra fifteen percent per show?"

"It's not about the money, Emerald. You already made a very generous offer. I just need a little more time."

"I know you're scared, but you are one of the hardest working dancers I know. This shit was made for you. Don't miss out on your calling because of a little fear. I'm gonna be calling you back."

"I know you will. Give Rhyon my love."

"I will. Tell your mom, granny, and Liv I said hi."

"I will."

We disconnected the call, and I fell back against Liv's couch. She sat on the other end with JJ in her lap, knocked out. He didn't care that her big belly was in the way. His head rested comfortably on her, drool falling from his lips. My mother walked in from the kitchen with a bowl of ice cream for her.

"Let me take him," she said, handing off the bowl before picking him up.

He squirmed a little, but once she was comfortably seated, he was right back to being sound asleep. I smiled. She was loving being a grandmother to Jamison's children, and they loved her too. Since Liv was getting bigger, she tired out quicker. Our mother volunteered to come cook dinner, and she didn't object.

"Thanks, Ma," Liv said, digging into the bowl. "I have to eat this before my husband gets home. He is obsessed with my sweet tooth, and I'm this close to snapping on him."

"You know he's just overprotective," I said. "You've met this family, right?"

She rolled her eyes. "I know, I know. As bad as it pisses me off, with these hormones, it gets me all hot and bothered too."

Our mother laughed. "You better leave that man alone."

"Tell him to leave me alone, Ma."

"Nah, you gave him the name big daddy," I reminded her. "You better do what he says before he spanks you."

"I have no qualms about him spanking me."

"At least you'll be in your own home, and neighbors won't see you fondling him," Mom said, looking over at me.

"Whaaaat!" I asked, my octave rising.

"Who were you feeling up, Ja?" Liv asked.

"Who else?" Mom asked. "Walker. For somebody who couldn't stand him a few weeks ago, they were awfully friendly at and after dinner."

"Wait, so you crashed dinner?" Liv asked.

"I guess you could say that."

"After you fussed about him coming to Sunday dinner?"

"Y'all are worried about the wrong thing," I said, deflecting. "And I wasn't fondling him—"

"Oh, you liar!" my mother said. "I looked out the window. Liv, if her hand had gone any deeper in his pants, she might as well have whipped it out and sat on it."

"Mama!" I exclaimed.

"Jorja!" She mocked me. "I told you. I told you this wasn't over between y'all."

"Maybe it's not... He asked me on a date tonight."

"A date!" Liv exclaimed. "Sooo... that situation?"

"Is dead."

"You mean Tyson?" Mom asked.

"You mean the cheater? The adulterous husband hiding his wife and daughter?"

"What the hell?"

"Yeah, Ma. He was married, perpetrating like he was single and looking."

"How are you feeling about that?"

I shrugged. "I was upset at first."

"Mama, she went over there," Liv said.

I glared at her. "You are such a snitch!"

"You went to confront him alone?" my mother asked. "You know better."

"I know, Ma. I was upset. He played in my face. He was taking me on dates, cooking for me, kissing on me. We... well, you know. I liked him, and he ruined it."

"Well you don't seem too mad now. I have to ask... what are you and Walker about to do, Ja? You two can't fall back into the same shit."

"I know. That's why I plan to bring it up on our date. I want to do things different."

Even if it meant that I had to abstain from sex with him, I'd do it. It would kill me... but I'd do it. Sex got us into this situation in the first place. I wasn't supposed to catch feelings, and neither was he. We weren't supposed to be hanging out, sleeping at each other's house, or traveling together. Even though we mostly traveled for my shows, we still made the most of the time together whenever we were in a new city.

We had all the elements of a relationship without the title.

The truth was, the more time I spent with him, the nicer it felt to have my own person. Watching Liv and Jamison and then Cartel and Adina softened my heart to real, unconditional love. I didn't want their experience, but I began to want a man to love me like that. Subconsciously, I found myself comparing Walker to them. I had internal conflicts with him, and it wasn't fair.

I wanted him to treat me like his woman. Instead of telling him what I wanted, I was petty in the things I said and did to get his attention, in hopes that he would get the hint. That was where I went wrong. He was a man, and he had flaws, but he wasn't a mind reader. The adult thing to do was have a conversation with him. For that, I could admit I was wrong.

I wouldn't do that this time.

If things with us progressed, I'd be open and honest about my feelings.

"Look at you growing up," my mother said with a smile. "I'm proud of you, Ja. I'm proud of both of you." She looked sad for a moment. "When your father left, it broke my heart. I kept feeling like I didn't do enough, or I wasn't enough. I gave him years of my life. I gave him two beautiful little girls, and he just left me to go make a family with another woman. I've never given another man a chance to love me correctly, and I wanted so badly for the two of you to find the love you deserve."

She looked at Aleviyah.

"You found a beautiful family that loves you so much. You made me a grandma, and I'm loving every second of it. The way Jamison loves and protects you is everything I wished for, for you, baby."

She turned to me.

"And you... my hot-headed child. You may not have seen it, but I've always known that Walker loved you, Jorja. I saw it in the way he looked at you. I see it in the way he supports your dancing. I see it in the attention he gives you. You, my love, were so focused on the bigger things that you didn't see the little ways he expressed his love for you."

"I guess you're right," I said, plucking my nails. "I could have been better. I see that now, and I promise I'll work on it." I looked up at her. "For the record, Mama, I think you deserve love too."

"Agreed," Liv said, scraping the bottom of the ice cream bowl.

"You are and always have been a baddie, Mama. If young men like Reese..." I pretended to gag, "if they are attracted to you, I know men your age are. You don't even have to try to be fine, girl."

She laughed as she waved me off. "I know I'm still youthful. And Reese, as young as he is, I'm flattered by his compliments."

"Please don't tell me you would consider dating him," Liv pleaded. "Ma, he's literally like our little brother."

"Girl, no! That boy still has Similac on his breath, and I would turn him out. I'm just saying, your mama has options, and I might start dating. Not right now though. I want to enjoy being a grandma for a little while."

She kissed JJ's forehead. His little eyes fluttered open. He looked over at Liv with a frown on his face.

"Hey, buddy," she said with a smile. "Did you have a nice nap?"

He nodded as he sat up, looking around. When he looked up at my mother, he smiled wide. She hadn't been here when he fell asleep.

"Grammy!" he exclaimed, throwing his little arms around her neck.

"Hey, Grammy's baby!" She smothered his cheeks with kisses, causing him to erupt in giggles. "I missed you."

"I miss you too. I go your house?"

"You wanna spend the weekend with me?"

He nodded eagerly.

"You're just gonna leave me, JJ?" Liv asked him. "Who else is gonna cuddle with me?"

He grinned. "Daddy."

"That's how we got this one," she mumbled, rubbing her stomach.

I still couldn't believe she'd gone from no kids to about to have five. Jamison's fertile ass was sure to give her at least one more before it was all said and done. He and the girls came home about an hour later. The first thing he did when he walked in was walk over to Liv and pull her to her feet for a hug and kiss before stooping to kiss her stomach and talk to his baby. He was such a sweet man, and I loved the way he loved my sister.

He sat her on his lap, rubbing small circles on her stomach.

"Baby?" she said.

"Yes, love?"

"You remember that bet we made a couple months ago?"

He looked over at me with a grin, and I was slightly confused.

"I remember." He turned back to her.

"Well, it's happening."

"You lying."

"I'm not. They have a date on tonight."

"Like a real date?"

"Yes, a real date."

I sat up. "I know y'all didn't make a bet at my expense!"

Jamison laughed. "Oh, we most certainly did. You aren't exactly in a position to fulfill your wishes, Liv."

"Maybe not now, but I intend to collect."

"Hold up now!" I interrupted. "What was the bet?"

"She bet me that you and Walker would get it together in six months. I said you'd still be playing games."

I pretended to be offended. "You had no faith in us, Jamison?"

"Can you blame me?"

I rolled my eyes. "So since you lost, what's the wager?"

Aleviyah grinned. "Handcuffs."

I laughed. "I hope she gets your ass good," I said to Jamison.

"Shit, me too."

I sat with them until it was almost time for me to start getting ready for my date. I said my goodbyes after promising Liv I would call her with details tomorrow. As I was driving down the road, I got a text from Walker. It was a picture of his haircut.

That Nigga: I'm getting fine, don't make me look bad.

Me: Boy, fuck you.

That Nigga: I'm joking. I know you're gonna step out looking like you need your back cracked.

Me: And is! I'm headed home to get ready.

That Nigga: I'll see you in a few. I love you.

Me: I love you too.

I smiled as I dropped the phone into the cup holder. It was going to take some getting used to, hearing him tell me that, but it made me feel all warm and shit inside. I was anxiously waiting to see what he had planned.

* * *

THE BURIAL OF A PLAYER

SIX FORTY-FIVE ROLLED AROUND, and I was putting the finishing touches on my outfit.

When I arrived at my apartment building, the receptionist handed me a big box with a beautiful bow on top. I noticed the label on it was from an expensive boutique in town called Elegance. They sold prom dresses and dresses for special occasions. I couldn't get to my floor fast enough to get the box open.

When I took the top off, the first thing I saw was an envelope sitting on top of the tissue paper. It was a handwritten note from Walker.

MY LOVE,

A BEAUTIFUL DRESS *for the most beautiful woman in my world. I hope tonight is the rebirth of something equally beautiful between us. I love you. I'm ready to commit to you and to us. Tonight is just the beginning...*

Love, Walker

I SMILED SO HARD when I read that. Inside was the most beautiful emerald-green, floor-length gown with elegant, silver beading around the bust area. The split went right up my thigh, and the dress itself hugged my curves to perfection. To match the dress, he'd also sent a beautiful pair of silver stilettos and a matching clutch and jewelry.

As I looked myself over in the mirror, I had to admit that this man outdid himself. He picked the perfect outfit, and now my mind was running rampant wondering where he was taking me tonight. I snapped so many pictures and sent them to the group chat I had going with Liv, Adina, and Alaina.

ALAINA: Oooo bitch you look fine as fuck!

Liv: Okay Walker! He better pull out all the stops! You look flawless!

Adina: Girl! If you don't give him some boonkey tonight! You look so beautiful, Ja!

Me: Thanks y'all. I have no idea where he's taking me but I guess I'm gonna have to act like I have a little class tonight. LOL.

AT SEVEN O'CLOCK on the dot, my doorbell rang.

Grabbing my clutch, I headed out of my bedroom to answer. When I opened the door, Walker was standing there looking so damn good, my panties were instantly flooded. He was draped in an all-black suit with emerald-green accents that matched my dress. In his hands were a bouquet of white roses. His eyes passed over me before a smile spread across his lips, showcasing his slugs. That made me grin wide, showing off mine as well.

"My nigga," he said, reaching out to dap me.

I laughed as I slapped his hand. Stepping aside, I allowed him to step into the apartment. He handed me the flowers before he leaned in and kissed my lips softly. He stepped back and twirled me around.

"Damn I did good," he said, grinning.

"You did amazing," I said, looking down at everything. "Seriously, Walker. Thank you. I know this wasn't cheap."

"Money has never been an issue, and it won't be. You deserve everything I'm coming with tonight. Why don't you put those in some water, and we can get going."

I smiled brightly as I headed into the kitchen to put the flowers in a vase. When I returned, he pulled me into his arms for a picture. After snapping a few cute ones, a few sexy ones, and a few ratchet ones, we got ready to go. He offered me his arm, and I slipped mine through it as we walked out the door. Ms. Cooler was peeking out her door as usual. When she saw us, she opened it wider.

"Well don't you two look nice," she said, smiling brightly.

"Thank you," we both said.

"It's good to see you together again. I knew it was coming. I guess I better get my headphones ready tonight."

I rolled my eyes. "Goodnight, Ms. Cooler."

"Baby, if she don't give you none, you come right on over here. I got something for your young, handsome self."

Walker's face turned red. "I wouldn't know what to do with you, woman."

He quickly ushered me to the elevator before she could get started. I roasted him about that shit the entire ride down. I finally stopped when he threatened to take me back upstairs. As we stepped out of the building, my eyes widened at the limousine waiting out front.

"You rented a limo?"

"Tonight is special," he said as the driver opened the back door. "I want you to always remember our first official date since you said the others weren't real."

I playfully pushed him before climbing in. The inside was beautiful. Rose petals littered the floor, and there was champagne and chocolate covered strawberries. Soft music played low on the speakers, setting a romantic mood.

"I can't believe you did all this," I said quietly as I looked around.

"You deserve all of me, Ja. I don't want to give you bits and pieces anymore. I'm gonna prove to you that I am worthy of being your man. You won't regret giving us a real chance."

He leaned over and kissed me as we pulled onto the street. I couldn't help but feel butterflies in my stomach. For the first time in a long time, shit felt right.

Twenty-Two

WALKER

JORJA WAS LOOKING fine as fuck in this emerald dress.

When I picked it out, I knew it would look perfect on her. Lucky for me, I was able to find a tie, vest, and pocket square in the exact shade. We looked so fucking good together. I hadn't been this clean since Jay and Aleviyah's wedding. We snapped a ton of pictures on the way to our destination. The drive to Grand Hills was about thirty minutes.

Being that Jorja was a dancer, I decided to take her to the ballet that was in town. We had front row tickets. When she first told me that she danced ballet, too, I thought she was joking. Then she took me to the studio, and I got to watch her perform. She moved so light and fluidly… so elegant. It was a complete contrast from the sexy dancing I'd normally seen her do. Hopefully, she would enjoy the show.

When we arrived at the Capital Concert Hall, her eyes widened at the banner outside.

"The ballet?" she asked, smiling.

"I thought it might be different."

"I haven't been in so long! Thank you." She leaned over and kissed my lips.

"You're welcome."

The driver opened my door, and I stepped out to help her. Linking her arm through mine, we walked inside. After presenting our tickets, we made our way into the space where the show was scheduled to take place. The place was filling up pretty quick, so we hurried to claim our seats.

"I've always wanted to perform here," Jorja said, looking around. "So many dancers got discovered here."

"You've been discovered, baby. You just have to take the job."

She sighed. "He called me again today, looking for an answer."

"What's holding you back, Ja? That's your dream."

"I know it is. I just... I've never been away from home so long. There's my mama and granny. Then there is Liv and the baby, the kids... you."

"You know we all support you, right?"

"I know."

"And we will be waiting for you to come home. I don't mind flying out when I can, to be by your side, but you have to do this for you. You're a beast on stage. That's where you flourish; it's your passion. You don't give that up for anything."

"I don't want to give it up. I'd love to dance for Emerald. I've known him since we were kids, and I know he'll look out for me."

"If I have to, I'll hire security to travel with you."

"I don't need all that. You know I can handle myself."

"I know. But whatever you need to take this opportunity, I'm here to help. I got you."

She smiled as she linked her fingers through mine. "I'm loving this side of you. All soft and shit."

I chuckled. "I can commit to being soft for you. Nobody else."

"Just be soft when I need it. I still love the joke cracking, shit talking, aggravating Walker Jareau. Make sure he never leaves."

"I got you, baby."

She cupped my chin, gently pressing her lips against mine as the lights went down. Once the show began, it was quiet between us. I watched the show, but for the most part, I was focused on her. I caught the smile on her face and the gleam in her eyes. Every time she pointed something out to me, her voice was filled with excitement. When she saw that two of the girls from her dance team were in the show, she fought back the urge to scream for them.

"That was my move," she said proudly. "I taught them that. They're doing so good! I have to see them after the show."

When they were done, she stood to give them a standing ovation. They waved at her with bright smiles and blew her kisses. As she returned to her seat, she grabbed my hand and pulled it to her lips. Softly, she kissed the back of it before resting her head against my shoulder.

I was glad that I could contribute to her happiness tonight. Months ago, I wouldn't have even thought to do anything like this. We used to split our free time between my family and hers. Sometimes, we'd hit up a club or a kickback or went to grab food. Nothing extravagant. This was a little out of my element, but this was pretty dope. I had to admit it... I was loving the softer side of her too.

* * *

THE SHOW CAME to an end after about two hours.

As everyone else made their way out of the concert hall, Jorja and I headed backstage to find her students. When they saw her, they rushed over to hug her.

"Ms. Jorja!" they exclaimed.

"Jordan! Camilla! You girls killed it," she said, squeezing them. "I'm so proud of you. Why didn't you tell me you were dancing?"

"Because if we sucked, we didn't want to embarrass ourselves in front of too many people we knew."

"What do I always tell you? You're highly capable; you just have to want it bad enough. This was huge for you guys."

"You saw we used a few of your moves?" Camilla asked.

"I did. Perfectly executed, by the way. I almost screamed, but I remembered where I was."

The girls laughed as they looked up at me.

"Who's this?" Jordan asked.

THE BURIAL OF A PLAYER

"That's Anais's uncle," Camilla said. "You remember? The cute one with all the tattoos from her birthday party last year."

"Oh! Hey, Mr. Jareau!"

"Aht, aht," Jorja said, playfully poking her. "This one is mine."

She slipped her arm around my waist.

"Okay, Ms. Jorja!" Jordan said, snapping her fingers. "I see you! He's much cuter than Millicent's uncle."

I snickered, causing her to elbow me.

"He's alright," she said, playfully pushing me.

"I hate to break this up," I said, looking down at my watch. "But baby, we are gonna be late for dinner."

"It was good seeing you girls." She hugged them once more. "I'll see you at practice on Monday."

"See you! Bye, Mr. Jareau."

"Bye, girls."

I grabbed her hand and led her back out toward the exit. I sent the driver a text that we were ready.

"Even your students—"

"Shut up!" she said, pinching my arm. "You've got me now, sir. Enjoy it. Once upon a time, this wasn't even a thought."

I kissed my teeth. "Lies. You know you missed me as much as I missed you. You just enjoyed being petty."

"Maybe just a little," she admitted. "Low key, it gave me great pleasure in watching you beg."

"You thought it was funny to have me on my knees?"

"Well, maybe tonight, I'll get on my knees for you, to make up for it."

I licked my lips as we came to a stop out front.

"Stop playing with me, Ja." I leaned in, whispering loud enough so that only she could hear. "I will assault that pretty little mouth of yours."

"Oooo... you know I love when you do that."

Fuck! My dick was bricking in my pants.

"You are pressure, woman."

"I know."

I shook my head at her cockiness. That was my baby. Cocky as a muthafucka.

* * *

WE MADE it to our dinner reservations with five minutes to spare.

Luckily, we were seated right after giving the hostess our names. I'd reserved a private table on the balcony. Normally, about five tables were available out there, but because I wanted privacy, I reserved the whole thing. It was set up with rose petals leading out to a candle lit table with her favorite wine chilling.

She gasped. "Walker... this is... oh my God!"

"I take it you like it?"

"I love it." She turned to me, placing a peck on my lips. "You didn't have to do all this."

"Yes, I did. I need you to know I can give you the type of treatment you deserve. I want to do this right, Ja. I love the physical aspects of you, but I know you crave more."

She looked around at the space. "Can we sit and talk for a minute?"

"Sure."

I grabbed her hand and led her over to the table. Pulling out her chair, I allowed her to sit before I pushed her in. I then took a seat across from her. She reached for my hands, and I placed them in hers.

She took a deep breath. "I need to apologize."

"For what?"

"For a while... I was comparing you to Jamison and Cartel. I saw the way they treated Liv and Adina, and I was angry that you didn't do that for me. Then I realized, I never told you what I wanted. I did or said petty shit, thinking maybe you would get the hint, when I should have been verbal. I was carrying around this anger towards you, when I never spoke up about my desires. I don't know if it would have made a difference back then, but I should have said something. For that, I'm sorry."

"While I can agree there, I shouldn't have brushed things off when you said some of the things you said. I got the hint, Ja. I just... I didn't think you were serious when you kept coming back after you cooled off. I guess that was the toxic shit."

THE BURIAL OF A PLAYER

"It was definitely toxic."

"You know what Margo told me?"

"The bald-headed chick with the fat ass?"

I chuckled. "I swear you and Reese said the same shit. She has a fade; she ain't bald. Anyway, she said toxic shit turns women on until it turns them off. I never thought about that."

"That's about right." She looked over the balcony, overlooking the city. "I remember the first time I realized it turned me off. It was the night Adina pulled that knife on that girl. Liv brought me home, and you were waiting for me. I remember feeling embarrassed. My sister... she's seen the many phases of Jorja. She's never judged me. In that moment, I knew she probably thought I was weak as hell.

"That I would let you into my apartment, we'd argue, we'd fuck, and it was fine. We'd had a whole conversation about me being tired of that shit, and there you were, proving our predictability. That was the moment I knew I didn't want to do that anymore. My hot girl phase came to an end that night."

That incident happened at least a year ago. I remembered leaving Jay's and making a beeline for her apartment. I didn't know if I was trying to save face in front of my brothers, but I brushed it off like I didn't care. Yet, I found myself at her apartment, trying to plead my case. We argued for hours, and she didn't speak to me for weeks. It wasn't until Cartel got shot did she finally come around.

When I got the news from my mother, the first person I called was her. She came straight over and drove me to the hospital. She pushed my Rover, doing a hundred the whole way. It was a miracle she didn't get a ticket. She was there to comfort me the entire time. Nights when I couldn't sleep due to worry, she sat up with me. Sometimes, we didn't say anything. She just let me lay on her while we watched TV.

She was gentle with me... loving in ways I didn't realize I loved or needed until I didn't have it anymore. How could I have missed what was happening between us? Following our last strife, my ego was bruised. I put on a façade, but inside, I was feeling the pain from that shit.

I sighed. "I'm sorry for the part I played in perpetuating that narrative. We can't change the past, Ja. We can't live there either."

"I know. We just needed to have this talk. I don't want to discuss it again. Let's just move forward and be better."

"We can do that." I kissed her hands. "I love you, Jorja."

"I love you too."

Our waitress finally came out to take our drink order and distribute menus. By the time she returned with the drinks, we were ready to order. Dinner went smoothly. The food was great. The vibe was vibing. I was enjoying her company. During dessert, one of the violinists came out, asking if we'd like some music. She was a beautiful melanated sista, and she and Ja hit it off.

She had that girl playing "Super Gremlin" by Kodak Black, and I had to give it to her; that shit was fire. They were dancing, rapping and all. I sat back, appreciating the smile on her face. She was genuinely happy, and it was over the smallest thing. She took pictures with her and posted a video clip to her IG, shouting her out.

I ended up giving ol' girl a nice tip for her entertainment. Jorja was all smiles as we left the restaurant.

"That was an amazing experience," she said, sinking into the cusp of my arm. "I'm about ready to get out of these shoes and relax though."

"You mind if we make a pit stop? I promised my mama I would bring her and Pops cheesecake."

"That's fine."

I let the driver know what address to take us to, and we were on our way. Forty-five minutes later, we were pulling up to my childhood home. I helped her out of the car. She'd already come out of her heels and was walking around in a pair of foldable flats. Hand in hand, we walked into my parents' house.

"Where y'all at!" I yelled.

My father came from the kitchen, a frown on his face.

"I'm about sick of you and that," he said, pushing me away from Jorja. He pulled her into a hug. "You look beautiful, baby girl."

"Thank you, Papa Jareau. Your son actually put together my whole outfit."

He raised an eyebrow. "By himself?"

Jorja laughed. "Yes, by himself."

"Don't sound so shocked, Pops."

He shrugged. "I'm just saying."

"I guess I'm gonna have to give Mama your cheesecake." I held up the bag.

"Let's not be hasty," he said, taking the bag from me.

"Oh, don't you two look good!"

My mother came through the back patio door with a smile. When she reached us, she pulled us both in for hugs and kisses. "I've always said you two make a beautiful couple. How was your night?"

"It was everything, Mama Jareau," Jorja answered. "He planned an amazing night."

"I can tell by the smile on your face." She looked over at my father. "Is that the cheesecake?"

"Yes, dear. I'm gonna plate it up. You two wanna join us outside? We're having a few drinks and listening to some music."

"We can't stay too long," I said. "The limo is waiting."

"Let them go. I'll call the car service to take you home."

"You don't have to tell me twice," Ja said. "I've been eyeballing a slice of that cheesecake. Please tell me you'll share?"

My father cupped her chin. "How could I say no to that pretty face?"

I rolled my eyes. "Let me grab our things."

I kissed her cheek before heading out to grab my jacket and her clutch and shoes. After tipping the driver, I headed back inside. I placed our things on the bench near the front door, then headed out back. I found my mother sitting on the chaise, killing that damn cheesecake. Jorja and my father were prancing around the yard, stuffing their faces and dancing to "Let's Stay Together" by Al Greene.

I took a seat next to my mother to watch them.

"She looks happy, son," she commented, looking over at me.

"She does... Tonight was a good night, Mama."

"I'm happy for you. I take it you two have talked about all your issues."

"Yes, ma'am."

"And?"

"And... we're giving this thing a real chance. No more bullshiting."

She slapped my arm. "Alright, now."

I laughed. "I'm just calling it what it was, Mama."

"It was definitely some bullshit."

"So you can say it, but I can't."

"I'm grown."

"I'm grown too, woman."

She pointed the fork at me. "You ain't that grown. *No juegues conmigo.*"

She told me not to play with her.

"Seriously though," she said, setting her plate down. "I'm happy you two worked things out. I wasn't prepared to like anybody else either of you brought into the family."

I had to laugh at that one. She loved her some Ja, and Ja loved her too. She relaxed into the chair with a sigh.

"Well that's three out of five. Now there's just Alaina and Reese."

"Reese I can handle. Alaina... nah. Sis can't date until she's forty."

"Y'all are going to let my child live."

"I'm sure she lived it up in Spain. I keep telling her she might as well move back. She's been here like every other month since Cartel was released."

"I know. It's been nice having her around more. She thinks she's slick."

"How?"

"Once upon a time, she was talking about renting an apartment for when she comes home to visit. She claimed she wanted her privacy. Now all of a sudden, she's more comfortable here when she's home. She thinks I don't know she still has a thing for Roosevelt."

"Rose is good people. Do I want him to date my baby sister? No. But he's a cool dude."

"He is good people. But Alaina isn't ready for that type of man yet. Sure, he's pretty, but he also has a child and priorities that can't always accommodate her and the attention she'll want from him. If she's not ready to make some changes, she needs to wait."

That hit home for me. She'd told me the same thing when Jorja and I started hanging heavily. The first time I brought her over for dinner, we had that conversation. I never brought women home, not even as a chap. She saw it before either of us did, just like Ms. Alicia. Then again, most parents saw shit we thought they were oblivious to. Paloma Jareau had a sixth sense about a lot of shit.

This was one time I prayed she was right in how she felt about Ja and me. I was one of those people. If my mama said it was okay, it was okay.

Twenty-Three

JORJA

I WAS SO DAMN TIRED.

Walker and I ended up staying at his parents' house for two hours. Papa Jareau and I spent much of that time dancing. The love I had for his parents almost matched the love I had for my own family. Mama Jareau was my girl, and Papa... well, Papa was the father I never had. My inner child came out anytime he called me baby girl. He was always so affectionate and loving toward me.

Until I met him, I didn't realize how bad I craved a father daughter relationship. Sometimes when Alaina came home, he'd gather all of us— her, Liv, Adina, and I—and take us out for lunch. He showered us with attention. He offered fatherly advice. He reminded us of how beautiful and worthy we were.

Days like that drained me at times. While it was what I needed, when I left his presence, I was reminded that I didn't have that bond with the man that created then abandoned me. Days like that, I usually ended up at my mama's house, curled up under her with her babying me. I could admit, at twenty-six years old, I was a big ass baby when it came to that woman.

"You good over there?" Walker asked, interrupting my thoughts.

We were a few minutes from my apartment.

THE BURIAL OF A PLAYER

"I'm good." I rested my head against his shoulder. "I had a really good time tonight."

He chuckled. "I think you enjoyed my parents more than the date."

"You know I love your parents. They are some of the best people I've ever met. I'm grateful for them."

He kissed his teeth. "They a'ight."

We shared a light laugh as the driver pulled up to my building. Walker got out and then helped me out as well. Hand in hand, we headed into the building, onto the elevator, and up to my floor.

"I guess this is goodnight?" I asked, pressing my back against my door.

"It is."

"You sure you don't want to come in?"

"As bad as I want to—"

I stepped into his space, placing my finger to his lips. "Walker... I want you here. I want you with me. I want *you*."

He inhaled deeply. Pulling out his phone, he called down to the driver and told him he was free to go. I smiled as I pulled out my key and unlocked the door. Inside, we headed for my bedroom. I locked the door behind me and stood against it. He stood next to my bed, his hands shoved in his pockets. For a moment, we gazed at each other.

The sexual tension in the room was suffocating. All night long, my attraction to him was peaking. I knew I said I could abstain from sex with him, but the way I craved him right now... that shit was out the window. I walked over to him and pushed the jacket from his shoulders. He let it fall to the floor. Slowly, my fingers worked to undo the buttons of his vest and dress shirt before I pushed them off as well.

His smooth caramel skin was littered with tattoos. My fingers traced the designs, admiring his toned body as well. They trailed down to his belt buckle. When it was undone, I slowly pulled it from the loop and dropped it to the floor. I unbuttoned then unzipped his pants and slipped my hand inside.

"Mmmm... I've missed that..." I whispered as I wrapped my fingers around his dick.

His hand came to my neck, giving a gentle squeeze.

"He's missed you too. What's that shit you said about getting on your knees earlier?"

I smirked. He leaned, blessing my lips with the sweetest, nastiest kiss that had me dropping to my knees in this expensive ass dress. I pulled his pants and boxers down, and his pretty ass dick sprang forward. Fuck, I missed this shit. I took him in my hand, allowing my fingers to trace the intricate lines of the pulsating veins.

Precum leaked from the tip of his dick. Hungrily, I stuck out my tongue to taste him. He inhaled deeply as my lips covered the tip, giving him gentle suction.

"Shit..."

Closing my eyes, I took him deep into my mouth. My throat welcomed him back by opening up to receive him. I sucked him slow, adding a generous amount of spit and hand grips. His fingers threaded through my tresses as he gathered my hair.

"Fucking beautiful ass..." He groaned as he thrusted his hips. "You look so fucking pretty with my dick in your mouth, baby."

My pussy tingled, and I knew the seat of my thong was saturated in my juices. I loved when he told me how pretty I was like this.

"Fuck! I've missed you, woman. You got my shit throbbing."

He pumped his hips faster, assaulting my throat in the most pleasurable way. I reached behind me to unzip my dress and pull the top down. With my titties freed, my hands moved to them, pinching my nipples. I couldn't help but to moan as sensations flooded my middle. While I didn't want to rush him, I needed him to cum so he could put my kitty out of her misery.

He pulled out of my mouth and held back, painting my swollen lips with his dick. Tilting my head back, he stroked himself as he looked in my eyes.

"Open."

A simple command.

I opened my mouth and immediately caught the stream of his nut. The last couple drops trickled down my chin. I swiped what I could with my tongue before scooping the rest up with my finger. He bit his lip as he watched me swallow his load and wipe my mouth clean.

"So fucking nasty... Bring your ass here."

He yanked me up from the floor and crashed his lips into mine. His kisses were so rough and sexy. He pushed my dress down over my hips, and it pooled on the floor. I felt myself being lifted into his arms where he wrapped my legs around his waist. He kicked off his shoes and pants with ease before placing me in the middle of bed.

"Mmm... mmm... mmm." He groaned as he stroked his dick. "Look at you... wet as fuck already."

He hovered over me, peering down at me lustfully. His finger trailed between my breasts and down my stomach. He gripped the band of my underwear and ripped them right off my body.

"Shit..."

Walker's fingers dipped into my wetness and right into my center. I gasped as my back arched from the bed. When he pulled his hand away, his fingers were saturated in my juices. Placing them to his mouth, he sucked them clean before guiding them back into me. Tediously, he teased me, bringing me almost to the edge before pulling his hand away again. His fingers gently gripped my throat as I followed the pull of his arm. He placed his fingers to my lips.

"Open."

Again, a simple command that had me eagerly opening my mouth and sticking out my tongue. I slithered my tongue through them, capturing my essence. I wrapped lips around his digits as he slowly worked them in and out of my mouth. A low moan escaped his lips.

"Mmm... I love how much you like that shit. Wet ass pussy... You know you taste so... fucking... good. Come put this shit on my face."

Walker rolled onto his back, beckoning me to him. I wasted no time climbing to my feet and standing over him. He licked his lips as I lowered my pussy onto his mouth. I braced myself against the headboard as his hands gripped my ass to hold me in place. The first swipe of his tongue caused me to gasp.

"Oooo... shit!"

He French kissed my pussy lips as he swirled his skilled tongue around my swollen clit. I looked down to find his eyes closed. He moaned into me like he was enjoying and savoring the taste of me on his pallet. Slowly, I rocked my hips against his mouth. The friction his tongue and lips caused felt so damn good.

I tossed my head back and closed my eyes. I cupped my breasts, pinching my nipples as I rode his mouth to a beat in my head. My hips wound back and forth against his mouth. When his tongue slipped into my wet canal, I didn't hesitate to bounce on it.

I moaned as I palmed the back of his head. "Eat this pussy."

Walker had a generous tug on my clit before shoving his tongue deep inside me.

"Oooo… that's a good boy. Show mama how much you missed this shit."

I balanced myself on my toes, sliding my pussy back and forth across his lips with a steady motion. He slapped my ass, and I couldn't help but to squirt a little. He lapped my juices with deep, purring moans.

"Mmmm…."

His eyes locked onto mine, and I couldn't force myself to look away. The deeper he stared into my soul, the more aroused I became. The more aroused I became, the wetter my pussy was.

"Oooo, fuck! You look so sexy with my pussy in your mouth. You want this nut, don't you?"

He nodded, his eyes and lips never leaving me. Another hard slap came to my ass, forcing me to speed up. At this point, I was actively fucking his face. He took that shit with no complaints, no breaks for air, and no backtalk. I tossed my head and pinched my nipples, feeling myself about to explode.

I cried out in pleasure. "Shit! I'm gonna cum… Fuck, I'm gonna cum!"

I couldn't hold back as my pussy released into his waiting mouth. His entire face was drenched as I came for and because of him. I sat there for a second, coming down from the high of my release as he sucked my lower lips. Finally, I rolled off of him and onto my back. He sat up and went into the bathroom, returning with a towel to wipe his face. With care, he wiped my inner thighs clean and tossed the towel aside.

He joined me in bed, planting his body between my legs. Hovering over me, he pulled one of my legs around his waist.

"I don't wanna fuck you," he said, pressing his forehead against mine. "I wanna make love to you, Ja."

He kissed my lips before migrating to my neck.

"I want you to feel every ounce of pleasure as meticulously as possible."

His head dipped to my nipples as he sucked them into his mouth one and then the other.

I moaned his name. "Walker..."

"Can I have you, Ja?"

"Y-yes... Take it."

His dick slid into me with ease. My arms went around him, clinging to him for dear life as he filled me. Slowly, he thrusted his hips, burying every inch of himself in me with every stroke. Whimpers escaped my throat as the tension between us built. I was so used to him fucking the shit outta me that I never knew this would feel so damn good. Nobody had ever made love to me. I never had the desire to be made love to either.

Yet this... this was magical... powerful... liberating.

"Walker... shit, baby!"

"Tell me you're mine, Jorja," he whispered in my ear. "I need you, baby. I can't be just your friend. I can't let any other nigga have you when you're supposed to be mine. Tell me you're mine, Ja."

"I'm yours... I'm all yours..."

I buried my face between his neck and shoulders. My nails sank into his back, clawing it up as his strokes deepened. Tears pooled in my eyes. He was loving me so... damn... good. He moved to drape my legs over his shoulders, pinning my arms to the bed. My pussy was wide open, his for the taking. He took it and made me take all of him in return.

With every stroke, my whimpers turned into soft cries.

"Oh God!"

"Yes!"

"Right there... fuck!"

At one point, I couldn't even make a sound. I just clung to him, allowing the sensations to run freely through my body.

"Fuck, Ja!" He growled in my ear.

His strokes quickened, and his thrusts deepened. I could feel his dick throbbing as he pummeled my walls. The sounds of my juices gathering filled the room. When his fingers wrapped around my neck, gently squeezing, I came undone. My walls clenched around him, and my mouth opened, expelling a guttural cry from deep within.

"Aaaahhhh!"

The orgasm that rippled through me knocked out my hearing for just a moment until he grunted loudly in my ear.

"Fuck!"

I felt his seed filling me... spilling out of me...coating my insides.

He stiffened, then dropped his weight on me. We lay there panting... dick throbbing... pussy pulsating. He lifted his head and brought his lips to mine, kissing me ravishingly.

"I love you," he whispered. "I'm never losing you again, you hear me?"

"I hear you... I love you too, Walker."

He rolled onto his side and pulled me into his chest. I wrapped my arms around him, resting my head against his chest. In no time, we were out for the count.

Twenty-Four

WALKER

I COULDN'T EVEN FORMULATE the words to describe how good a nigga was feeling right now. After that mind-blowing first round, Jorja and I took a good forty-five-minute nap. When we woke up, we spent the next two hours getting reacquainted with each other. I fully remembered why I had to size up any nigga that looked at her the wrong way. Our sexual chemistry had always been through the fucking roof.

She liked freaky shit, and I did too.

After managing to pull ourselves out of bed, we ended up in her jacuzzi tub for a hot soak. She decided to do her nightly facial, so here she was, perched in my lap as she gazed in the mirror behind us. I peppered the tops of her breasts with kisses as my hands glided up and down her back. When her nipple brushed against my lip, I sucked it into my mouth.

She laughed as she shoved me away. "Boy, stop! You're gonna fuck up my routine."

"You don't need that anyway. Your skin glows naturally."

"And that's because I take care of it. You should let me give you a facial."

I chuckled. "I think you gave me enough of a facial earlier."

She looked down at me and rolled her eyes. "I'm serious, fool."

"I don't know what's in that shit."

"If it were dangerous, do you think I'd be using it on my face? Just sit back and shut up."

"Stop trying to Deebo me."

"Lay your damn head back."

I chuckled as I followed her instructions. She started with cleansing my face and placing these cucumber patches over my eyes. While I couldn't see what she was doing, I was aware of all the different textures and tools she was using.

"I'm not gonna lie; this is relaxing," I admitted.

"So you're gonna let me do this more often?"

"I might. I guess I could get used to this." I gently massaged her thighs. "I have to get some sleep after this."

"Sleep? After this, I need a snack."

"Woman, you ate a three-course meal plus two slices of cheesecake with my parents."

"And you burned every calorie of that off in the last couple of hours. Don't act like you aren't gonna eat some of this cookie dough dip."

My ears perked up. That was our guilty pleasure for late night snacking. We typically used graham crackers to scoop it up. Whenever she made it, she made a pretty big bowl because we'd eat the whole thing before we stopped.

"Well you didn't say it was that," I countered, slapping her ass. "I missed that shit. I tried to make it one night. It wasn't anywhere near as good as when you make it."

She plucked the cucumber peels from my eyes. "So you missed me for my snacks?"

I grinned. "Partially. Mostly... I just missed you. You were the highlight of many days. I'm sorry it took me so long to see that, but I see it now."

She smiled as she pressed her lips against mine. After replacing the cucumber slices, she continued with my facial as we reminisced about our night. After another thirty minutes or so in the tub, we let the water out and hopped in the shower to wash up. While she made the cookie dough dip, I changed her sheets, placing the cum covered ones in the washer on a cycle. By the time she was finished, I'd just finished fixing the bed to her liking.

Pulling back the covers, I climbed in. She made herself comfortable between my legs, resting her back against my chest. I turned out the light and turned on the television to find us a movie. We got about halfway through *Shaft* when I heard her light snores. I chuckled as I pulled the bowl out of her hands, placing it and the crackers on the nightstand. After turning off the movie, I rolled her onto her side, sliding up close behind her.

With her resting in the curve of my body, I closed my eyes to go to sleep. She shifted, turning so that she could face me. Her arm draped around my waist and her leg over my thigh.

She yawned as she said, "I love you."

I placed a kiss on her forehead. "I love you too."

* * *

"SOOO... HOW WAS YOUR DATE?" Margo asked.

We had some time in between clients today, so we decided to hit the gym for a run on the treadmill. She was the one who recommended the shop where I bought Jorja's dress. When I told her about the date, she congratulated me on growing the fuck up. Those were her exact words.

I chuckled. "Margo, we have to get you a name tag."

"What? Why?"

"'Cause every time I mention your name, you're recognized as the bald-headed chick with the fat ass."

She playfully tried to push me, and I almost busted my ass.

"That's what you get. I can't help what my mama gave me. And I'm not baldheaded!"

I laughed. "I told them you have a fade."

Again, she pushed me. She kissed her teeth. "How was the damn date?"

"It was dope. She really enjoyed herself."

"You see what a little effort can do for you?"

I kissed my teeth. "You just wanna be right."

"I am right!" She slowed to a job before stopping completely. "I could teach you a few things on how to keep your woman."

"You probably could," I said, coming to a stop myself. "How long have you and Lacey been together?"

"Seven years. I cater to her, she caters to me. We have a mutual respect for each other. All of that yelling and cursing at each other when we're mad, we don't do that shit. Breaking up and making up is exhausting. Love isn't supposed to feel like that. It's supposed to be one of the most natural feelings in the world. When two people genuinely love each other, it's so simple to show that shit. It doesn't always have to be verbal. Do little things. Acknowledge subtle changes like when she gets her nails or eyebrows done. Women *love* to know you're paying attention to them, and I'm not talking about ass and titties, Walker."

I stopped midway from wiping the sweat from my brow.

"I didn't even say anything, bruh. You are just like my siblings, always jabbing at me."

"Well you certainly work my nerves like an older brother. If I wasn't a lesbian, you could not be my man. I would have to shoot you. You might like that toxic shit though."

"I haven't had a women shoot at me before, you know."

"Don't sound so intrigued. It's no fun."

"Who's been shooting at you?"

"I've had an ex or two. I say this is the humblest way. I'm the type of woman whose presence would leave a void if I took it away. I have my flaws, but I am a good woman and a good person. Good people are hard to replace. An ex or two realized that a little too late. Once I'm done with you, I'm done. Our purpose in each other's lives have been fulfilled, and I'm gone."

"So you never gave a second chance?"

"I've never dated anyone who deserved a second chance or that I desired to give things a second chance. Lacey is it for me. No second chance needed."

"That's some lovable shit. I like that."

Margo rolled her eyes as we headed back toward the offices. "You just better make the most of this second chance."

"I hear you. You're a good friend, Margo."

She smiled as she stuck her nose in the air. "I know. I'm an asset in every capacity."

I playfully pushed her. "You a'ight... bald-headed ass."

She swung at me, catching me in my left shoulder.

"If your big ass keeps pushing me, I'm gonna lay you the fuck out. And keep calling me baldheaded. Me and my fiancée are gonna take your girl and make her ours."

"You would do that to me, Margo? All it would take is a good meal and a fat blunt."

"I'm so telling her you said that."

"Don't do that. You're trying to put me back in the doghouse I just crawled out of. I'm tamed now."

"Mmm hmm. We shall see, Mr. Jareau. If you'll excuse me, I'm gonna go freshen up before our next client gets here."

She sashayed down the hall to her office, and I slipped into mine and settled behind my desk. I pulled my phone from my bag and saw that I had a message from Jorja. When I opened it, it was a video of her in the studio. She was dressed in her ballet uniform, dancing to "ICU" by Coco Jones. The caption read, *Feeling inspired.*

I watched attentively as she moved fluidly around the space. Her passion for dance itself was inspiring. She had to take this choreographing job. I understood that she was afraid of missing out on so much at home, but shit like this didn't drop from the sky on the regular. Emerald was a big star. He could take her places that little ass South Carolina couldn't. She worked hard, and she deserved that.

Pressing her contact info, I called her.

"Hello?"

"Hey, baby."

"Hey, boo. How's your day?"

"Pretty decent. I worked out with Margo for a little bit in between clients."

"Mmm hmm. You trying to sneak a peek at that ass? It's okay. I looked too."

"Girl, stop. Margo is literally like another sister to me. She flames my ass just as bad as the rest of my siblings. She did tell me she was gonna take you if I called her baldheaded again."

Jorja giggled. "She'd have to come with something pretty substantial to make me switch teams."

"You still at the studio?"

"Yeah. I just woke up this morning and felt like dancing. I've been here for hours just getting it out. I went live on my Instagram account, and here came Emerald."

"Why are you playing with that man's time, Ja?"

"I'm not playing—"

"Take the job. This can put you in rooms with people that can open even bigger doors for you."

She whined. "I know! I'm scared, Walker."

"What are you scared of?"

"Of getting out there and failing. Dancing locally or going out of town for a show here and there is different. Coaching is different. I know I want this. I prepared for this moment my entire life. Now that it's really happening, I'm scared. Being on stage in front of thousands of people night after night, city after city... it scares me. I don't want to be a back-up dancer all my life."

"Baby... the man offered for you to not only dance but to be his choreographer. He sees greatness in you, and I do too. Please take the job, Ja. You'll never forgive yourself if you don't."

She was quiet for a moment. I heard her sniffling on the other end of the phone.

"Okay... okay, I'll do it."

I smiled. "That's my girl. Dry your eyes."

"Thugs don't cry."

"You're the biggest baby of a thug I've ever met, and I love you."

"I love you too. Are you going straight home after work?"

"Yeah. I'm gonna need a shower. You coming over?"

"I can. The girls have practice after school today. After that, I'm tapped out."

"Well just pack you a bag and come on over. I'll run you a bath and get you something to eat."

"Look at you being a good boyfriend."

It took a second for it to register what she said. I shook my head.

"Damn... I am your boyfriend, ain't it?"

"That better be what you were asking me when you were balls deep in my pussy the other night, nigga."

I laughed loudly. "Yeah, it was. I'm your boyfriend. Damn, that sounds foreign to me."

"Don't go getting cold feet. I'm beating your ass next time. On my mama, I'm stomping your fucking chest in."

"Calm down, killa. I got you. I'm your man. You're my woman. I love you, stink."

She laughed just as loud, and I had to smile.

"I love you too. Get back to work. I'll see you tonight."

"Okay. See you then."

We disconnected the call, and I sat there for a minute with a huge grin on my face.

"Awww, look at you!" Margo said from the door. I hadn't even heard her come up.

"How long have you been standing there?"

"Long enough to hear you cupcaking."

I threw the stress ball lying on my desk at her. "Don't you have work to do?"

"I was coming to tell you our two o'clock is here." She paused for a minute, smiling at me.

"What?"

"Happy looks good on you. You were moping around here for a while. It's good to see you smile like that."

"It feels good, Margo."

It really did feel good. I'd never been a mushy ass nigga. I loved to talk shit. Talking cutesy shit with Ja had me feeling all warm inside. It was crazy how embracing our true feelings for each other sparked a change in the way we interacted. It was still that aggressive shit I liked, but it was indeed cute. Who would have thought?

Twenty-Five

JORJA

"FIVE... SIX... SEVEN... EIGHT!"

Coach Love and I stood back watching the girls hit the routine we'd been practicing for the last hour. The sounds of Aaliyah's "Try Again" blared through the speaker as they danced. I smiled big. They'd been asking to dance to this for the longest, and we finally came up with a routine that was appropriate. A few of them got beside themselves while we were working it out. They wanted to shake their asses, and I wasn't having that. The last thing I needed was somebody's parents asking me what the hell I had their daughter doing.

"That was perfect!" I said, clapping as they finished. "I'm so proud of you girls."

"So am I." Coach Love agreed. "You've been working hard, and it shows. With this routine, you are sure to place at the competition on Saturday."

They looked around at each other, smiling and whispering. This was the second competition of the school year. After doing so well at the first one, they were pumped to get back out there. Coach Love and I promised them that if they kept their grades up and showed continued improvement during practice, we would allow them to compete again. I was proud to say that they took it to heart.

Coach Love looked at her watch. "That's enough for today. Pack up and head out."

"Have a good evening, girls."

As they dispersed, Anais came over to me. I pulled her in for a hug.

"I see you out there leading the pack. You're doing an amazing job as captain."

"Thank you, Auntie. I really love it. I think I want to follow in your footsteps."

That made me smile, but it also made me sad. Eventually, I wouldn't be able to commit to coaching, depending on Emerald's tour schedule. I wasn't sure how I was going to break the news to the team.

I clasped my hands together. "Well, I can always get you into my old dance academy if you want to take this seriously. Take some time to really think about what you want to do with the rest of your life. While I would love to have you as my protege, I want you to be certain that dance is what you really want. I've known girls who danced for years and years during school and never danced again. That's the difference between dancing for fun, dancing as a hobby, and dancing as a career."

"I hear you. I'll think about it."

"Hey, you two!"

I looked up to see Liv waddling toward us with JJ holding her hand. When he saw me, he smiled brightly. She released his hand, and he sprinted toward me.

"JaJa!"

I laughed because he couldn't quite say Jorja.

"Hey, Peanut!" I scooped him up and swung him around. "How is Auntie's baby? You've been a good boy?"

He kissed my cheek. "I been good."

"Hey, sissy." I pulled her in for a hug before rubbing her stomach. "Hey, TiTi's baby!"

"TiTi's baby has been on Mommy's bladder. I feel like I'm gonna piss myself at any moment."

I laughed. "Do I need to get you a diaper?"

She playfully shoved me. "You're lucky my kids are here; otherwise, I'd have a few bad words for you."

"No bad words, Mama," JJ said, wiggling his finger at her.

"That's right, nephew."

Liv rolled her eyes. "How was practice?"

"It was great." I cupped Anais's chin. "Our girl is a natural born leader. Wait until you see her killing those moves on Saturday."

"Trust me, even if I don't always see it at home, I hear her and that music. And don't let some of the girls come over. They jump around for hours in her room."

"Practice makes perfect, Mama Liv," Anais said, matter-of-factly.

"Then you, my dear, should be as close to perfect as you can possibly be."

Light laughter passed between us as the gym doors opened. In walked Tyson with a little girl in his arms. She had his entire face. How could he ever deny such a beautiful child? I felt a scowl form on my face as he walked over to Coach Love to sign Millicent out.

"Bastard," I mumbled under my breath.

He glanced in my direction. His eyes shifted from his daughter to me. Quickly, he ushered Millicent out of the gym.

"Ugh!" I shook my head. "I can't believe I gave him the time of day."

"Well, no need to beat a dead horse," Liv said. "You've got your man now... He is your man, right?"

A smile broke out on my face. I couldn't believe I was blushing and shit over Walker.

"Yes, he's my man."

Anais squealed. "Yes! I knew it would happen. I hear wedding bells!"

I held up a hand. "Slow your roll there, cupid. Let us get used to being a couple before you marry us off."

Liv laughed. "She might be right. I mean, she did call her father and me from the jump."

"A blind man could have called that."

"Oh, whatever! I'm still waiting to hear about this date."

"Umm... Anais, why don't you take JJ to the car while I talk to Liv?"

"Aw, man. I wanted to know about the date too."

"We had a very good time. Go to the car."

"Ugh! Come on, JJ."

I placed him on his feet, and she grabbed his hand and the keys. Once they were out of earshot, I spoke to Liv.

"So first of all, the dress you saw, he bought it. The dress, the shoes, the jewelry... all Walker."

"Okay, bitch! Brownie points!"

"He picked me up in a limo. Girl, when I opened the door and saw his big fine ass... instant waterfalls. Bitch, he looked so fucking beautiful. He took me to the ballet and then out to dinner. I met the most amazing violinist. She was so dope. After dinner, we had to drop cheesecake off to his parents. We ended up spending about two hours over there. You know I love Papa Jareau's old fine ass. We were just laughing and dancing, and it felt so good. Then... boo... he took me home, and that man made love to me. I've never had no shit like that."

"You are blushing hard as hell right now. I have never seen you like this, especially not over him."

"He's... He's different, Liv. I can't explain it, but this thing between us... it feels different. Like, once we put it all out there, shit became clear. I've never felt this good about a man."

She pulled me into a hug. "I'm so happy for you. I told you, you deserve this. Damn, I can't wait to cash in on this bet."

I laughed. "I always knew you were a damn freak," I said, grabbing my bag. "What are you gonna do to that man while he's cuffed up?" We headed for the exit doors.

"I don't know... Maybe a little candle wax. Oooo, maybe a paddle! Do you think he'll let me gag him?"

I stopped walking. "Bitch... does Jameson look like the type of man to let you gag him?"

"You're right. I'll just let him gag me."

"Please drop this baby first. I don't need you going into premature labor."

"Girl, I'm so ready to drop this little boy. He stays crip walking in here. There isn't that much room. And..." She held up a finger. "Sex is becoming uncomfortable. Jay can't be as rough as I'd like him to be. He choked me the other night, and I damn near passed the hell out."

I laughed loudly. "Stop it!"

"I'm serious." She shook her head.

"You never told me what he wanted, if he won the bet."

She grinned. "He wanted his own personal rose party with me."

My eyes widened. "What does the doctor know about a rose party?"

"Chile... I'm gonna find out."

"Y'all are gonna traumatize those damn kids."

"That's why we have the basement. It's been our spot ever since he claimed me that night."

She licked her lips as she seemingly went back to that night in her head.

"Mmm... mmm... mmm." She blew a breath. "Let me get these two home. I love you, sissy."

"I love you too, boo."

We shared a hug and kisses before she got into her Suburban. I stood back and watched them drive away before I climbed into my own car and headed home to pack a bag.

* * *

THIRTY MINUTES LATER, I was pulling into the driveway of the house that had previously been my third home. Walker lived in a beautiful four-bedroom, three-and-a-half-bath home with a three-car garage. His backyard was equipped with an inground pool that I loved to dip my pretty ass in, a jacuzzi, and a lounge area with three flat screen TVs and surround sound. I loved this house. Many times, I dreamed of it one day being my home as well.

Grabbing my things, I climbed out of my car and headed to the front door. As I raised my fist to knock on it, it opened. There stood my man with a smile."

"Hey, punk." He snaked an arm around my waist, pulling me into him.

"I got your punk."

He grinned as he lifted me with ease with one arm. My legs immediately locked around his waist. He took my duffel bag and draped it over his shoulder.

"You love picking me up like a chap," I said, locking my fingers behind his head. "You better not drop me."

"Girl, hush. Nobody is gonna drop you. Don't come in here starting your shit. If you want to start something, start by giving me a proper greeting."

I giggled as I slightly maneuvered my way up his torso, just enough to put us at eye level. With both arms wrapped tightly around his neck, I pressed my lips into his. It was a soft and gentle kiss, the kind I'd begun to love from him.

"You ready to relax?" he asked.

"Yes."

"Your bath is ready and food has been ordered."

I smiled. "Look at you on top of things. Thank you, Walker."

"I got you, love."

He carried me up to his bedroom. After placing my duffel bag on the bed, he walked me into his bathroom, one of my favorite spots. With the overhead lights off, the space glowed with the lighting from several candles. Soft music played through the Bluetooth speaker. Beside the claw foot tub was a small table with wine chilling in a bucket and a glass waiting for me.

"Baby..." I whispered. "You didn't have to do all this."

"I know, but I wanted to. I'm your man, right?"

Again, I smiled. "Yes, you are my man."

"Then let me take care of you." He gave my ass a hard slap as he placed me on my feet. "Undress and get in. I'll be right back."

He pecked my lips before leaving the bathroom. I quickly stripped down and climbed into the tub. As the water engulfed my body, I expelled a relaxed breath. Finally submerged, I reached for the wine bottle and poured myself a glass. He'd gotten my favorite. I rested my back against the tub as I sipped the wine and sang along to the sounds of J. Howell and Dondria's "Why You Love Me."

That man could do no wrong with his vocals.

The potent smell of weed infiltrated my nostrils as I heard Walker's footsteps approaching. He walked into the bathroom, now dressed in nothing but his sweats and socks, with a blunt hanging from his lips. After taking a long pull, he leaned forward and blew me a shotgun before passing the blunt off to me.

"Oh, that's that good shit," I said as he sat on the edge of the tub. "I really needed this after a long day."

"Glad I could be of service."

"You want to hear something funny?"

"Amuse me."

"Liv and Jamison placed a bet on us."

"Get the fuck outta here!" He laughed loudly. "A bet, on what?"

"She bet him that we would get together within six months. Your brother had no faith in us, and he lost."

"Serves his ass right. Wait until I see him. So what does Liv get since she won?"

"She wants to handcuff him."

"I knew your sister was a freak. I keep telling Jay she's gonna work him over one of these days."

"I'm sure he's beating her back out. She doesn't call him big daddy for nothing."

He pretended to gag. "I don't want to think about that. I'm just happy they're happy. I really have mad love for Liv. She brought my nigga back to life." He cupped my chin. "She brought me you."

He leaned forward and kissed me softly. When he pulled away, the sound of the doorbell echoed.

"That's probably the food," he said, standing. "You finish soaking and I'm gonna go get it."

"Okay."

He pecked my lips once more and then left the space. I leaned back into the tub, allowing the smooth sound of John Legend and Ledisi's "Good" relaxed me. It wasn't long before my body was so relaxed that I drifted off to sleep. It wasn't until I heard Walker calling my name did my eyes open.

"You are gonna fuck around and drown, falling asleep in here," he said, holding out a towel. I noticed he'd laid out my pajamas and brought my hygiene products in.

"I'm not gonna drown. I wasn't sleeping that hard."

"You can also pass out from being under too long. Even if you don't die, that shit can still cause brain damage."

"Okay, I get it, dad. I won't fall asleep in the tub. I'm just tired. I put in work today, babe. My body is sore."

He reached down to help me stand, then wrapped the towel around me. He brushed his lips across mine.

"How about a massage after we eat?"

"That would be love."

"I brought the food up here."

"Okay. Well, give me a second, and I'll be out."

He nodded as he left the room. After letting the water out, I hopped in the shower for a thorough wash. When I was done, I slipped into my pajamas and headed back into the bedroom. Walker already had our food laid out on trays. My stomach growled a very audible *"Thank you"* as I climbed into bed.

"Have you called Emerald?" he asked.

"Not yet. I was busy today, but I'll call him tomorrow. I promise."

"Good. You nervous?"

"I'm... anxious. I think I'll be okay once I know what the tour schedule is. You think your dad's lawyer can look over my contract?"

"I'm sure he will as a favor for my father."

"I know Emerald is fair, but I don't know his reps. I'm not trying to get hoodwinked and bamboozled, because I will act up in Cali."

"I'm sure Isaac will be thorough. I guess I better soak up whatever time we have before you leave out, huh?"

"You encouraged me to do this—"

"I know, and I want you to do it. I'll push you every step of the way. I'm just gonna miss you. We're finally getting shit right when you might be leaving soon."

I was quiet for a moment. "Do you think we're making a mistake?"

"No. I wanna be with you, Jorja. I didn't beg and plead for months to let something like distance keep us apart."

"What about when I'm gone for months at a time? Are you gonna be able to keep your dick in your pants?"

"Don't do that. Like I told you, my dick hasn't been in anyone but you for the last two years. I'll just have to beat my shit until you come home or I come to you. Hopping on a plane is nothing. What about you? Don't go out there and get one of those industry niggas fucked up. It's nothing to cop a flight, you know."

I rolled my eyes. "You know I can handle myself, right? Don't come to my shows looking to fight anybody, or you're gonna have to fight me."

He chuckled. "Fuck around and get folded up."

"You like folding me up, don't you?"

"Hell yeah, I do. Watching my dick slide in and out of you is a form of art, woman."

I shook my head as I forked a helping of Sesame Chicken into my mouth. I didn't mind being folded up. Sex with Walker was anything but boring. He knew my body. He knew what I liked and how I liked it. During the months without him, none of my toys brought me the amount of pleasure he did. Tyson, while he worked magic, was nothing like this caramel-coated, tattooed-bodied man next to me.

In fact, I could honestly say that no man I'd been with measured up to Walker in the bedroom—not stamina, not in his stroke game, not in his ability to completely deplete my energy and put me straight to sleep. The dick might have been what initially got me, but truthfully, I found my best friend in him. When things between us were good, they were great.

Aside from lack of commitment, we didn't have many other issues. Now that commitment wasn't an issue, I prayed we could move forward. I didn't want to end up heartbroken. That was one of my biggest fears... to love a nigga then have him shit on me the way my sperm donor shitted on my mama. She was right all those months ago when she said I exercised control of my heart with my pussy.

If I didn't feel anything toward a nigga, he couldn't hurt me. When I realized I was falling for Walker, I also realized I no longer had control. I was already deep in it. The harder I tried to fall back, the deeper I fell. If this didn't work out... I feared it may crush me. I was going to need every prayer my mama and Granny could pray over me.

Twenty-Six

WALKER

"I HAVE a bone to pick with you, my nigga."

I playfully nudged Jamison as we strolled into the gym for Anais's competition. I missed the first one, but I made it my business to make it to this one. The whole family was here to cheer her on.

"What did I do?"

"I heard you and your wife made a bet at my expense."

He laughed. "Oh, that? Had it been a few more days, I would have won."

I playfully punched him. "You had no faith in me, Jay?"

"I have plenty of faith in you. It's just when it comes to Ja, your mouth says one thing, and your actions show another. We all knew you two wanted each other. Maybe it was physical at first, but we literally watched you fall in love when you weren't looking. I'm proud of you for stepping up and claiming your woman."

"Yeah, well, I had to grow up sometime. You got married. Cartel is practically married. Maybe it's time for me to start—"

"Roll that back!" Liv turned her ass around. "Start what? You thinking about marrying my sister?"

"Damn, Liv. You nosy as hell," I jested.

"I don't care. That's my sister, my baby. Now answer the question."

I shook my head. "If you must know... I was just saying, maybe it was time I got serious. I love your sister. I know I never want to lose her again, so I have to move and handle her differently than I did before. I promise you, I'm giving her my best these days."

"Good. She deserves that. Ja may put on a hard exterior, but she's soft inside. When she loves you, she gives you everything in her. Don't take that for granted again. Next time... I'm not gonna mind my business. I love you, and I'm coming to you from a place of love. If you hurt my sister... if you fuck her over in any way, you and I are gonna have beef. I don't wanna have beef with you because that's gonna cause issues between me and my husband. I don't want issues with this man."

"What my wife is saying is, don't do anything that's gonna get your ass whupped," Jamison said, guiding her onto the bleachers.

"That's exactly what I meant. Thank you, baby."

She puckered up for a kiss, and he happily gave it to her. I shook my head. They were sisters all right. I raised my hands in surrender.

"I hear you, and I respect that. I don't want no smoke, sis."

She smiled as she pulled JJ onto her lap. "I wish you two the best of luck. I need some nieces and nephews to come out of this."

"Slow your roll there. We aren't ready for kids just yet. Let us survive dating first."

She rolled her eyes. "I guess."

We settled in the stands, waiting for the show to start. I toggled between people watching and scrolling through my phone. When I looked up again, my eyes landed on that clown ass nigga Tyson. He was walking with a woman and a little girl who looked just like him. They made their way up the stairs, having to pass the area I was sitting in. His eyes landed on me.

I smirked as I shook my head. He glared at me for a moment as they waited for people to pass so they could get by. I noticed the wedding ring that wasn't there before. The woman I assumed to be his wife noticed the stare off between us. This had to be Francesca. She must have thought he was staring at Ms. Alicia, who was seated next to me, glaring at him too.

"Is that another one of your whores?" she asked.

THE BURIAL OF A PLAYER

Ms. Alicia looked at me. "Who is she talking about? 'Cause I know it ain't me."

"Yeah, you. Why are you looking at my husband? You sleeping with him too?"

Liv slid JJ onto Jamison's lap and stood up.

"I know you aren't talking to *my* mama," she said, pointing at her.

Jay handed JJ off to our father and stood to sit her down.

"Tell your mother to look at men her own age."

Ms. Alicia stood, and so did I, pulling her behind me.

She looked around me as she spoke to him. "Tyson... get your wife. I will embarrass both of you in front of all these people. Find you someone safe to play with, baby."

"Go find your seat, bruh," I warned him. "I already owe you one. I'd hate to have to show my ass in here."

"So what? You went from the daughter to the mom?" he shot back at me.

It was Reese's turn to jump in. "Watch ya mouth. Don't get yoked up in front of your wife and kid."

"Y'all, stop it!" Granny snapped. She pointed at Tyson. "Young man, take this woman and move along. You know what you did, and apparently, she does too. That's business between the two of you. This family will not engage with this foolishness any further. Good... bye."

Behind me, Ms. Alicia cracked her knuckles. "I *want* you to say something to her," she said in a threatening tone.

Granny rested a hand on Ms. Alicia's shoulder and sat her down.

"He's not going to say anything. He's going to go about his business, and we are going to focus our attention on my grandbabies. Isn't that right, Tyson?"

Tyson frowned as he looked around at all of us. Saying anything out the way to Ms. Oleena was a guaranteed ass whupping, no matter the time or place. Instead of responding, he grabbed his wife's hand and snatched her the rest of the way up the bleachers, arguing the whole way. Reese and I reclaimed our seats. No sooner than I sat down did my phone vibrate with a text from Ja.

I looked up to see her staring in our direction from the door. A scowl was present on her beautiful face, and she pointed at her phone. I shook my head as I opened my message thread.

Thugga: What the hell was that?
Me: Nothing you need to worry about.
Thugga: Then why do my mama and Liv look like that?"
Me: It's handled.
Thugga: Walker if that muthafucka said something—

I didn't bother to read the rest of the message. Instead, I called her. Immediately, she started going off.

"If I have to come from backstage to hand out an ass whupping, I'm gonna make it worth it."

"Everything is fine, Jorja."

"I don't like the look on their faces, Walker."

"Ja, calm your nerves."

"Don't tell me to calm my nerves. I don't play with people fucking with them. I will—"

"You ain't finna do nothing but what you came here for. Your mama and sister are surrounded by family. You already know they're protected."

She huffed. "I know but—"

"But nothing, baby. I promise you, they're good. Focus on your team and their performance. If you have bad energy, they are gonna feel that too. All the hard work y'all have done will be for nothing if they can't perform at their best. Just take some deep breaths, calm down, and refocus."

She glared at me, folding her arms.

"Fix your face, love," I said, softer. "You're too beautiful to have frown lines."

"Don't butter me up. I'm pissed."

"I know you're upset. But everything is fine. Jay's got Liv. I've got your mama. If worse comes to worse, Reese is more than happy to comfort her."

Ms. Alicia slapped the back of my head, causing Jorja to laugh.

"That's what you get."

"You laughing while your mama is abusing me?"

THE BURIAL OF A PLAYER

Ms. Alicia shoved me with a grin. "Boy, shut up. Nobody is abusing you. I'm good, baby. Do like he said and calm your nerves."

"You heard that?" I asked.

"Yeah... I heard it. I don't want to, but I'll let it go."

"Good. Get back to the girls. We'll be right here when it's all over."

She sighed. "Okay."

"I love you, big head."

"I love you too."

I disconnected the call, and almost immediately, I could feel all eyes on me. When I looked up, my family was staring at me, amusement written all over their faces. I realized that it was the first time they heard me actually verbalize to Ja that I loved her.

"What? Y'all never heard a man tell his woman he loves her?"

The eye rolls were unanimous and damn near in sync; however, they remained quiet... all except Reese, that is. He shook his head as he elbowed Cartel who sat next to him.

"Cap ass nigga," he mumbled, smirking.

"*Big* capping ass nigga," Cartel agreed. "Ol' *'That ain't my girl,'* head ass."

"Y'all leave my baby alone," my mama said. She wrapped her arms around my neck from behind and kissed my cheek. "He's growing up, and I'm proud of him."

"Thank you, Mami."

That really did make me feel good. I was trying to change my ways. I could take the jokes in stride because I knew what kind of man I had previously been. I just hoped that they could eventually see me for the man I was becoming.

* * *

AFTER THE SLIGHT DRAMA, things chilled out, and the show got started.

To say my niece showed out was an understatement. Anais danced her ass off. Liv, the kids, and my mama were on their feet, yelling and cheering for her the entire time she performed. Her improvement was abundantly clear over the last year, and I knew that was thanks to Ja. There was the unexpected portion of the coaches battling it out.

When I say Ja mopped the floor with all of them... she did the damn thing. The crowd was on their feet giving her a standing ovation.

"That's my sister!" Liv screamed.

Riley stood on the bleachers. "That's my auntie!

JJ climbed up next to her. "Go JaJa!"

Jorja smiled big as she looked at us in the audience. I kissed two fingers, raising them up to her. She blew me a kiss before disappearing from the floor to join her team. They all greeted her with hugs and smiles. I knew she was going to miss them when she left to go on tour, but I also knew she would constantly be checking in.

The show had come to an end, and it was time to announce the winners. Ja and her team ended up winning first place. The girls were screaming, crying, and hugging each other when it was announced. I could see the pure joy on their faces as they stepped forward to claim their trophies.

While the photographer snapped pictures, the crowd began to disperse. We waited in the stands for Ja and Anais. About fifteen minutes later, they ventured into the stands.

"There's my baby," Jay said, opening his arms for my niece. She went to him, hugging him tightly. "You did so good, baby girl."

"Thank you, Daddy."

She made her rounds, gathering love from everybody.

"You were beasting out there, lil bit," I said, kissing her forehead as I hugged her.

"Thank you, Uncle Walker. Let's not forget the mastermind behind it all, though." She pulled Ja forward. "Thank you for believing in me, Auntie Jorja."

"Always, baby."

They shared an embrace. When she let her go, Anais pushed her toward me. She smiled as I reached for her hands.

"You did amazing, love. I'm so proud of you."

"Thank you."

I pulled her into my arms and pressed my lips against hers. She must have forgotten where we were because she wrapped her arms around my neck and slipped her tongue into my mouth. There was our family in the background, making comments.

"All that damn playing, now look at them."

"I don't know who they thought they were fooling."

"Alright now!"

"Yasssss, sis!"

I broke away from Jorja to look at them. "Y'all are real embarrassing right now."

Reese laughed. "This is what you signed up for when you turned in your playa card. You simping right along with Frick and Frack over here." He pointed to Cartel and Jamison.

Cartel slapped the back of his head. "Shut your ass up."

I grinned. "Nah, bruh, you were just laughing. It's funny 'til it's you, right?"

He rolled his eyes. "Ja, get your newfound man."

"Nah, y'all love coming for both of us. We got time today."

"Alright, children," my father said. "Enough being petty. Anais, baby, how do you wanna celebrate? It's on me."

"Can we go to Copper Pavilion?"

"Oh, you have expensive taste today? I guess you deserve it after that performance. I got you, baby girl."

"Thank you, Grandpa."

Cartel pulled out his phone. "I know the owner, so I'll call ahead and reserve us a space."

We waited until he confirmed they had room for all of us. It was just our luck they did. Jorja and Anais went to change clothes. Once they returned, we dispersed to our cars. I opened my front door, allowing Jorja to climb in. As I went to shut it, she stopped me.

"What is it?" I asked.

"Nothing... I'm just really happy right now. My girls did so good..."

"They did amazing."

"I can't believe I have to leave them."

I could see the tears forming in her eyes. I cupped her face as I spoke to her.

"Don't think of it as you're leaving them. You're taking an opportunity of a lifetime. They will understand. I promise, they will root for you as hard as you root for them. You're fully stepping into your purpose. Nothing but great things are coming your way, love."

I swiped a tear from her eye and pulled her into my chest.

"I'm right here with you. I'll be with you every step of the way. Dry your eyes, put a smile on your pretty face, and let's go eat. You know how much you love that."

She pulled back, playfully pushing me. "Shut up and get your ass in the car."

I grinned as I shut her door. I rounded the driver's side then got in, cranked up, and fell in line with our family that was pulling out.

Twenty-Seven

JORJA

IN A PRIVATE ROOM at Copper Pavilion, the Jareau and Sandifer families were getting kind of loud. It was a lot of us, so there was a lot of talking over each other and side conversation. I sat between Walker and my mama. While each of them had their own conversation going on, I quietly sat, picking at my food. I was trying to figure out how I was going to tell them I'd be leaving soon.

Following my promise to Walker to call Emerald, I finally accepted his offer. He sent the contract via e-mail the very next day, along with his tour schedule. Isaac had gone through it with a fine-tooth comb and said everything looked legit. The moment I signed it, I cried real tears of happiness. My dream was finally coming true.

A light nudge to my side broke my thoughts. My mother leaned into me.

"Are you okay?" she asked, grabbing my hand. "You're awfully quiet."

"I'm just thinking, Mommy."

"About?"

"I have something I need to tell everyone."

"Are you pregnant?" she asked in a hushed whisper.

"What? No. It's good news, Mama. Nothing involving my uterus."

"Oh." She looked a little disappointed.

I shook my head as I stood, tapping my spoon against my glass. The room slowly fell quiet as I looked around.

"I have something to share with you all."

"You pregnant too?" came Cartel.

"Walker, you done put a baby in her already?" That was Reese.

"Would y'all shut up!" Walker snapped. "We are not having a baby. That's not what this is." He gave my ass a light tap. "Go on, love."

I giggled as I continued.

"As most of you know... I was offered the opportunity of a lifetime to not only dance behind but choreograph for one of the biggest singers right out of little old South Carolina. I um... After much convincing... I've decided to take the job."

The small room erupted with cheers and congratulatory claps. I couldn't stop the tears forming in my eyes. There was so much genuine love in this space, and it was a bit overwhelming. For so long, all I really had in this world were my mama, my sister, and my granny. Now, I had a second mother in Mrs. Jareau, a father in Papa Jareau, brothers, and two extra sisters. I had nieces and nephews galore, and I had my man.

The changes in Walker would never go unnoticed. He wasn't the same guy looking to get me into his bed. I wasn't the same girl looking to get him into mine. We were both growing up, even if it had been at a different pace to begin with. Growth and change were both so scary, but the results... the results were so beautiful.

As my tears fell forward, Walker stood to comfort me. He wrapped his strong arms around me, pulling me into his chest. Gently, he stroked my back as I cried inaudibly. It soon became apparent to everyone that these weren't just tears of joy. The room soon quieted down. I felt the soothing arms of my mother come around my waist.

She kissed the back of my head as she whispered a prayer over me. I closed my eyes to receive it. As she spoke, I could feel my body begin to relax and my racing heart began to even out. When she ended the prayer, I slowly opened my eyes.

"You good?" Walker asked, wiping my face.

I nodded. Slowly, I turned to face my mother. She smiled as she kissed my cheek.

THE BURIAL OF A PLAYER

"I'm so proud of you, baby. You've been working toward this for so long, and you deserve it. You tell Emerald he better treat you good and do right by you before I call his mama."

I giggled. "I knew you'd have my back."

"Always, girl. Mama don't play about her babies."

"And her babies don't play about her," I said, snapping my fingers.

"Period, point, blank," Aleviyah chimed in.

"Oh, we saw that earlier," Cartel said grinning. "I thought we were gonna see you act up, Ms. Alicia."

My mother shook her head as we sat back down. "I don't like to get out of character, but I don't mind letting people know I'm not the one or the two. There are very few things that get me riled up, but over these three right here..." she pointed at me, Liv, and Granny, "I'll do hard time."

Reese grinned. "Now you know you are too fine for that orange jumpsuit."

"Still not happening, Reese."

"Damn it." He shook his head. "You are gonna miss this when I get a woman."

"Somehow, I think I'll survive."

I threw my napkin at him. "How many times do I have to tell you my mama don't want you? You are not destined to be Mr. Alicia Sandifer."

"That does have a nice ring to it," he jested.

"Alright, Reese. Shut the hell up."

That was his mother. They began going back and forth, and before long, the whole table became one big roasting session. They were flaming each other, and it was so damn funny. We were lucky we had a private room; otherwise, we'd probably have gotten put out for disturbing the peace. When the celebratory dinner ended, we all shared a round of hugs and kisses before saying our goodbyes.

"Where to?" Walker asked as we settled into his Range and pulled into traffic. "Your place or mine?"

"Can we stop by my apartment? I need to grab some clothes."

"Sure. You know you can just leave your shit at the house, right?"

"I know... I was just trying to ease into it."

"Nah, don't ease into shit." He reached into his center console and handed me a set of keys. "Come home. You're gonna be gone a lot. There's no need to keep paying bills at your place and wasting money."

I giggled. "You paid my rent for the year, so *I'm* not really wasting anything."

He kissed his teeth. "Well when you get the money back, keep it. Use it for your traveling expenses or pocket money. I don't care. When you come home, I want you to come home to me."

"Are you asking me to move in?"

"I'm asking you to make the house a home. It stopped feeling right without you a long time ago, Ja. I miss your clothes in the closet. I miss your shit on your side of the vanity. I miss your wigs scaring the fuck outta me on that damn stand."

I had to laugh at that one. I almost gave him a heart attack one day when I was curling my wig. I'd left it on the stand in the bathroom to go check the laundry. He had motion sensor lights in the bathroom, so when I left out, they turned off. When I heard the *"What the fuck!"* come from him, I thought something was wrong. I'd rushed back into the bathroom to see him posted against the wall, holding his chest.

"My point is," he continued, "I miss your presence. I know it might be soon in asking, but we've wasted enough time. If we are gonna do this, I want to be all in."

I felt the tears rushing to my eyes. He was giving me everything I wanted. It was clear the time we spent apart was needed. We came back stronger and more mature, and Lord knows we needed the maturity. We were young but still too old to be moving through life with the mindset we once had.

I nodded. "Okay."

"You'll move in?"

"I will. Just promise me something, Walker."

"Anything."

"Promise me we won't go back to the way we were. I don't have it in me to go through the petty, toxic shit again. Coming to terms with my feelings was hard for me. Feeling love for a man outside of family relationships is foreign. I know it won't be perfect. I know we'll have our share of ups and downs. Just promise me... at the end of the day, we'll always remember to put love first."

He grabbed my hand as we came to a stoplight.

"I promise. I commit to being a better man... a better boyfriend... a better person in general. If I've learned anything in the last six months, it's time ain't waiting on you to get it right. I lost you once... I won't make that mistake again."

He leaned over and kissed me softly.

"I love you," he said, cupping my chin. "I'm so sorry it took me this long to get here."

It took both of us a while to get here, but now that we were, I was confident we would finally stay on the same page.

* * *

IT WAS SUNDAY.

Family dinner was hitting a little different today. It was the grand reopening of *Abundance of Soule*. Cartel had been working diligently to get the restaurant rebuilt and decorated in time for today. We all knew how important this day was for him. Adina's husband tried to take so much from them, and by the grace of God, they were both still here. Watching them stand in front of that big ass ribbon with their daughters was a beautiful moment.

His smile was big, and so was hers.

They were surrounded by everyone they loved. His family, my family, and hers were all in attendance, along with everyone in the community who loved his cooking. Cameras and television crews were all over the place. In an effort to support his philanthropy, he was donating half of tonight's profits to a local women's shelter. People were waiting up and down the street to support him.

Our families were settled around a huge table in the back, eating and laughing, just celebrating him on his big night. He'd been busy in the kitchen, but every so often, he came back to check on Adina and the kids. He always left her and their babies with a kiss before heading back to work. The last time he came out, he headed to the stage where the live band he hired for tonight was playing.

"Can I have everyone's attention, please?" he said into the microphone.

The restaurant quieted down, giving him their full attention.

"Can I have my beautiful family come up here?"

He motioned for Adina. With both babies cradled in her arms, she made her way to the stage. A round of *"Awwws"* went up as he grabbed Carmella from her.

"First, I just want to thank each of you for coming out to support and celebrate this night. It's been a long time coming." He grabbed Adina's hand as he held Carmella and the mic with the other. "This beautiful woman standing beside me is the one who motivated me to push forward with rebuilding. For a while there, it almost didn't happen. I was prepared to take this loss and move on with my life. But she told me that I had a purpose, and *Abundance of Soule* wasn't just a restaurant. It was a family, and we take care of family."

A round of applause went up around the restaurant.

"She pushed me to reopen the same way she pushes me in every other aspect of life. Adina, I am so grateful for you. I'm grateful that I'm still here to wake up to you every single morning. I'm grateful for your love and support. I'm grateful for this life that we have built together with our beautiful girls. I know the journey hasn't been ideal. I know it's been rocky. I know that everything has conspired against us, to keep us apart. But we're still here. We still have each other. And you know that having you is all I've ever wanted."

Adina smiled and nodded as she wiped a tear from her eye.

"I love you. I know we decided that we would wait with everything that was going on. But I can't wait any longer."

He reached into his pocket and pulled out a small black box. Adina gasped as he dropped to one knee and opened it.

"I've always told you that you were gonna be my wife. So tonight in front of all of our family, I want to make good on that promise. Will you do me the honor of becoming my forever, love? Will you marry me?"

Tears streamed down her face as she nodded.

"Yes! Yes, I will marry you."

Cartel slipped the ring on her finger and stood to his feet. The room erupted with cheers and applause as they shared a passionate kiss. There wasn't a dry eye at our table. I leaned into Walker, and he wrapped his arm around my shoulder. Much to my surprise, he dropped a tear too. I knew how much he loved his siblings. He had his flaws, but this man loved his family. Their happiness meant the world to him.

When they came down from the stage, he reached for one baby, and I reached for the other. They were almost three months now and getting so big. Carina looked up at me with wide eyes. I couldn't lie. I said I wasn't ready, but the baby fever was real.

"Hey, pretty girl." I cooed, fingering her chubby cheeks. She smiled at me, and my ovaries melted. "Maybe one won't hurt."

Walker's head jerked around at me. "You serious?" he asked, bouncing Carmella.

"Maybe. Give me a year or so, and I'll be ready for the first one."

"The first one? How many are we talking, woman?"

"No more than three. At least two years apart."

"We'll see what my soldiers have to say about that."

"You're gonna wrap that shit up."

He kissed his teeth. "My mans don't even know what a condom is with you anymore. If I put that shit on, he's likely to recoil. What does my frat say? Meat to meat."

"Is your frat gonna help take care of these kids?"

"Absolutely. My son will be a legacy. They got him for life."

"And what about your daughter?"

"My princess will always be my princess. She can live with us until she's forty, and Daddy will take care of her."

"I think the fuck not."

"What are y'all going on about?" Alaina asked. She'd gotten in early this morning to make it to the grand opening.

"Your brother seems to think we will have a forty-year-old child in our house, still taking care of them. And no, I'm not pregnant."

"I plead the fifth on that one. I'm about to be living with my daddy again."

Everyone at the table looked at her. The only person who didn't seem surprised was Adina. The two of them were super close, so she probably already knew.

"I was going to announce it tonight..." Alaina said, waving her hand. "Then big head over here stole the show with that beautiful proposal. But yes, I'm coming back to the states. My things are packed and shipped. I really missed you guys. Our family is growing, and I feel like this is where I need to be."

"We're glad to have you home, baby girl," Papa Jareau said, standing to hug her. "I've been praying for this moment for a long time. I don't know what made you leave, but I trust that you've worked it out."

"I have. I'm never leaving again."

Papa Jareau kissed her forehead and hugged her tighter. If this man did nothing else, he was a damn good father to his children. Hell, he was a damn good surrogate father, too. I would forever love the man for all he had been to me.

"Excuse me. I hope we aren't interrupting a private moment."

I looked up to see Roosevelt and his beautiful daughter standing at our table. They looked adorable in their matching colors. Alaina's eyes lit up when she saw him.

"Not at all," she said, flashing him a flirty smile.

He smiled back. I didn't miss his eyes passing over her where she stood. I also didn't miss every Jareau brother sitting up straight.

"Juniper and I wanted to congratulate Cartel on his grand opening as well as his and Adina's engagement." He held out a hand to Cartel, who shook it. "Congratulations, brother. If anybody deserves this kind of happiness, it's the two of you."

"Thanks, Rose." Cartel pulled him in for a brotherly hug.

He whispered something in his ear, causing his eyes to drift to Alaina, who was staring at him. He smiled and nodded as he pulled away.

"I got you," he said.

"Y'all are welcome to sit with us for a spell," Mama Jareau said.

"Thank you, but I have to get baby girl home and ready for school tomorrow."

"Well, thank you for coming out." She turned to Juniper, who was holding tightly to her father's jacket. "Thank you for coming, Juniper. You look so pretty."

Juniper blushed, and it was adorable.

"Thank you. You look pretty too."

"Aren't you the sweetest? Rose, you have to bring her by so she can play with my grandbaby. She and Riley are about the same age."

She pointed Riley out to Juniper. Her ears perked up at the mention of a play date, and she was smiling big. She loved making new friends.

"You can meet Piggy!" she exclaimed.

"Who's Piggy?" Juniper asked.

"Her fat little furball," Cartel answered.

Riley frowned. "He's not fat. He's fluffy. Don't listen to Uncle Cartel. He's just mad because Piggy doesn't like him."

The table erupted with laughter. Cartel and that dog were forever going at it. He would fuss at Piggy, and then Piggy would bark at him. By the end of it all, he gave him treats, and they would be the best of friends.

"Can I, Daddy?" Juniper asked.

"I don't see why not. We could set up a play date sometime soon. Right now, we have to get you home. Say goodbye."

"Bye, everybody!"

"Y'all have a good night," Roosevelt said, grabbing her hand. "Ms. Alaina... it was a pleasure to see you again, as always."

Alaina blushed. "The pleasure was all mine."

Roosevelt subtly bit his lip as he walked away. Alaina's eyes followed him all the way out the door.

"Girl, you got it bad," I said, breaking her stare.

Walker chimed in. "That's really why you wanted to come back home."

"What? No!" The elevated pitch of her voice said otherwise.

Reese playfully pushed her. "You lying like a rug. The way you were gawking at that man just now. You think we didn't see the way he looked at you? I don't like it."

"Me either," Walker agreed.

Alaina scoffed. "I am twenty-six years old, and neither of you can tell me what to do. That goes for you two as well." She pointed at Jamison and Cartel.

"Pops, are you gonna let her go after that man?" Reese asked.

Papa Jareau sighed. "I don't like the idea of my princess being with any man. But Rose is a good one. And I know my baby can handle herself. She used to beat your ass, Reese."

"And still will," Alaina shot at him.

Reese kissed his teeth. "That ain't changing the fact that you still have four of us to go through for approval, little girl."

"You are so lucky that our parents are here, because otherwise, I'd tell you a few things. You and our brothers have no control over my love life. I am not a child anymore. I know who I am and what I want, and I want him. Kid and all. If there is any chance of that, and any of you ruin it for me, I will never forgive you."

Mama Jareau intervened. "Okay, okay, let's calm down. Alaina is an adult. If she and Roosevelt want to pursue something, nobody is going to intervene unnecessarily. All I'm asking is you be respectful of that man's time, baby. He has a child."

"I know, Mama. I'm perfectly capable of dating a man with a kid. Juniper and I might become the best of friends. Besides, I have the perfect sister in-law to go to for advice." She smiled at Liv. "Watching you care for my nieces and nephews has been inspiring. I love you so much more than you know."

Liv started fanning her already glossy eyes. "You're gonna make me cry! Y'all know I'm super emotional right now. My hormones are all out of whack."

"You'll be back to normal in a few weeks," I said. "Then you can cash in on that bet."

She and Jamison both grinned at that.

Mama Jareau raised an eyebrow. "What bet?"

"Nothing!" they both answered.

"Mmm hmm, just don't end up pregnant at that six-week checkup."

I laughed. "I don't know, Mama Jareau. You know your son is pretty fertile."

Her head snapped in my direction. "Don't get me started on you and Walker. I'm surprised we don't already have a baby from the two of you. Something tells me we're gonna see you dancing on stage, big belly and all in a couple of months."

"Y'all are gonna stop invading my womb!" I exclaimed. "I love being auntie, but I'm not ready to get pregnant just yet."

"If you ain't ready, you better get ready," Granny stated. "I've been dreaming about fish."

I sighed. "Granny, that's just a superstition."

"Maybe to you, but the ancestors have never steered me wrong. You mark my words. Somebody here is having a baby." She smiled as she looked between Walker and me holding the twins. "They do look good on you two."

Granny must have been sipping that good wine. There was no way I was pregnant or getting pregnant right now. Absolutely none.

Twenty-Eight

WALKER

TIME REALLY DIDN'T WAIT for anybody.

The weeks seemed to fly by.

In preparation for her tour, which was set to begin in just a month, Jorja had moved out of her apartment and was officially moved in with me. Surprisingly, things had been going well with us. Everything felt so right... so natural these days. I didn't hesitate to show her love, no matter the time or the place. Falling into the couple routine was effortless. We did the same shit we'd always done, except this time, we weren't trying to convince people that there was nothing between us.

With all the excitement of the upcoming tour and finishing out her stint as Anais's dance coach, I wanted to take her somewhere she could relax. I found a beautiful villa in Yabucoa, Puerto Rico, someplace she'd talked about visiting for the longest. When I gave her the tickets, she literally screamed. Then she cried. Then she tried to suck the skin off my dick as a thank you.

For the entire almost five-and-a-half-hour flight, she was excited. My baby hadn't been out of the country, so I was honored to be the person to give her that. She wasn't happy about me blindfolding her in the rental car. She wanted to see the city, but I wanted to surprise her with the villa. I promised her we could go sightseeing later.

THE BURIAL OF A PLAYER

"Are we there yet?" she asked.

"Almost."

"You said that fifteen minutes ago."

"And you are just as impatient now as you were then. Are you always gonna be this hard surprise, woman?"

"You know I'm anxious."

"I know, but trust your man. I got you."

She huffed and crossed her arms. Being submissive when needed was a challenge for her. She loved to talk back, but she was getting better at it. It didn't take nearly as much fight to pull off this surprise as it would have months ago. She knew I was up to something, but she didn't pry as much as she would have.

I pulled into the driveway of the beach bungalow I rented out for the next four days. While we waited on our rental car, I ordered groceries to be delivered. They had been confirmed delivered just five minutes ago. I had no plans for leaving this house much. Shit, I barely planned to put on clothes. The house was located in a secluded area with private beach access. We were all alone, just how I wanted it.

"We're here?" she asked impatiently when the car shut off.

"Yes, Ja, we're here."

She moved to take off the blindfold, but I slapped her hands away.

"Wait, woman."

"I'm gonna fuck you up."

I laughed as I climbed out of the car and rounded the passenger side to her door. I took her hand and helped her out.

"On three. One... two..."

She was giddy with excitement, and it was so damn cute.

"Two and a half..."

She elbowed my gut. "Walker!"

"Don't make me start over."

She stomped her foot. "Baby!"

I chuckled. I loved fucking with her.

"Three."

She snatched off the blindfold and gasped at the sight of the house before us.

"Oh my God... It's so beautiful!"

I wrapped my arms around her waist and kissed her temple.

"This is all us for the next four days. I wanted to make sure you had some time to relax before you headed off. And I wanted some time away with you. We're always surrounded by people, and I just wanted to be with you, no interruptions."

She turned to face me, wrapping her arms around my neck.

"Thank you, baby. This was sweet and thoughtful. I appreciate it and you."

She kissed me softly before pressing her forehead against mine and closing her eyes.

"We've come such a long way, Walker..." she said quietly.

"We have."

"I'm gonna miss you when I leave."

"It's not for long. The first stint is only two months. I'll be at a couple of shows with you."

She pouted. "I know, but you'll always have to say goodbye."

I laughed. "You're gonna miss me that much?"

"Yes. We've been together every night for the last six weeks. I've got to get used to not sleeping next to you."

"And I've got to get used to not hearing you snore."

"I don't snore."

"You're a damn liar. You snore like a motherfucker. I don't mind though." I slapped her ass. "Let's get inside."

We parted ways and grabbed our things from the trunk. After getting them placed into the bedroom, we grabbed the box of groceries on the front porch and put everything away. Once that was done, we ventured out onto the back balcony area. The view of the beach was beautiful with its white sands, clear blue waters, and peaceful ambiance. Nothing surrounded us but the sounds of nature at that moment. The birds chirped, leaves rustled, and waves crashed against the shore.

"I could get used to this," Jorja said, leaning against the railing.

"We could always get a timeshare with our siblings, with the whole family. I could get on board with a week's vacation with everybody once or twice a year."

"That would be nice. I can see the kids running around on the beach... bonfires... beachside barbecues. I like the idea." She turned to face me, and she pressed her back against the railing. Her gaze became lustful as her eyes passed over me. "You know what else I like the idea of?"

"What's that?"

"Us... bringing in our vacation right here."

She gripped the hem of my shirt and pulled it over my head. She then pulled off her own, exposing her hardened nipples through the lacy fabric of her bra. I yanked her to me by the belt loop of her shorts.

"You trying to have these people hear you acting up over this dick?" I asked, unbuttoning them.

She bit her lip and nodded as my hand slipped past her thong to cup her pussy. Her lips were already slick. If surprises made her this wet, I needed to surprise her more often.

"Tell me how you want it," I said, stroking her pearl.

She gasped. "Ooo... I want you to eat my pussy... Shit! Then fuck me while the sun sets."

I smirked as I pulled my hand away. My fingers were saturated in her juices. As I licked them from my digits, she opened her mouth to catch them as they dripped from my tongue. Hungrily, she licked her lips before capturing mine, sucking the remaining essence from them. Tucking my thumbs into the sides of her thong, I slipped them and her shorts off in one swift movement.

I pulled up a chair in front of her and sat before my favorite meal. Her arousal greeted me as it did anytime I prepared to feast on her. She didn't need any instruction as she braced herself against the railing and draped both of her legs across my shoulders. Face to face with her clean shaven pussy, I inhaled the mouthwatering aroma. Her swollen clit peeked out at me.

I sucked it into my mouth, releasing it with an audible *plop*.

"Mmmm..." Jorja moaned, tossing her head back. "Suck that shit, baby."

Greedily, I captured it between my lips again, sucking ever so gently. My tongue slithered in and out of her slit, collecting juices as they expelled. I spit it back out her clit, before covering and sucking her entire pussy into my mouth.

"Fuck!" she cried out, thrusting her hips forward to fuck my face.

Her nails racked over my waves to the back of my head, pushing my face in deeper.

"Oooo... baby! You eat this pussy so well... Such a good boy..."

I loved when she got to talking that shit with her pussy in my mouth. It made my dick hard and made me want to give her the performance of a lifetime, every time. With a free hand, she pushed her bra up over her titties, exposing those hardened buds. She hissed as she pinched one between her middle finger and thumb.

I slid my middle and ring finger into her wetness as I sucked and flicked my tongue over her clit. With every thrust, her walls clenched them. Ja had that *"Hello, nice to meet you"* grip. I loved sliding up in her and watching that tight ass pussy grip my shit. I couldn't wait for her to cum so we could get reacquainted.

"Shit!" she screamed, squirting just a little.

That wasn't enough. I wanted her to spray my face. I wanted that shit to run down my chest and drip onto my stomach. I ate her pussy for my pleasure too. As I continued to feast on her, I released my dick from my sweats. My erection was painful, and I needed to get this one off before I slid in her walls. Feverishly, I stroked him with my free hand.

"I'm about to cum... fuck! Oooo shit! I'm cumming!"

Baby almost drowned me, and it was so worth it. We came together in a beautiful, wet, messy bliss. Her body trembled uncontrollably as she rode out the wave of her orgasm with my fingers still stroking her.

"Mmm... you know I love when you wet my face, baby. You gon' wet this dick up just like that?"

She panted. "Yes..."

"Assume the muthafucking position."

She dropped her legs from my shoulders and turned around, propping one of her legs up on the railing. She looked back at me and slapped her ass.

"Come fuck this pussy."

That sentence alone made my shit brick even more. Dick in hand, I stood and pushed the chair back. I didn't even need to lube my shit up with her. She was always so wet that I slid in with ease every single time.

"Mmmm..." I moaned as I buried my rod inside her. "Take it... all of it."

She was a snug fit.

I slapped her ass as I hit her with long, deep, and steady strokes. Her pussy graciously coated me as it talked back.

"Fuck, Ja!"

One hand crept around her throat as the other palmed her right breast. I pulled her back until her back rested against my chest.

"I love your ass so fucking much..." I declared, licking her neck.

"Oooo, baby! I love you too! Fuck, I love you!"

Before us, the sun was beginning to go down. My goal was to make her cum as the reflection disappeared at the water's edge. My strokes deepened, and my pace quickened. The hand cupping her breast slid down her stomach and between her thighs to her clit. I strummed it with the same rhythm. Gasp after gasp expelled from her lips. Before long, they turned into whimpers, and the whimpers into cries of pleasure. I was sure anyone within earshot could hear her calling my name.

"Walker! Don't stop! Fuck, don't stop!"

The sun was almost down. I fisted her hair, forcing her to look out at the ocean.

"There it goes, baby," I whispered. "You gon' let the sun beat you?"

"N-no..."

"Cum for me, Ja."

"Fuck, it's so beautiful..."

"Not as beautiful as you. Cum."

I didn't have to tell her again. Her muscles contracted, and when they released, so did she.

"Aaahhhh shiiiiit!"

She came hard, and I was right behind her, depositing my load deep in her. With one final thrust, I rested my forehead against her back, allowing my dick to throb inside her as the last of my seed spilled out.

I panted. "Shit, that was good!"

I finally pulled out of her, and the mixture of us seeped onto the wood flooring. She dropped her leg but remained hovered over the railing. She turned her head slightly, and laughter fell from her lips.

"What's funny?" I asked.

"We had an audience."

She pointed, and my eyes followed to see a woman standing on the balcony two houses down. She clutched her chest with one hand and fanned herself with the other.

"Hey!" Jorja yelled, waving.

"That was so damn hot!" the woman yelled back.

This time, both of us laughed.

"Let's get back inside before she gets any ideas," I said, grabbing our clothes.

"I don't know. Knowing she was watching is kind of exciting. Maybe we should give her another show."

I shook my head. "Get your ass in this house. No more freebies for her."

She laughed as we headed back inside. The peep show was over... at least for today.

Twenty-Nine

JORJA

PUERTO RICO WAS SO BEAUTIFUL.

Even though Walker didn't have plans of leaving the house, I wanted to explore the area. After my best convincing head, we spent our days painting the streets of Yabucoa red and our nights fucking each other senseless. If I hadn't gotten on birth control when I did, I was sure I would have left the island pregnant.

On a serious note, I felt like we grew even closer during our stay. During the moments when we were simply laid out on the beach, sipping drinks, and soaking up sun, I felt so close to him. He couldn't keep his hands and lips off me. I never imagined being so openly in love could feel like this, least of all with him.

It was a welcomed change from meaningless hook ups and lonely nights in my bed. When he told me he wanted to be all in, he put action behind those words. The day after he asked me to move in, I'd contacted my leasing office to terminate my agreement. Since he had a house full of furniture, I donated most of mine to Adina's nonprofit. A mother in need would be getting almost an entirely furnished home and that made me feel good.

Sunday dinners resumed with my mom and Granny. They were happy to have us, and the neighborhood kids were excited to have their ice cream plug back. Every Sunday like clockwork, they ran Walker's pockets, and he happily pulled out his wallet. Watching him run around, playing with them and our nieces and nephews, was really softening my heart toward waiting to have kids. He was a natural with children, and I knew he would spoil our future babies with so much love and attention.

As we stood in line at the airport, waiting to board our flight home, my phone rang. I pulled it out and saw that it was my mother.

"Hey, Mommy."

"Hey, baby. I know you are about to board the plane, but I wanted to let you know that Liv went into labor."

I screamed in excitement, causing several people to look at me.

"You trying to burst my damn eardrums!" my mama scolded.

"I'm sorry! I'm so excited! We're coming to the hospital as soon as we land."

"Okay. Have a safe flight. I love you. Give Walker my love."

"I will. I love you too." I disconnected the call and turned to Walker. "Liv's water broke!"

"Oh shit! Damn, we gotta hurry up and get back."

"I can't wait to meet my little peanut! I'm so glad the tour didn't start before she had him."

"I know. You are about to spoil this baby, just like you spoil the rest of them."

"And is. Don't act like you aren't gonna be on the same shit. He is gonna run your pockets too."

He chuckled. "I won't deny that."

Just then, a woman came over the speaker, announcing that our flight was now boarding. We grabbed our carry-ons and headed into the terminal. Even seated, I couldn't be still. My body was riddled with excitement. My baby was having a baby!

* * *

EDWIN JALEN JAREAU, AKA EJ, was such a handsome little fella.

I couldn't stop smiling as I stared at him. Liv had given birth fifteen minutes after we arrived. I got to be in the delivery room with her, along with Jamison and our mother. My poor brother-in-law had worry etched in his handsome face as she was pushing. I could tell the moment took him back to his deceased wife. I didn't know what to say to reassure him Liv would be okay. All I could do was hold his hand as we both held hers while she pushed.

That man damn near broke my fingers.

When EJ gave his first cry, he released the biggest breath of relief. Now that she was settled in her room, he couldn't stop loving on her. Right now, he was seated behind her in bed, massaging her shoulders as she looked on.

"He's so perfect, Liv!" I said, kissing his little fingers. "That's TiTi baby! You so handsome, man!"

"Stop hogging him, Ja," Walker fussed. "I wanna hold him too."

I waved him off. "You'll get your turn."

He kissed his teeth.

I sighed. "Here, take him. But don't keep him too long."

He rolled his eyes as he took his nephew from my arms.

"Hey, big man," he said, cradling him in his arms. "Your auntie thinks she's the only one who gets to love on you. What's wrong with her?"

"Y'all aren't gonna be fighting over my son," Jamison said, chuckling. "We are gonna be calling you two to hold him when he doesn't wanna be put down."

"That ain't no problem," I said, fingering his chubby cheeks. "I need to soak up all the love I can while I'm here."

"You are only gone for two months, Jorja," Liv reminded me. "Besides, I know you. You're gonna FaceTime me every day to see him."

"I'm glad you know this."

"Don't overdo it," my mama chimed in. "My baby still needs her rest. Come here, Grammy's sugar pie."

Walker was reluctant to give him up. He looked over at me.

"You were right."

"About?"

"One won't hurt."

I giggled. "I need a ring on my finger before I pop out any of your big-headed babies, sir."

Alaina agreed. "You better say that! My girl said make her a wife. You better get that ring size, Walker."

"I know her ring size, thank you."

I raised an eyebrow. "Do you now?"

He bought me jewelry, but never a ring.

"What is it?"

He grinned. "I guess you'll have to wait until you get a ring, won't you."

I playfully pushed him, and he grabbed my arm, pulling me into his chest. Softly, he pressed his lips against mine.

"Y'all have become absolutely sickening," Cartel jested.

Walker shot him a look. "Fu—forget you. Between you and Reese, I don't know who our biggest hater is."

Reese threw up his hands. "I ain't even say nothing!"

"Yet," we said in unison.

"See, I was gonna let y'all live. I was gonna keep my comments to myself. I ain't said nothing about y'all punk faking each other for the last two years. I even kept quiet about this nigga practically crying on my couch cause Ja wouldn't talk to him."

"Ain't nobody been crying!" Walker defended.

"You did shed a few tears, baby," Mama Jareau said.

"Mama!"

"What! It's the truth!" She shook her head. "That's all in the past though. You two are growing beautifully together, and I love it. You're my baby, and I just want you to be happy. Jorja makes you happy. It's good to see you two embrace your love for each other instead of running from it."

The room sounded with agreement.

I had to admit, they were all rooting for us, even when we were sabotaging things at every turn. This year had been a learning experience. We learned to communicate. We learned to be unselfish... We learned to love in a capacity neither of us knew was possible. If that wasn't growth, I didn't know what was.

Epilogue

WALKER

Three Months Later

THE ARENA WAS PACKED.

It was the last leg of Jorja's tour with Emerald, and this was the final show. I'd successfully attended five out of fifteen shows, in support of my baby. Every time she got on the stage, she killed that shit. I couldn't lie and say I wasn't cheering for her off stage. Emerald had been gracious enough to allow me to watch the show backstage. On the occasions when Reese or Alaina joined me, they were welcomed as well.

While the crowd cheered for him, we cheered for Jorja. Every time she walked off stage, she ran into my arms to hug and kiss me. I always expressed how proud of her I was because I damn sure was a proud ass nigga. Emerald was a real one for giving her, her props after every show when he gave his thank yous. Five shows in, she told me that other artists had been hitting him up to get her contact information.

While she hadn't committed to anything yet, she was considering it. We were in the process of finding her a manager. Isaac recommended an excellent entertainment lawyer, and I set her up with my accountant. If she was going to be legit, she had to be all the way legit. Nobody was going to fuck her over in this industry if I could help it. One thing my father instilled in me was to stay ready so I didn't have to get ready.

"Thank you, Columbia!" Emerald yelled into the microphone. "It was only right to close out this tour in my city."

He gave his shoutouts, as always, saving Jorja for last.

"Last but certainly not least, I want to thank the woman responsible for these amazing dancers behind me, Ms. Jorja Sandifer!"

Cupping my hands around my mouth, I yelled, "That's *my* fucking woman! You the shit, baby!"

She and Emerald looked over at me, both of them grinning.

"Looks like Jorja has her own personal fan club. Y'all know she's homegrown, too, so show her some love!"

The crowd erupted with cheers. A few of her former students from the dance team were in the front row with signs, screaming their heads off. Anais was right there with them, cheering her aunt on with a proud look on her face. She blew Jorja a kiss, and Ja blew one back.

Emerald wrapped up the show and said goodnight before they all dispersed from the stage. Jorja came straight to me.

"You just couldn't help yourself, could you?" she asked, her hands on her hips.

I grinned. "I had to let them know." I pulled her into my arms and kissed her softly. "You were amazing as always, love."

"Thank you, baby. And... I get to come home tonight, so you know what that means."

She discreetly grabbed my dick.

"Don't get fucked up in front of all these people," I mumbled.

She giggled as she pulled her hand back. "Let's go grab my shit so we can get out of here.

"Actually, I have a surprise for you."

"A surprise?"

I pulled the blindfold from my back pocket, and she groaned.

"Baby... you know I hate that thing."

"You'll live for a few minutes." I put it over her eyes and grabbed both her hands so she couldn't take it off. "Follow me."

"Like I have a choice!"

THE BURIAL OF A PLAYER

I maneuvered us through the crowd backstage to the private room I had reserved, unbeknownst to her. After typing in the access code, I opened the door and let us in. Everything was in place. The room was flooded with flowers and balloons. There was a basket of her favorite after show snacks and a few gifts for her, but the biggest surprise was yet to come.

"Be still," I said, chuckling as I stood behind her to remove the blindfold.

"I'm anxious!"

"Keep your eyes closed. On the count of three, you can open them. One... two... three."

She opened her eyes, and they immediately widened.

"Walker... baby..."

She turned to face me, only to find me on one knee with a beautiful two-carat, emerald-cut diamond engagement ring. Her hands flew to her mouth, and tears flooded her eyes. I took her hand in mine.

"I know we've shared so much of our life and relationship with others, so I wanted this to be a moment just for us. Jorja Monae Sandifer... you really fucked me up, love. I wasn't looking for anything serious, and then you came along... the blue-haired beauty that stole my heart before I thought I was ready to hand over the reins. I've loved you since before I could admit it to myself. You're my best friend... my lover... my partner in crime.

"Thank you for making me grow up. Thank you for opening my eyes to everything that was and had always been right in front of me. Losing you once taught me that I could and would never lose you again, Ja. You make me better, and I always want to give you the best of me because, baby, you deserve it."

I waved my hands around the room.

"You deserve your flowers every day. I had to play catch up, but there is a flower in here for every single day you've been a part of my life. I love you, Jorja. I love you, and I want to spend the rest of my life loving you. I know I haven't always been deserving, but I'll spend eternity showing you that giving me a second chance wasn't a mistake. Will you marry me, Ja?"

Tears freely streamed down her face. Her hand dropped to her chest, and she nodded.

"Yes... yes..."

I slipped the ring on her finger. "Would you look at that? A perfect fit. I told you I knew your ring size, woman."

She giggled as I climbed to my feet and pulled her into my arms. She cupped my face and kissed me passionately. I couldn't begin to describe how good that shit felt. She'd always been mine to have, and now she would forever be mine to keep.

The sound of my phone ringing broke the kiss. I pulled it out, knowing that it was our family. They'd all gathered at my parents' house to live stream the show. After getting the blessing from Granny and Ms. Alicia, I told them I was going to propose, so I knew they were anxiously waiting for an answer.

I answered the FaceTime call from Alaina's phone. When it came to view, I could see everybody in the background with smiles.

"Well!" Alaina said. "Did she say yes?"

Jorja grinned as she held up her hand. "I said yes."

Cheers and tears of joy were the only thing that could be heard on the other end of the phone.

"Y'all hurry up and get here!" my mother said. "We have to celebrate!"

"We're on the way, Ma."

I hung up the phone and slid it into my pocket.

"There may be a party at my parents' house for us."

Jorja laughed. "What if I had said no?"

"The way your granny and Ms. Alicia prayed when I asked for their permission... I knew you'd say yes."

"You... you asked for permission?"

"Yes. I needed the blessing of two of the most important people in your life. I even went as far as asking for permission from *my* father, 'cause you know that man loves him some you."

"He does." She smiled brightly. "And I love *me* some *you*. Let's get out of here. Once we leave your parents' house, we are having our own little celebration."

THE BURIAL OF A PLAYER

She kissed me again, this time slow and sensual.

I won't lie; a nigga's heart was so full right now. Who would have thought Walker Jareau would be getting married? This was the final end of an era... the burial of a player.

The End

Afterword

Thank you for reading *The Burial of a Player*. I hope you enjoyed Walker and Jorja's story as much as I enjoyed writing it! Please leave a review if you enjoyed this novel. Feel free to connect with me on Facebook, Twitter, and Instagram! Don't forget to sign up for my mailing list for sneak peeks, giveaways, and more!

Much love,

Kimberly Brown

Facebook: https://www.facebook.com/authorkimberlybrown

Facebook Readers Group: https://www.facebook.com/groups/kimberlyscozycorner

Instagram: https://www.instagram.com/authorkimberlybrown

Twitter: https://twitter.com/AuthorKBrown

Website: https://www.authorkimberlybrown.com

Also by Kimberly Brown

Pretty Caged Bird

Tame Me

With Everything in Me

Beyond Measures: An Urban Romance

More Than Words

After All Is Said And Done

Power Over Me

The Sweetest Taste of Cyn

I Could Fall in Love

Something In My Heart

It's Gotta Be You

Before I Let You Go: A Novella

Where Hearts Lie: A Christmas Novella

When Love Takes Over

Pick Up Your Feelings

Something She Can Feel

After All Is Said and Done

Liberated: An Erotic Short

The Last Sad Love Song

This Very Moment

The Point of Exhale

For His Pleasure: Virgin Territory

When Secrets Collide

A Naughty Offer: A Two For One Special

Where Love Blooms: A Jareau Family Novel (Book 1)
Deep In My Soul: A Jareau Family Novel (Book 2)
Signed, Sealed, Delivered: A Jareau Family Wedding

With Love This Christmas

Tethered Love

Thank You

Thanks for reading! If you enjoyed this book, please leave a review on Amazon and mark it as read on Goodreads. We hate errors but they do happen. If you catch any, please send them to us directly at blovepublications@gmail.com with ERRORS as the subject.

Love publications
Heart Piercing Swoon Worthy Black Love Stories

Made in the USA
Columbia, SC
21 October 2024